'I have a proposition for you,' he said, choosing his words carefully. 'I would like you to listen to what I have to say and think before you give me [illegible]

Rosa smil[illegible] turned serious as [illegible]

'I think we should marry.'

Rosa almost choked as he said the words.

'Don't jest, Thomas,' she said. 'I know I am unmarriageable, but please don't poke fun.'

'I'm completely serious.'

'Why would you want to marry me? You're not in love with me. You barely know me.'

All very good points, but he knew enough.

'You need to marry, and soon, or the child you carry will be illegitimate for ever.'

'That's not what I asked. I know why I'm in desperate need of a husband.' Rosa grimaced. 'But no man in his right mind would take me on.'

'Maybe I'm not in my right mind.'

She regarded him in silence, almost warily, until he spoke again.

'Just listen and I will explain.'

Author Note

I never thought I would write a romance in which one of the protagonists lives under the shadow of the threat of an inherited disease! It isn't a subject that immediately lends itself to images of happiness and passion. However, complex neurological disorders are an issue very close to my heart, and when I found myself wondering what it would be like to live two hundred years ago with one of these diseases I couldn't let the idea go.

Although not identified in the book, the disease running in Thomas Hunter's family is Huntington's disease—a hereditary disorder of the central nervous system. If a parent is affected, his or her children will all have a fifty per cent chance of developing the disease. This we know today, from modern clinical research, but in 1820—when genetics and theories on modes of inheritance were far into the future—a disease that ran in the family would often be thought of as a curse. There was no way of knowing if you would be affected, and when I was planning this book I couldn't let go of the thought of the unimaginable strain that lack of knowledge would put someone under.

I have tried to be as accurate as possible in Thomas's descriptions of the disease his father and brother died from, but as with many illnesses it affects people differently. What I hope *is* accurate is Thomas's journey to accepting the uncertainty his future holds, and allowing himself a little happiness on the way.

A RING FOR THE PREGNANT DEBUTANTE

Laura Martin

Published in Great Britain 2017
by Mills & Boon, an imprint of HarperCollins*Publishers*
1 London Bridge Street, London, SE1 9GF

ISBN: 978-0-263-92595-1

Our policy is to use papers that are natural, renewable and recyclable products and made from wood grown in sustainable forests. The logging and manufacturing processes conform to the legal environmental regulations of the country of origin.

Printed and bound in Spain
by CPI, Barcelona

Laura Martin writes historical romances with an adventurous undercurrent. When not writing she spends her time working as a doctor in Cambridgeshire, where she lives with her husband. In her spare moments Laura loves to lose herself in a book, and has been known to read from cover to cover in a single day when the story is particularly gripping. She also loves to travel—especially visiting historical sites and far-flung shores.

Books by Laura Martin

Mills & Boon Historical Romance

The Governess Tales

Governess to the Sheikh

Linked by Character

An Earl in Want of a Wife
Heiress on the Run

Stand-Alone Novels

The Pirate Hunter
Secrets Behind Locked Doors
Under a Desert Moon
A Ring for the Pregnant Debutante

Visit the Author Profile page at millsandboon.co.uk.

For Luke and Jack. You keep me smiling.

Chapter One

Rosa lifted her head from the pillow as the door opened and looked at the unappetising bowl of stew before turning her gaze to her odious cousin. He watched her as she dismissed first the dinner and then him, a cold contempt behind his eyes.

'You should be grateful for the scraps I bring you,' Antonio Di Mercurio sneered as he flung the bowl of brown slop on to the rickety wooden table. 'Whores don't deserve to eat with the rest of the family.'

'Would it hurt you to be civil?' Rosa replied in her broken Italian. She tried to remain aloof, but could already feel the anger threatening to take over. Her cousin had been needling her for the past four weeks, trying to provoke some kind of reaction, and Rosa knew it wouldn't be long before he succeeded. There were only so many insults she could turn the other cheek to before retaliating.

'Civil? Maybe you should work on being less civil. Might save the family from further shame in the future.' Antonio laughed heartily at his joke, made the protective sign against the evil eye with his hands and turned to leave.

Rosa picked up the bowl Antonio had just set down and flung it at her malicious cousin, but he was already out of the room and the dinner splatted against the closed door. Letting out a growl of annoyance, Rosa flopped back on the bed and tried to relax. She knew she shouldn't let Antonio upset her so much, but it was difficult being in a foreign country with people she didn't know. The Di Mercurios might be her family on her mother's side, but they didn't act warm or loving. In the four weeks she'd been staying in the villa in Italy not one of them had said a single kind word towards her.

Rosa suddenly sat up straight and looked at the door. In Antonio's haste to avoid her flying dinner he might have forgotten to lock it. She didn't remember hearing the click or the grating of the metal key in the ancient lock. Hardly daring to hope, Rosa stood and crossed the room. She gripped the handle, wondering whether it was a trick, an unkind ruse planned by her cousin to give her the hope of freedom.

Knowing she couldn't give up on even the slightest chance of escaping her imprisonment, Rosa pushed down on the handle and nearly cried out with happiness as the door opened. Quickly she glanced out into the corridor and saw it was deserted; the Di Mercurio family had no need to station a guard outside her door when they kept it locked all day and night.

Rosa carefully closed the door and rested her head against the rough wood. This was her one and only chance to escape. For twenty-three hours a day she was locked in this small chamber, only let out for one hour's exercise around the grounds daily. When outside her room she was always watched closely by one of her numerous uncles or cousins, all intent on keeping her hidden from the world so she wouldn't bring shame to their family. So now really was her only chance and she wouldn't let the nerves that were bubbling away inside her spoil it.

Grabbing her travelling cloak, Rosa collected together the few items she felt she couldn't leave behind and made a neat bundle. Just before leaving the room she pushed her hand under her mattress and removed the small purse of money she'd managed to keep hidden throughout her journey to Italy and subsequent imprisonment in the villa. Then, without a backwards glance at the room that had been her prison cell for the past month, Rosa darted out into the courtyard.

The garden was shrouded in an inky blackness and it took Rosa's eyes a few minutes to adjust. Luckily she knew this part of the grounds from her daily exercise excursions from her room and as she felt her way along the villa wall an escape route began to form in her mind.

'Don't be like that, Maria.' Antonio's voice carried through the night.

Rosa stiffened, her heart pounding in her chest so loudly she thought the whole world must be able to hear.

'I never promised this would be anything more than a few nights of fun. You're only a maid after all.'

Rosa couldn't hear the words of Maria's reply, but she understood the gist of her feelings from the tone. No doubt Antonio had implied he would give the servant much more than a quick fumble. Normally Rosa would have stormed over and confronted her cousin, but tonight she had to be selfish. She couldn't bear to be locked up for another five months, but more importantly she wouldn't let the Di Mercurios snatch her baby away and send it to live with some other family.

Going forward, Rosa would have to be selfish, it wasn't just her own future she was fighting for now.

Creeping softly through the night, Rosa moved further away from the villa, making sure she kept the perimeter wall to her right. She was heading for a huge lemon tree at the southern-most corner of the grounds. There she was confident she could make it over the wall and to freedom, and even the most vigilant of her family wouldn't be able to see her climbing the tree that far from the house.

With the lemon tree looming above her Rosa checked she hadn't been followed before testing out the branches. There was no movement from the villa, even Antonio and his disappointed maid had fallen quiet and Rosa concluded they must have returned inside.

Rosa had been climbing trees since she was a little girl, but concern for the baby inside her made her pause and evaluate for a moment longer. Knowing she had no choice, she hiked up her skirt and began to climb. Within two minutes she was sitting on the stone wall, regarding the drop on the other side. It was further down than on the villa side of the wall, due to a sloping of the land, maybe six or seven feet. There was a rough path running alongside the wall with nothing to cushion her drop. She could probably jump without doing herself too big an injury, but the tiny life inside her was another matter. Maybe if she lowered herself slowly whilst holding on to the top of the wall she would be safe.

She was still contemplating her options as she heard movement coming along the path. Footsteps and a low whistling became gradually louder as Rosa pressed herself into the stone and wondered what to do. At this height whoever was approaching might not see her, but if they happened to look up for any reason her escape attempt would be ruined.

The whistling got louder and Rosa knew there was nothing for it but to climb back over the wall until the man had passed. It went against every instinct to return to the grounds of her prison, but she kept telling herself it was only temporary. In a few minutes she would be back on top of the wall and on her way to freedom.

As she swung her legs over she felt herself toppling slightly. With the extra weight she was now carrying around her middle her equilibrium was off just slightly and as she windmilled her arms to try to regain her balance Rosa knew it wasn't going to be enough. With a scream she fell backwards, wrapping her arms protectively around her belly and praying for a miracle.

* * *

Thomas felt his breath knocked from his lungs as something careened into him from above. One moment he'd been walking along lost in thought and the next he was flattened, unable to move.

'Oooh…' a soft voice moaned on top of him.

Thomas reached up and his hand met soft fabric. If he wasn't much mistaken there was a woman lying on top of him, but he had no idea where she had come from.

'Excuse me,' he said in Italian eventually when the woman made no attempt to move. He almost laughed at the stiff formality of the words—even after three years of living abroad you still couldn't remove his innate good manners.

There was some wriggling, then fingers digging into his ribcage as she manoeuvred herself upright. Thomas watched in a daze as the young woman ran her hands over her body as if checking for bumps and bruises, caressing her abdomen through the material of her dress.

'Are you hurt?' she asked eventually, once Thomas could see she was satisfied she had not injured herself in any obvious way. She spoke in Italian, but there was an accent that made him wonder if she was not native to this part of the world.

Testing out his theory, Thomas replied in English, 'Just a little winded.'

'You're English.'

He could hear the note of fear in her voice and noticed how she begun to lean away from him as if he were about to do her harm.

'Yes,' he replied tersely. 'Would you mind letting me up?'

'Oh,' the young woman said, mortification in her voice as she looked down and realised she was still straddling him. Quickly she stood, but as she transferred her weight to her left foot she cried out in pain. From his position on the ground Thomas saw her stumble and then come lurching back towards him. This time it was her elbow that caught him in the stomach and a slender knee in the groin area. For a moment Thomas felt the whole world blur with pain before he was back on the dusty country road with a woman on top of him.

'I'm sorry,' the young woman mumbled, too focused on her own pain to realise the extent of the damage she had inflicted on him.

Thomas just grunted, lying still until the ache had subsided, before gripping the young woman around the waist and firmly setting her on the road beside him.

Before deciding what to do next, he regarded

the woman in front of him for a few moments. She was dusty and dishevelled, and at the moment her face was screwed up with pain, but if Thomas wasn't much mistaken this was no common thief or intruder trying to escape the Di Mercurio property. She was too well dressed, her bearing and her speech too polished.

'Why did you jump off the wall?' Thomas asked.

Immediately he saw the young woman bristle.

'I didn't jump. I fell.'

'Let me rephrase the question. Why were you climbing over the wall in the first place?'

'That is none of your concern,' she said primly.

Thomas watched her for a few seconds and then shrugged nonchalantly. He wasn't about to browbeat the information from her, but she would tell him.

'Would you like me to escort you back to the Di Mercurio villa, or fetch someone to come and get you?' he asked lightly.

He actually saw the pallor bloom on her face as the blood drained away.

'Please do not concern yourself,' she said. 'I'll just get on my way and you can continue with your evening.'

'You will need my help…' he motioned to

her left ankle '… I'd wager you won't get far on your own.'

'Truly, please do not let me detain you further,' she said with exaggerated politeness. Thomas could see he was beginning to irk her, but found himself unable to stop with his goading. He was enjoying this interaction more than he had any for months now.

He looked on with interest as she tottered to her feet, grimaced and bit down forcibly on her lower lip, presumably to stop her crying out in pain as she tried to put weight on her left foot. Thomas's concern turned to amusement as she began hopping down the road and he had to stop himself from laughing out loud.

'I don't think anyone has ever gone to such lengths to avoid my company before,' he mused loudly as he pushed himself upright and began to stroll along beside her.

She didn't even spare him a look, just hopped resolutely onwards.

'I hope you didn't need to be somewhere in a hurry. You're rather slow at hopping.' This did earn him a glance, but no conversation.

Suddenly she stopped, changed direction and hopped unsteadily to the side of the road. Thomas watched with interest as she hefted a heavy fallen branch from the ground and tested it as a makeshift crutch. It didn't look that helpful.

'So let me guess,' he said as she staggered onwards. 'You're a disgraced maid and you stole the family silver.'

'Don't be ridiculous.'

Two more steps, then she rested, looking back over her shoulder and appearing disappointed with how little progress they'd made.

'You're being forced to marry one of the unpleasant Di Mercurio boys and you're fleeing on the eve of the wedding.'

'That would be a very good reason to run,' the young woman muttered under her breath.

'I've got it,' Thomas exclaimed. 'They were going to offer you up as a ritual sacrifice to the devil.'

'Why are you following me?' she demanded.

'I thought you might need some assistance.'

She stared at him with wide eyes and motioned to the nearly useless crutch. 'You're not providing any assistance so will you just leave me alone.'

'I *could* provide you with assistance,' Thomas said with a charming smile, 'If you ask nicely. And tell me what you were doing climbing over the wall.'

She had a stubborn streak running through

her, Thomas mused as she limped a few more paces with her head held high before relenting.

'I was being held prisoner. Now, please will you help me?'

'Well, that wasn't the most gracious of pleas, but a gentleman can overlook these things.' Thomas scooped her up into his arms, hiding a grin at her squeal of surprise and the initial stiffness of her body. 'Where to, my lady?'

No reply was forthcoming and Thomas could see the thoughts tumbling through her head. For some reason she had felt she was being held prisoner by the well-to-do Di Mercurios and had manufactured her escape, but he would wager his entire inheritance that she hadn't really planned beyond getting over the wall.

'Maybe to the residence of the local magistrate so you could report your imprisonment?' Thomas suggested, suppressing a smile as she tensed. 'Or we could go straight to the *governatore*, the man in charge, seeing as they are such an influential family in the region.'

Still no reply from the woman in his arms.

'What's your name?' he asked.

'Miss Rosa Rothwell.'

'Well, Rosa,' he said, enjoying her scowl of indignation at his use of the overfamiliar form of address, 'it is decision time. What's the plan?'

'I would be grateful if you would take me to a local *pensione*,' she said decisively.

'I don't like to criticise a well-thought-out plan, but won't the village guest house be the first place the Di Mercurios look for their runaway?'

'I will ask the owner to be discreet.'

'It will all come down to who has the bigger purse, you or the wealthiest landowners around the lake.'

Rosa fell quiet again and Thomas adjusted his grip on the pensive young woman in his arms.

'Are you sure you can't sort this feud out with the Di Mercurios?' Thomas asked softly, the levity gone from his voice. 'It would be the easiest way.'

'No.' The force behind that one short word told Thomas all he needed to know about Rosa's predicament. She was in trouble, real trouble, and it wasn't going to be sorted with an apology and a friendly handshake. He couldn't imagine the Di Mercurios had actually kept Rosa locked up, they were a respected and important family, but he was well aware he didn't know the details.

'I need to get away from here,' Rosa said quietly. 'I need to get back to England.'

Thomas quickened his pace along the dusty road and felt Rosa squirm in his arms.

'Where are we going?' she asked.

'I'm renting a villa about a mile from here,' Thomas said. 'You will stay tonight and arrangements can be made in the morning.'

'I'm not sure that is an appropriate—'

'You don't really have a choice,' Thomas interrupted her. 'It's this or the Di Mercurios finding you within the hour.'

'I am a young woman of a good family,' Rosa said stiffly.

'Trust me, there is nothing further from my mind than ravishing you. You'll be perfectly safe.'

Not that she wasn't pretty enough, in a wholesome, innocent sort of way, but Thomas had not been tempted in a long time and he wasn't going to let this dishevelled young woman be the reason he stepped off his predestined path.

Chapter Two

Thomas set her down gently on a wooden chair positioned on the terrace to the rear of his rented villa. Rosa was momentarily mesmerised by the view over the lake to the mountains beyond, the inky blackness of the water giving way to the solid outlines of the snowy peaks silhouetted against the starry sky. Although she'd been in Italy for a month she hadn't seen past the walls of the Di Mercurio villa since her arrival.

'Beautiful, isn't it?' Thomas commented as he caught her looking at the view.

She regarded her host for a few moments, trying to decide what she thought of him. He was confident and arrogant, a man used to getting his own way. She had bristled earlier when he'd made the decisions about her immediate future without really consulting her, but she'd bitten her tongue because…well, because she didn't have anywhere else to go.

'Who are you?' Rosa asked as she took in the expensive furniture and no doubt expensive view.

'Hunter. Lord Thomas Hunter. It is a pleasure to make your acquaintance, Miss Rosa Rothwell.' Her name sounded seductive on his tongue.

'Do you live alone here?' Rosa asked.

'Don't worry,' Thomas said, flashing her a lazy grin, 'I meant what I said, your virtue is safe.'

Rosa instinctively laid a hand on top of her lower abdomen, stroking the fabric of her dress and thinking of the growing life that was to be her ruin. She'd lost her virtue long ago, but that didn't mean she couldn't hold some moral values. Staying in a house alone with a single, rather attractive gentleman was certainly on the list of *Things a Young Lady Must Never Do* that her mother had often recited to her when she was younger. Nevertheless, here she was, without any other option and ready to put her fate and her already sullied virtue into the hands of Lord Thomas Hunter. Her mother would be appalled.

Lord Hunter disappeared for a few minutes

before re-emerging from the villa holding a bottle of wine and two glasses. Rosa watched as he pulled out the cork and filled both glasses, before pushing one towards her.

'So, tell me, whatever have you done to make the Di Mercurios lock you away?' He held up a hand as he took a mouthful of wine. 'No, no, no. Let me guess. It's more fun that way.'

'It's a private matter,' Rosa said, watching as Hunter leaned back in his chair and swung both feet on to the table.

'Did you steal something?'

Rosa refused to be drawn in and focused instead on her wine glass.

'Something more scandalous, then,' Hunter mused. 'Did you insult one of the old women, the ones that look like mean English Bulldogs?'

'Those *old women* are my grandmother and great-aunt.'

'Oh, I am sorry. Well, maybe you won't be quite so wrinkly when you're older. All is not lost.' He paused, then pushed on, 'So they're family, are they? The plot thickens.'

Rosa took a sip of wine and felt the warmth spreading out from the throat and through her body. It was warming and delicious and already a little intoxicating.

'I was sent here in disgrace,' she said eventually.

'Your family sent you all the way to Italy? You must have done something pretty unsavoury for that amount of distance to be required.'

She supposed getting pregnant before marriage was pretty disgraceful, her mother at least had enough to say on the matter. Rosa was *a disgusting harlot*, *an ungrateful wretch* and *as bad as a common streetwalker.* The strange thing was, despite having been brought up with her mother's strict set of moral values, Rosa didn't feel disgusting or unsavoury, and she couldn't summon anything but warmth for the small life blossoming inside her.

Uninvited tears sprung to her eyes at the thought of the venom in her mother's voice as she'd told her she never wanted to see Rosa, or her child, ever again. They'd always had a difficult relationship, but the finality of her mother's goodbye had hurt Rosa more than she would have imagined.

What had hurt even more had been the look of shock on her father's face when Rosa had admitted her pregnancy. She and her father had always shared a close and loving relationship. It was her father, not her mother, who had played with her as a child, who often would call her into his study so they could spend hours discussing books. So when he'd been unable to rally on hearing the news that his only daughter was expecting a child out of wedlock Rosa had felt her heart rip in two.

Dipping her head, Rosa quickly blinked away the tears. She would not cry in front of a stranger, not about something that could not be changed.

'I suppose it was unsavoury,' she said, smiling sadly.

'The Di Mercurios were meant to look after you?' Hunter asked and Rosa was glad of his change of direction.

Rosa shrugged. She didn't know what their instructions had been, but as soon as she had arrived it had been made clear she was not a welcomed guest.

'They locked me in my room for a month.'

'And fed you gruel, no doubt.'

She looked at him sharply, wondering if he was mocking her, but saw the joviality that had filled his eyes earlier had gone.

'Well, sometimes they treated me to stew and a stale piece of bread.'

'How generous. No wonder you wanted to escape.'

Rosa looked past her host, out over the dark water and to the night beyond and knew she would have put up with the cruelty if it hadn't been for the threat of losing her child. On one of her daily walks around the grounds a maid had sidled up to her and whispered, 'Don't worry, *signorina*, the family they have chosen are kind and loving. Your little one will be well looked after.'

The girl had risked a beating for just talking to her and the words had meant to be reassuring, but Rosa had felt her heart fill with dread and known there and then she needed to escape. No one would take her child from her. She would fight with every ounce of strength and determination in her body and nothing would keep them apart.

'So what is the plan, Rosa Rothwell?' Hunter asked.

'I will seek passage to England.'

'Back to the family that sent you here?'

Rosa grimaced. She had no doubt her mother would pack her straight back to Italy the moment she turned up on the doorstep.

'I have a good friend who will take me in, I just need to get to her.'

Rosa was aware of Hunter's eyes scrutinising her. He did it brazenly, as if he didn't even consider it would make her uncomfortable, or he wasn't concerned if he did. Roaming eyes taking in her every movement, her every expression, making her feel exposed and as if he knew all of her secrets.

'Time for bed,' Hunter said abruptly, standing and draining the dregs of wine from his glass.

Rosa was just about to say she would stay on the terrace a while longer when Hunter's strong arms whisked her up from her seat and carried her over the threshold into the villa.

'What are you doing?' Rosa asked indignantly.

'Taking you to bed.'

'Put me down.'

He ignored her, manoeuvring round the furniture in a plushly decorated living room before kicking open the door to a bedroom. Quickly he strode into the room and deposited her on the rather inviting four-poster bed.

'I might not want to go to sleep,' Rosa said.

Hunter shrugged. 'You're here now.'

Rosa clenched her jaw to stop the flow of uncomplimentary phrases that were trying to escape.

'Only because…' Rosa began, then stared in surprise as Hunter left the room, closing the door behind him. It was difficult to have an argument with a man who refused to listen half the time.

Rosa nearly struggled to her feet, thinking

she would hop back out on to the terrace just to show she couldn't be ordered around and sent to bed like a child, but her body was already sinking into the soft mattress and freshly laundered sheets. Tomorrow she would stand up to Lord Hunter, tomorrow she would thank him for his assistance but firmly insist she go her own way from now on. Tonight she was going to enjoy the comforts of Lord Hunter's guest room and rather welcoming bed.

Chapter Three

Thomas tossed and turned, throwing the light sheet from his bed with a growl of frustration. It was nearly dawn yet he hadn't slept for more than a couple of hours and now he felt groggy and unsettled.

Reaching out to the small table beside his bed he picked up the well-read letter, the real reason for his disturbed night. Every time he read the now-familiar words his conscience collided with his more selfish needs and he came away uncertain as to what course of action to take. And if there was one thing Thomas didn't like it was uncertainty. With a sigh he sat up in bed and started to read again, wondering if he was just punishing himself or hoping for divine inspiration, a new point of view, knowing the words and the pleas would still be the same as all the other times he'd read it.

My darling son,

I hope you are well and are finding what you need to soothe your soul on your travels. It has been three years and eight months since I last set eyes on you—one thousand three hundred and forty-five days since you left. You must know I don't blame you for leaving—I actively encouraged you to go—but I miss you every minute of every day that you are gone.

I am keeping as well as can be expected. My friends ask when I will come out of mourning...when I will start to move on. They don't understand what it is like to lose a husband and a son. I don't think anyone does, apart from you.

Ever since you left I have tried to be patient, tried to allow you to grieve and come to terms with the uncertain future in your own way. You know I have never pressured you to return, never pushed your responsibilities or the estate's need for a master. I truly hoped you would find peace on your travels, revel in new experiences and return to me with a renewed passion for life, but three years and eight months is a long time to wait and now I want my son home.

I'm lonely, Thomas. I'm surrounded by

friends, by extended family, by servants I have known for half my life, but without you it all seems empty. So I have decided to be selfish. I know you have lost a father and a brother, and I know you've needed to come to terms with a possibly cruel and difficult future, but now I ask that you think of me.

Come home to me. Fill the house with laughter once again. Allow yourself to think about the future, to hope. A wife and child might be too much to ask, I know that, but please consider returning home and taking up your birthright.

I live in hope that I might embrace you in my arms one day soon.

Your loving mother

He wanted to put the letter out of his mind, to forget the hurt and loneliness that must have triggered his mother to write in this way after allowing him to fulfil his own wanderlust for nearly four years without a word of protest. She had been the one who'd encouraged him to leave in the first place, who'd urged him to travel and experience a bit of the world so he would have no regrets about his own life. Thomas knew soon he would have to return to England, return to the memories and the half-empty family home. He was not cold-hearted enough to refuse a direct plea from his mother.

A swim, that was what he needed, a bracing and refreshing start to the new day. Maybe then he could find it in himself to start planning the long journey back home. Thomas jumped out of bed, grabbed a towel and tucked it loosely around his waist. He padded barefoot through the villa, resolutely not looking at the closed door to the guest room, and out on to the terrace. Even though the sun's rays were just beginning to filter over the horizon Thomas could already feel the heat in the air. It would be another scorching day, the type that sometimes made him long for the cool breezes and cloudy skies of England.

It only took him thirty seconds to reach the lake, two more to stretch and brace himself for the icy shock of the water and then he dropped his towel to the ground and dived in. The blackness consumed him immediately and as Thomas glided deeper he could barely make out the shape of his hands a few inches in front of his face. The water skimmed over his skin, washing away the remnants of the restless night and invigorating him for a new day. Forty seconds in and his lungs began burning, but still he glided deeper. Fifty seconds and he felt the tremor in his muscles from lack of air. Sixty seconds and little grey spots began to appear before his eyes. One more pull of his arms, and then another, the ultimate test of his mind's control over his body. Only when his head began to spin did Thomas relent and kick powerfully to the surface, breaking free of the water and taking in huge gulps of air.

He floated on his back for a while, allowing his body to recover and his breathing to return to normal. As the sun started to rise over the hills and reflect off the water's surface Thomas began to swim. He took long, leisurely strokes, propelling himself through the water at a moderate speed and focusing on the horizon.

This was his favourite time of day, whilst he was powering through the water he could plan and reflect without any distractions. It was just him, the early morning air and the silent lake.

He swam for about fifteen minutes before turning back, the villa now the size of a model house on the banks of the lake. It was still peaceful, but there were signs of life stirring around the edge of the lake. A farmer's cart trundled along the dusty track, kicking up a plume of dirt. A young boy chased an eager dog down to the water's edge and further away to his left the sleepy village was beginning to show signs of activity.

As Thomas reached the edge of the lake he paused, turning to look out over the murky blue water before pulling himself up the old wooden ladder on to the shore.

It was getting light when Rosa awoke and for a few moments she allowed herself to lie in bed and watch the soft light of dawn streaming in through the windows. She wasn't a natural early riser—at home she would often indulge in breakfast in bed late in the morning—but these last couple of months she had found herself waking early with an entrenched sensation of nausea that could only be cured by a cold glass of water and something to eat.

Rosa knew she was lucky, many women at her stage of pregnancy spent their days vomiting and confined to their beds. A little early morning nausea was not something that stopped her from getting on with her day at least.

Rising slowly, Rosa straightened her dress, aware of the creases from where she'd slept fully clothed, and patted the loose strands of hair into place. She took a moment to examine her ankle, which had swollen overnight and had a purple hue to the stretched skin. Even placing it lightly on the floor made her wince in pain, but she gritted her teeth and managed to hobble to the door, leaning heavily on furniture as she went.

Outside her bedroom the villa was quiet and Rosa sensed she was alone. Of course Lord Hunter would be an early riser, he was just the type to be cheery at an ungodly time in the morning. Rosa was just about to admit defeat and flop into a chair when she spotted an ornate walking cane leaning up against the wall next to her bedroom door. Hunter must have put it there after he'd bid her goodnight, ready for her to use this morning.

Grasping the carved knob, Rosa tested the cane out, finding she could walk a little better with the extra balance it gave her, although the pain was still there. She would have to remember to thank Lord Hunter for his kindness.

Not wanting to rummage through his cupboards, but desperate for something to eat, Rosa ventured outside on to the terrace. She recalled from the night before the large orange tree overhanging the seating area and her empty stomach growled at the thought of a juicy orange to start the day.

Rosa had to stretch to reach even the lowest branch, but her efforts were rewarded when she began to peel a ripe and fragrant orange and popped the first segment into her mouth. Chewing slowly, she savoured the sweet juice, licking the remnants off her fingers before biting into a second segment. She had to stop herself from wolfing the whole orange down in a few seconds as she peeled the remainder of the skin from the flesh it was so delicious, but somehow she managed to resist the urge. With the first orange gone Rosa stretched up and plucked a second from the branches of the orange tree, grasped hold of her cane again and limped to the edge of the terrace.

As she looked out over the lake, admiring how the sun reflected off the smooth surface making the water look blessed by the gods, her eyes came to rest on the small figure propelling himself towards the villa. He was swimming quickly, but in a way that looked as though it required hardly any effort on his part. As he got closer Rosa realised it was her host, Lord Hunter. She almost laughed—she'd known he would be a morning person, he probably swam a mile first thing every morning whilst she would normally be languishing in bed.

Rosa watched as he approached the shore, mesmerised by the rhythmic movement of his arms and the effortless way he glided through the water. She'd felt the hard muscles of his arms and chest when he'd picked her up yesterday and wondered if this was how he stayed quite so toned.

With a final pull of his arms Hunter reached the small wooden jetty that jutted out from the grounds of the property. Rosa could see his shoulders bobbing up and down as he gripped the ladder and began to pull himself out.

Time slowed and Rosa found she couldn't look away. Inch by inch Hunter's body rose from the water, his chest, his abdomen, the water pouring off him and leaving his skin shimmering. Rosa felt the heat begin to rise from her core as her eyes locked on to Hunter's naked form. Only when he pulled himself fully out of the water did Rosa realise he wasn't wearing anything at all, but still she couldn't look away. He stood, indifferent to his nakedness, seemingly unconcerned that anyone might see him, and brushed the water from his skin before picking up a towel and wrapping it around his waist.

Only then did he glance up to the terrace. Rosa knew the moment he saw her, the moment he realised she must have been watching him the entire time. For a fraction of a second his whole body went still, like a wolf catching sight of its prey, then he raised a hand and waved cheerily at her.

She wished she could just disappear, that an

earthquake would open up the ground underneath her and she could fall inside. He would think that she had been watching him. Well, she *had* been watching him, but not purposefully. She wasn't to know he swam naked, but now she looked like a shameless voyeur.

'Good morning,' Hunter said with a smile as he approached the terrace.

'Good morning,' Rosa managed to mumble, trying to look anywhere but the expanse of exposed skin at her eye level. He was tanned, wonderfully so, his skin a deep bronze hinting to the length of time he'd spent in warm climes.

'Did you sleep well?'

How could he ask such a mundane and ordinary question when he was standing there half-naked in front of her?

Forcing herself to look up and meet his eye, Rosa smiled.

'Very well, thank you.'

Her cheeks were burning so much it felt as though she'd just stepped out of a blacksmith's forge and her heart was beating so loudly she was sure it could be heard for miles, but if Hunter refused to be embarrassed by his lack of clothing then she would not let her discomfort show.

'Isn't the view beautiful first thing in the morning?'

Unbidden, her eyes flicked down to where the towel was tucked around his waist and Rosa heard him utter a low chuckle.

'I find the early morning light to be the most flattering,' Rosa said, watching as Hunter's grin widened.

'Everything looks even better from the middle of the lake,' he said, moving a step closer, 'You should join me next time. A swim can really get the blood pumping at this time of day.'

Rosa was sure he knew exactly what he was doing, no young woman from a good family would feel comfortable standing here talking about the weather and the view with a man she'd just seen emerge naked from the lake, but Hunter was pushing her, seeing how much it would take to make her flee in embarrassment or swoon. Well, she'd never swooned in her life and a little bit of naked flesh wasn't about to make her run. Even if it was particularly smooth and sculpted flesh.

'I can think of better ways to exert myself so early in the morning,' she said with a sweet smile. Without glancing at his face Rosa limped back over to the orange tree and plucked another of the round fruit from the branches. Carefully she began to peel it, worked a segment free and only when she was about to pop it between her lips did she look up and meet Hunter's eye. 'Can't you?'

It was, oh, so satisfying to see him lost for words, his eyes glued on the orange segment as it passed her lips. Allowing herself a small, triumphant smile, Rosa turned and headed back to the villa, her walk of victory only slightly spoiled by the clicking of the cane on the tiles.

Chapter Four

'Last night you were telling me about the disgrace that had your family disowning you,' Thomas said as he helped Rosa up into the curricle.

'No,' Rosa said pointedly, 'I wasn't.'

'Well, we've got an hour's ride to the village of Malcesine, and it will be a terribly dull journey if you sit in silence the whole way.'

Thomas had suggested a day trip to the next sizeable village around the lake when Rosa had talked about seeking a passage back to England. The Di Mercurios would no doubt be searching for their runaway prisoner and there was no point in making it easy for them. In Malcesine they would find the date and time of the next coach leaving for one of the port cities where Rosa would be able to buy a fare home.

'You could tell me what you're doing hiding

away in Italy,' Rosa suggested with that sweet smile she used when she was determined to get her own way.

'What if we play a game?'

'I'm listening.'

'We each get three questions. The other has to answer truthfully and fully.'

'I get to go first?' Rosa asked.

'Ask away.'

She sat in silence for a while, watching the countryside passing by and pressing her lips together as she thought. Thomas glanced at her every now and again. Ever since he'd caught her looking at him as he emerged from the lake he'd felt a spark of excitement, a slowly building intrigue at the woman hiding beneath the composed façade. He felt he needed to be close to her, to touch her, to find out what was really going on behind those calm, cool eyes. It wasn't often Thomas met a woman he could fully engage with intellectually. So many of the debutantes his mother had introduced him to before he'd fled England had seemed to want to appear less intelligent than they actually were, wittering on about the weather or the latest fashion. Admittedly he didn't know Rosa well, but there was something more to her—something bold, something that refused to back down.

'Why do you live in Italy?' Rosa asked eventually.

'I like it here.'

She shook her head and actually wagged an admonishing finger at him like some disapproving elderly aunt. 'You're breaking the rules,' she said. 'You said we had to answer truthfully and fully. Why do you live in Italy?'

Thomas broke out into a grin. 'You caught me. I will try to be more honest,' he said, trying out a contrite expression and finding it didn't sit well on his face.

The intensity of her gaze was a little unnerving as she waited for him to speak.

'The past four years I have travelled as far east as India, as far south as Turkey, stopping at various places for a few weeks, maybe a couple of months. I've been here beside the lake for six months, the longest I've stayed anywhere. I suppose I feel at peace here, waking up to such beauty every day is humbling. It makes you admit how insignificant your problems are.'

Although he had never set out to be quite so honest Thomas realised it was the truth. He could have settled anywhere, but he'd chosen Lake Garda to make his home at least for a while.

'Why do you feel the need to move around so much?'

'Is that question number two?'

Rosa nodded.

'When I first left England I didn't know what I wanted to see, I just knew there was a whole world out there waiting for me to discover it. I marvelled at the ancient temples in Greece, climbed an active volcano in Italy, was stalked by a tiger in the jungles of India and spent three glorious weeks floating adrift in a rickety old boat in the Black Sea.' He paused to see if Rosa looked as though she believed him. It was partly the truth, but it did not explain his need to run from his fate, a strange compulsion to keep moving, as if staying in one place too long might let the disease he was so afraid of catch up with him. 'Once I started discovering new places I was like a laudanum addict, I needed to see more, experience more. It was like an illness—if I didn't keep moving on I would become restless and anxious.'

'So why have you stopped now?'

Thomas pulled on the reins to slow the horses as they rounded a tight bend and considered Rosa's question. In truth he wasn't quite sure. The answer he'd given earlier, talking about the humbling beauty of Lake Garda, was true, but he'd visited many beautiful places in the past few years. He wasn't sure what had made him slow, what had made him start thinking of home, yearning for the green fields and grey skies and all the places he had known as a child.

He thought of the letter from his mother, asking him to return, and knew that even without her plea it wouldn't have been that long before he boarded a ship and sailed for England. Something was pulling him home, but he wasn't sure what.

'I suppose everyone needs a rest now and again.'

'You're being flippant again,' Rosa challenged him.

'Sorry. I suppose I don't know. For a while I grew tired of new places, not knowing anyone, never being sure of where I would rest my head from one day to the next.'

'So will you stay here, in Italy?'

Thomas smiled and shook his head. 'That's question number four, Miss Rothwell. You've had your turn, now it's mine.'

Rosa stiffened as if actually nervous about what he would ask, but nodded for him to continue.

'How many months pregnant are you?' He hadn't meant to be quite so blunt and as the shock and hurt flashed across her eyes he cursed his clumsy handling of the question.

'What makes you think I'm pregnant?'

'Look how you're sitting,' Thomas said softly.

Rosa glanced down and grimaced as she realised one hand rested protectively against her lower abdomen.

'I suppose it's natural, a mother's instinct,' Thomas said. 'You've had a hand on your abdomen throughout most of the morning, and every so often you will look down fondly when you think I'm not paying attention.'

She nodded, mutely. They continued in silence for nearly ten minutes before Rosa spoke again.

'Four months, nearly to the day.'

Thomas did a few quick sums in his head, and realised things didn't quite add up.

'And that was why you were sent away in disgrace? You must have known pretty early on that you were pregnant.'

It wasn't a subject Thomas was well schooled in, but he did have a vague idea that most women weren't sure until they were about three or four months along in their pregnancy.

'I knew as soon as I missed my courses, by that time I was only about a month gone. I spoke to the father a week later, confessed to my mother the same evening and the next day I was packed off to Italy.'

That explained the timings a little more.

'What if you were wrong?'

Rosa shrugged. 'I suppose my mother thought it easier to recall me if it turned out I wasn't pregnant than to explain an ever-growing bump.'

Thomas detected a note of bitterness along-side the sadness and wondered if the relation-ship between mother and daughter was a little strained.

'It took five weeks by boat, a couple more overland, and then the Di Mercurios kept me locked away for a month. That makes four months.' She said it in a matter-of-fact voice that belied the pain on her face.

'What about the father?' Thomas asked, won-dering if that was who she was running home to.

Rosa gave a bitter, short bark of a laugh and shook her head instead of answering.

'What do you plan to do, Rosa?' he asked, aware that this game of theirs had become very serious very quickly.

'Stop the horses,' Rosa said sharply.

Thomas glanced at her in puzzlement.

'Stop. The. Horses.'

He pulled on the reins, slowing the horses down to a gentle walk before coming to a com-plete stop. As soon as the curricle had stopped moving Rosa slid down, grabbed her cane and began to limp away. Thomas frowned, wondering exactly what it was about his question that had caused so much offence.

'Rosa,' he called, jumping down after her and jogging to catch up.

'Leave me alone.'

Thomas realised she was crying and slowed as he approached her.

'I'm sorry. I never meant to upset you.'

She shook her head, turning her back to him.

He stood undecided for a moment, unsure whether to step back and give her space or take her into his arms and comfort her.

'Shh…' he whispered as he wrapped her in his arms and gently pulled her head to rest on his shoulder.

He felt the sobs rack her body, her shoulders heaving as the tears ran down her cheeks and soaked through his shirt.

'I'm sorry,' she said quietly.

Thomas didn't reply, instead tightening his hold on her, running a hand over her raven-black hair and murmuring soothing noises.

'Come back to the curricle,' he said as her sobs died down.

'I don't know—' she started to say, but Thomas interrupted her with a shake of his head.

'I'm not a man who is used to having his requests refused,' he said in an overly serious tone and felt supremely satisfied when Rosa broke into a smile. It was small and uncertain, but a smile all the same.

Giving her his arm to lean upon, Thomas led her back, placed his arms around her waist and lifted her easily back into the seat.

'No running off whilst I climb up.'

'I'm sorry,' Rosa said as he took his place beside her. 'I never cry.'

'Half a day in my company and already you're breaking habits of a lifetime.'

'It's just so frustrating, so completely unfair. Every person who has found out about my predicament has expected me to give my child up. To be thankful for the suggestion that a nice family could raise my baby and no one will ever know.'

The thought had crossed his mind, and although that hadn't been the question he'd asked, it had been the answer he'd been expecting.

'So what are you going to do?'

Rosa took a deep breath, raised her chin and straightened her back. 'I will raise my child myself.'

It was an admirable idea, but not an easy one to fulfil.

As soon as the words had passed her lips Rosa deflated again, her chin dropping closer to her chest and her eyes focused on the ground beneath them as if searching for answers there.

Thomas thought of all the arguments against her plans, thought of all the struggles she would face raising a child alone. It wasn't so much her practical ability to care for and love a child he doubted, or the fact that she would be raising it without a father—many women raised large families after they were widowed. No, the struggle for Rosa would be how she would be shunned and hounded from society. Right now she might not think she cared about other ladies gossiping and pointing, snubbing her in the street and not inviting her to any of the social events of the year, but Thomas knew too well how lonely solitude could be. It would be a miserable existence.

'I know,' Rosa said softly. 'You don't have to tell me how difficult it will be. I will be an outcast, even my child might be an outcast, but I believe that love can make up for all of that. And I will love this baby much more than any family paid to take him or her.'

He nodded mutely. Who was he to disagree with her, his choices hadn't exactly been well thought out or well reasoned these past few years. After his father's and brother's deaths he'd more or less fled the country. He'd been halfway to France before he'd even stopped and thought about his decisions. If Rosa wanted to return to England to find a way to raise her child, then he had no business judging her.

Rosa wondered if he was judging her and then realised she didn't much care. It was true, she had thought of all the drawbacks to raising her child herself, but every single negative point was outweighed by the overwhelming love she already felt for the small life inside her.

'Do you think you'll ever go back?' Rosa asked, trying to change the focus of their conversation back to Lord Hunter.

'To England?' For a few moments he looked off into the distance as if he were deep in thought. 'I have a mother,' he said eventually.

Rosa laughed, she couldn't help herself. 'We all have mothers.'

Hunter sighed. 'Mine is particularly loving and understanding.'

'How awful for you,' Rosa murmured, thinking of her own mother's parting words to her. They had not been kind.

'She's lonely, rattling round in our big old house, and she's asked me to go home.'

'Will you?'

'She hasn't asked a single thing of me since…' He paused for a moment. 'Since I left England.'

'You might find you enjoy being back home, surrounded by the people who know and love you.'

Hunter grimaced, as if the idea was completely unpalatable. Rosa wondered if there was something else that made him reluctant to go home. All his talk of restlessness, of wanting to see the world and discover new places, was all very well, but she was astute enough to know it was a pile of lies. Hunter might feel all of that, but it wasn't the reason he was so unsettled, so reluctant to return home, Rosa could see it in his eyes. Something much bigger was keeping him away.

She was just settling back on to the seat of the curricle, making herself comfortable for the rest of the journey ahead when a movement to the side of the road caught her eye. She leaned forward, peering into the undergrowth to see whether it was some sort of animal or a person loitering where they shouldn't be.

'Alt!' a man shouted in Italian as he jumped from the bushes in front of the curricle. *Halt.*

Hunter didn't have many options. It was either rein in the horses or trample the tattily dressed young man.

Rosa felt her heart begin to pound in her chest and she had to keep her hands in her lap to keep them from trembling. She didn't recognise the man standing in front of the restless horses, but he must be there for her. In her month-long imprisonment in the Di Mercurios' villa she hadn't laid eyes on this man, but she had learnt that the Di Mercurio family was vast and the number of young men she could call cousin reached well into double figures. This must surely be some relation come to take her back.

Just as Rosa was about to grab hold of the reins and urge the horses forward she saw the pistol in the man's hand and paused for a second. Not because of the gun, not really. Of course the man could aim and fire and hit one of them, but hitting a moving target was difficult and she reckoned they had a good chance of getting away without injury to either of them. Rosa paused because of the strip of fabric covering the lower half of the man's face, as if he didn't want to be recognised.

'Don't move or I will shoot the lady,' another voice came from behind the curricle.

Rosa spun round and saw three more men similarly attired.

She glanced at Hunter, saw the expressions of irritation and disbelief flit over his face before it settled back to a stony, unreadable façade.

'Sorry, gentlemen, I don't speak Italian,' Hunter said, in an exaggerated, loud voice. 'English.'

Rosa frowned. She knew he spoke Italian, or at least she thought he did. She opened her mouth to translate for him and got a sharp dig in the ribs from his elbow. Quickly she closed her mouth again and moved a little closer to Hunter. She wasn't going to succeed in escaping from the Di Mercurios only to be killed by bandits on a dusty Italian road.

'Denaro!' the chief bandit shouted, then slowly, working his mouth around the unfamiliar word, 'Money!'

The three bandits from behind the curricle edged closer.

'I'm afraid I don't carry much with me,' Hunter said a little too flippantly for Rosa's liking. They were being threatened by four men with pistols and swords and here he was pretending not to understand them and refusing to hand anything over.

'Money,' the chief bandit demanded again.

A squat, swarthy man with the complexion similar to that of a toad jabbed Rosa lightly with the tip of his sword and leered at her, giving her a perfect view of his three remaining teeth, all black and rotten in his lower jaw.

Rosa fought the nausea that rose up from her stomach, desperately trying to suppress the gag that threatened to escape from her throat. Although she reasoned vomiting over a bandit might not be a bad way to get him to leave you alone.

'Money,' the toad man repeated, his accent thick and his eyes roaming over Rosa's body.

She felt Hunter shift in his seat beside her and wondered if he was reaching for his coin purse. Thinking of the small amount of money she'd been able to keep safe throughout the journey to Italy and her subsequent imprisonment, Rosa felt her fear melting away and a white-hot fury consuming her instead. They had no right to steal her money, no right to ruin her plans for the future.

Leaning forward, Rosa made to stand and give these bandits a piece of her mind when she felt a restraining hand on her arm.

'Sit down,' Hunter said calmly, as if he were talking about the weather at a garden party. 'Or you'll get us both killed.'

'At least I'm trying to do something,' Rosa hissed.

'Something reckless and stupid.'

'They will not get my money.'

'Is that small purse of yours worth your life?'

Rosa hesitated. He didn't understand. That small purse *was* her life. Without it she wouldn't have a way to fund her passage back to England.

She wouldn't even have a way to feed herself. She'd be forced back to the Di Mercurios, forced to throw herself on their mercy. No doubt she would be locked away for another five months and once she'd given birth they would take her child away from her.

Rosa was saved from having to answer by the toad man grabbing her by the waist and squeezing in a lascivious manner. With a squeal of outrage, she thumped him on the head and was just steadying herself to throw another punch when there was a flurry of movement beside her.

Hunter leapt from his seat, barrelled into one of the bandits, sending him crashing into the second man. Whilst the two criminals struggled to disengage from one another Hunter softly grabbed both their flailing pistols and fired a shot towards the chief bandit, making him dive back into the bushes.

Rosa watched in disbelief as Hunter sprinted after the man, leaping through the air as he reached the undergrowth and throwing a punch that sounded as though it hit its mark. There was a distinct crunch of bone and a yelp of pain, followed by a few moments' silence. Eventually Hunter hauled himself up out of the undergrowth with a casual grin.

The two men he'd disarmed moments ago

glanced at one another, then rushed towards him and Rosa heard herself gasp as Hunter sank to the floor and kicked out with a foot just as they reached him. Both men tripped, sprawling to the ground with shouts of pain. Quickly he aimed both pistols and fired a shot from each towards the bandits' heads.

Rosa squeezed her eyes shut, not wanting to see the explosion of blood and brains from the two bandits, but as she pressed her lids together she heard a low whimpering. Cautiously she peeked and saw a spasm of movement from the ground. For a moment she wondered if Hunter had missed from such a short range, but then realised he'd aimed a few inches above the men's heads.

'Run,' Hunter ordered. 'Now.'

Rosa watched as the two bandits wobbled to their feet and ran, not sparing a backwards glance for their compatriot left behind.

As Hunter turned slowly Rosa could feel her pulse beating in her throat, a warm, rhythmic reminder of how alive she felt right now. He strolled nonchalantly back towards the curricle, as if he was out for an evening walk and hadn't just single-handedly bested three armed bandits. In the mid-morning sun his blue eyes sparkled and Rosa had the sense he was enjoying himself.

Beside her the toad man hesitated, looking over his shoulder as if checking for possible escape routes.

'Run,' Hunter repeated, his voice low and dangerous.

For a moment Rosa thought the toad man would obey, but she saw the flash of defiance in his eyes just a second before he looped his arm around her waist and pulled her body tightly against his. She felt the cool metal of the pistol against her neck and knew this scared man holding her captive was very dangerous. He had been abandoned by his comrades and could see no way out. One false move and he would probably fire out of fear.

'There's no need for that,' Hunter said, keeping his tone soothing. 'Let the lady go and you have nothing to fear from me.'

Everyone present knew Lord Hunter was lying. He'd taken three men out without even breaking a sweat in the mid-morning sun, Rosa couldn't see a situation that worked out well for the toad man.

She felt the tremor of the bandit's hands, sensed his uncertainty as he shifted from one foot to the other.

'What's your name?' Hunter asked in flawless Italian.

'Er-Er-Ernesto,' the bandit stuttered.

'Well, Ernesto, why don't we make a deal? You let go of my friend here and I will let you walk away.'

'Walk away?' Ernesto asked in surprise.

'That's right. You haven't hurt either of us, haven't taken anything. I see no reason you can't just walk away from this.'

'I'm not stupid,' Ernesto said with a sneer. 'You'll kill me as soon as my back is turned.'

'Like I killed your comrades?'

Ernesto the toad man hesitated.

'Just start backing away. If you see me raise my pistol before you get out of range then shoot me, but I give you my word I will not harm you unless you make me.'

Rosa studied Lord Hunter's calm demeanour and reassuring expression. It was hard not to trust him, she realised.

'The money?' Ernesto asked, but Rosa could tell his heart wasn't in it.

'No, Ernesto. We leave here with our money. You leave with your life.'

Ten seconds passed, then twenty. Rosa could hear a soft mumbling as Ernesto reasoned his options out to himself. After what seemed like an eternity his grip on her loosened.

'Keep your pistols low,' Ernesto said. 'Or I'll shoot.'

Slowly he began backing away down the road, his eyes fixed on Thomas. Thomas stood still, his arms relaxed by his side, watching the bandit calmly. Rosa couldn't quite believe his heart wasn't pounding or his hands slick with sweat, but he looked completely composed.

As Ernesto got to the bend in the road he stopped for a moment before turning and running. They could hear his heavy footsteps for at least thirty seconds after he'd disappeared.

Rosa felt her body begin to shake and immediately Lord Hunter was by her side.

'Sit,' he commanded. 'Take deep breaths. You were very brave.'

As she attempted to limp back to the curricle Hunter gripped her gently and scooped her into his arms. The contact between their two bodies was a welcome comfort for Rosa and she held on tightly to his shoulders. As she felt his firm body pressed against hers Rosa glanced up and caught him looking down at her. He could feel it, too, she was sure of it. That need for physical touch, that desire for intimacy. She told herself it was just the shock, the stressful situation they'd been through together, but as he held her a little tighter Rosa wondered if that was all it was.

She half-expected her body to tense, to remember the last time a man had held her so closely, encircled her with his arms, but instead she felt her breathing become more steady and her racing heart slow as she was reassured by Lord Hunter's touch.

'You let him go,' she said as he placed her gently on the seat of the curricle.

'I gave my word.'

'You let all of them go.'

Hunter shrugged, but Rosa could see there had been a reason behind his decision. Most men would have inflicted maximum pain on bandits who threatened them and Lord Hunter had disarmed and bested them all without much effort. Rosa wouldn't have blamed him if there were four dead bodies strewn on the road right now.

'They would have killed us.'

Hunter chuckled. 'Bloodthirsty wench, aren't you?'

Rosa managed to smile.

'I don't think they would have killed us,' Thomas said simply. 'They were desperate, driven to do something terrible.'

'How do you know they were desperate?'

'Did you see the way they were dressed? How gaunt they were? These weren't successful criminals. And none of them knew how to fight.'

Rosa fell silent, contemplating what Hunter had just said.

'Circumstances can drive decent human beings to do almost anything,' Hunter said, looking off into the distance. 'And I suppose hunger is a real motivator.'

'Surely there have got to be better ways to make money than stealing, though?'

Hunter shrugged. 'Of course. But if you've been turned away from work, unable to provide food for your family, who knows what you might do.'

He moved away from her and began checking over the horses, murmuring soft words to soothe the skittish animals.

As she sat and watched him Rosa felt a new respect blossoming for the man who had saved her twice now. He might be a little arrogant and unapologetic at times, but there was something more to Lord Hunter. Rosa knew most men would have either panicked at being surrounded by bandits or become so furious they showed no compassion or mercy. It was rather refreshing to see a man think with his heart and not his fists.

'Where did you learn to fight like that?' she asked.

'Here and there.'

'In India?'

'Amongst other places.'

She wondered why he was so reticent talking about where he learned to defend himself so effortlessly.

'Ready?' he asked as he vaulted back up beside her.

Rosa nodded. Although they had come out unscathed she felt more than a little shaken by the encounter and was keen to be on their way.

Lord Hunter urged the horses forward and soon they were gliding through the country lanes. As Rosa felt her anxiety levels begin to drop she began to relax into the man beside her. It felt good to have even the slight physical contact of thigh against thigh after her months of isolation.

As her thoughts started to run away from her, tentative hopes spiralling out of control, Rosa forced herself to pull away. She'd lost her virtue and her future to one man, she would not lose anything else to another.

Chapter Five

'Tell me about the father,' Hunter said as he leaned back in his chair.

They were sitting on a terrace in the bustling village of Malcesine, sipping a rather delicious concoction of juices from tall glasses.

Rosa started in surprise at the bluntness of his question and coughed as the juice tickled her throat.

'The father?' she asked. She knew exactly what he was talking about, but she couldn't believe he'd asked the question so directly.

Hunter gestured to her abdomen and Rosa quickly laid a protective hand on the growing bump beneath her dress.

'The father of your baby. Who is he?'

'No one you would know.'

'An unsuitable suitor? A dastardly married man? A dashing young footman?'

'Shall we set about our enquiries?' Rosa asked.

'Sit back, relax. You've had a stressful morning. We can ask about a passage to England in an hour, nothing will change between then and now.'

'Except my desire to murder you,' Rosa muttered under her breath.

'What was that?'

She smiled sweetly and took another sip of her juice. It really was delicious. She could taste orange and a hint of lemon, but there was something else there, too.

Rosa tried to ignore Hunter's intense gaze as she drummed her fingers on the table, shifted in her chair and traced the condensation as it ran down the edge of the glass. He didn't ask the question again, just sat watching her, as if he knew she would crack and tell him eventually.

'What beautiful trees,' Rosa said, gesturing to a cluster of short trees near the water's edge.

Still Hunter said nothing, but that lazy smile she had begun to know well danced across his lips. She wondered how she could find a man so irritating, but still so attractive. It was his eyes, she pondered, you couldn't stay annoyed at a man whose eyes sparkled and glimmered with amusement all day long.

Again she shifted, trying to focus on watching the locals strolling arm in arm along the waterfront. It was unnerving, having someone watch you for such a length of time, and Rosa felt her composure slowly beginning to slip.

'Do you come here often?' she asked, trying to force a response out of Hunter.

'No.'

'You should. It truly is a beautiful spot.'

Silence again.

'Have you always been this annoying?' she asked with a sigh.

'My mother tells me I'm persistent.' Hunter gave a small shrug.

'That's a nice way of putting it.'

'Tell me about the father.'

'Why do you want to know?'

Hunter shrugged again. 'I'm interested. And it'll take your mind off our encounter today.'

That was true, Rosa hadn't thought of the bandits for a whole five minutes.

'He's our neighbour, a boy I grew up with.'

'Boy?'

Rosa grimaced. 'Man. He must be twenty-seven or twenty-eight by now, I suppose.'

'Old enough to behave better.'

'You don't know how he behaved.'

'You're here in exile in Italy rather than happily married in some country house in England.'

It was the truth, but that didn't mean it didn't

hurt. For a long time Rosa had imagined a life with David. A home of their own filled with beautiful children, the life she had been brought up to expect.

'So what happened?'

Rosa shook her head. She really did not want to talk about this. Even uttering David's name had the bile rising up in her throat and knots of tension forming across her shoulders.

'How about you?' she asked, desperate to change the subject. 'Any great loves in your life.'

Hunter smiled and shook his head, 'I've never found that special someone.'

'But you've looked?'

'Some people aren't destined to settle down.'

It was an odd statement, one that made Rosa pause and study the man in front of her for a moment.

'But you're titled, you have an estate. Isn't there a need for an heir?'

He shrugged. 'The estate will pass to some distant relative when I die.'

Although it was said casually she could see the pain in his eyes at the idea. Whatever he might say, this was an uncomfortable subject for Hunter.

'You wouldn't rather it went to your son, your own flesh and blood?'

'That is never going to happen so there is no point in mourning what never could be.'

'Why—?' Rosa started, but a small hand tugging at her sleeve cut her off.

'Please, miss, spare some money. I haven't eaten for three days.' A small girl stood looking up at her with large brown eyes in a skinny face.

Rosa hesitated and then reached for her coin purse. She might not have much money, and what she did have she needed for the passage home and her new life, but it was hard to ignore the real pleading in the young girl's eyes.

'Rosa, no,' Hunter shouted, trying to grab her hand, but it was too late. As soon as the coin purse was out in the open an older boy swooped in and grabbed it from her palm. At high speed both he and the girl ran in different directions, weaving through the crowd.

'No,' Rosa whispered, her heart plummeting as she realised her whole future had just been ripped away from her.

Hunter was on his feet immediately, darting after the boy, but Rosa could see straight away he would never be able to catch him. Hunter might be fast, but the boy knew the streets and was small enough to slip between the crowds.

Gripping the edge of the table, Rosa felt her breathing become shallower and could hear a harsh rasping coming from her throat. Without any money she was doomed. She had the choice of life on the streets in a foreign country or crawling back to the Di Mercurios.

'I can't go back,' she whispered. 'I won't go back.'

She looked down at the dress she was wearing, that would fetch her a small sum, but her modest jewellery had been taken from her by her grandmother when she had arrived at the villa. She owned nothing else in the world except the clothes she was wearing.

'I'm sorry,' Hunter said, returning to the table, his face flushed from exertion. 'I lost him in the crowd.'

Rosa shook her head, unable to get any words out. She'd been so pleased when they had escaped the bandits with her purse intact, she'd never thought it might be at risk here in this idyllic village.

'Was that all the money you had?' he asked. Gone was his normal jovial tone, replaced by concern and compassion.

'Everything.'

Hunter raked a hand through his short hair, causing tufts to stick up at the front.

'I can't go back to them,' Rosa whispered again to herself.

Anything would be better than that. Maybe she could find work somewhere, save up the money for a passage home. As soon as the idea entered her mind she dismissed it. If there was no work for able-bodied young men then no one was going to employ a pregnant woman.

'Rosa, look at me,' Hunter said, taking her hand in his own.

As his fingers gripped hers Rosa felt some of her panic begin to subside. It was as if Hunter was tethering her to reality, stopping her from plummeting into a deep despair.

'We will figure something out. All is not lost.'

'That was all my money. Everything I own.'

Gently he stroked the back of her hand with his thumb. Rosa looked up and met his eyes and realised that whatever he said she trusted him. It was ridiculous, she'd only known the man a day, but if he said all was not lost then maybe it would work out.

'Come,' he said, pulling her to her feet. 'I need to think.'

She allowed him to tuck her hand into the crook of his elbow, lay down a few coins for their drinks and lead her away from the riverside tavern. She leaned heavily on his arm, tapping the cane against the cobblestones for a little extra support, but out here in the heat of the day her ankle ached.

'I'm ruined,' Rosa murmured as they weaved their way through the crowds. Not ruined in the sense of a loss of virtue, that had happened many months ago, but all the way through her ordeal she'd had some hope, a plan to make things better.

Hunter didn't say anything, just continued down towards the water's edge.

'Look out there,' he said as they reached the promenade that ran along the edge of the lake.

Rosa looked, following the direction his extended finger was pointing in. The sun glinted off the water and in the distance the hills surrounding the lake were shielded in a thin heat haze.

'What am I looking at?'

Hunter didn't answer, he was looking down at his hand in horror. Rosa followed his gaze, but as soon as he noticed she was looking, too, it was as if a mask came down over his face and his hand promptly dropped to his side.

'What's wrong?' Rosa asked.

'Stay there,' he ordered her, not giving her a chance to answer before striding off along the promenade.

He had to get away. Away from the crowds, away from Rosa's concerned enquiries and away from the stifling heat that threatened to consume him. Forcing himself to walk and not run, Thomas headed away from the village.

'Lord Hunter,' he heard Rosa call in the distance, but her voice barely registered in his mind.

I will not look.

Resolutely he kept his eyes fixed on a tree in the distance, willing himself not to look down.

His resolve cracked within thirty seconds. The first glance was fleeting and brief, but when he saw his hands weren't moving rhythmically and of their own accord he managed to gain control of himself a little and take a second look.

Sinking down on to the stone wall that ran along the lakefront, Thomas held his hands out in front of him. As he had pointed out over the lake there had been a definite tremor, an uncontrolled shaking of his hand. It had been small, probably unnoticeable to anyone but him, but he could not pretend it hadn't been there.

Now his hands were steady and unmoving as he studied them. Thomas exhaled, trying to calm his racing heart and dampen the nausea that rose from his stomach. For a few moments he had thought it was the beginning of the end, that the disease that had claimed his father and his brother was starting to develop in him.

It always began this way—a minor tremor, an

uncontrolled movement. Followed by memory loss, personality change and the ever-worsening rhythmic jerky movements and a loss of co-ordination. His older brother Michael had developed his first symptoms when he was just twenty and died at twenty-eight. Thomas's age now. Their father had been a little more fortunate, surviving into his forties. It was a well-kept secret, the Hunter family curse, but generation after generation showed signs of affliction.

Maybe I'll be one of the lucky ones.

It was what Thomas prayed for every day, that he would be one of the few the disease skipped. Not every member of the Hunter family was affected, but there was no way to know if you would succumb until the day you died.

Thomas rested his head in his hands and closed his eyes. Every morning he inspected his body for any unnatural movements, any clue that he might be developing the thing he feared the most. For a moment there he had been convinced that was it for him, that his time on earth was up. One thing Thomas was sure of was that he wouldn't let this disease rob him of his dignity and his hope. If he was ever sure his turn had come, then he would find a more dignified way to depart this world, even if it was considered a mortal sin to commit suicide.

'Lord Hunter,' Rosa said as she approached him slowly, warily.

She'd followed him. Of course she had.

'What's wrong?'

He took a second, flashed a charming smile and stood. 'Nothing, nothing at all.'

'Then why did you run off?'

'I have a proposition for you,' he said, knowing it was the only way to get Rosa to drop the subject. 'Let me escort you home.'

He had to smile at Rosa's shocked expression: the gaping mouth, wide eyes and rapid blinking of her eyelids. Over the years he had become a master of concealing his fears of the illness that might one day claim him and distraction was a great technique.

'Home?'

'Back to England. To whatever friend you hope will take you in.'

'Why would you do that?'

Thomas shrugged. He'd made the suggestion impulsively, but the more he thought about it the more he warmed to the idea.

'I need to return home. I owe that much to my mother. It wouldn't be gentlemanly to abandon you in your hour of need, so why not combine the two objectives?'

'It's too much, I could never ask that of you.'

'What other options do you have?'

Rosa fell silent. She was in no position to turn down the offer of assistance in whatever form.

'You are sure you're happy to return to England? I wouldn't want you to return solely on my account.'

Thomas thought about it before answering and found he was. It would be pleasant to stroll around his estate and reminisce with his mother. He knew he would not stay there indefinitely, but a few weeks, maybe a month, and then he could pick a new destination for his travels. Thomas found the idea of revisiting the home he had once been so happy in rather appealing and knew if he wanted to return for a short period he should do so soon. Who knew if he would get another opportunity?

'Quite sure.'

Rosa shook her head in disbelief, then threw her arms around him.

'Thank you,' she whispered.

He had never heard two words uttered so sincerely or with such relief.

'I will find a way to reimburse you any expenses accrued once we get back to England.'

Thomas waved a dismissive hand—the cost of a passage on a ship and a few weeks in various guest houses was the least of his worries. It wasn't as though he would be able to take his money with him when he died.

'Thank you, Lord Hunter,' Rosa replied. Thomas could see she was struggling to hold back the tears.

'Call me Thomas. We're going to be spending much time together.'

'Thomas,' she repeated, smiling up at him.

'And I shall call you Rosa.'

'You do already.'

He grinned, took her hand and kissed her just below the knuckles. It felt good to have a purpose after all this time.

'This afternoon we shall return to the villa. There are a few things I will need to tie up before we depart. I will arrange for us to leave early next week.'

He would terminate his lease on the villa. As much as he loved the comfortable dwelling and beautiful views, he realised it was time for him to move on. The momentary fear that he might be entering his last few months of healthy life had jolted him into action. There was more of the world to see, more to experience. He would travel home with Rosa, visit his mother for a few weeks and then spin the large globe that sat in his father's study. *His* study. Wherever his finger landed, that would be where he travelled next.

As they walked back along the promenade Thomas tried to summon some of his normal excitement when contemplating a new adventure, but this time his heart was not really in it. His mind was preoccupied with thoughts of home: the rolling green hills, the woods he'd played in as a boy, even the peaceful spot right at the edge of the estate where his father and brother were laid to rest.

Chapter Six

Dearest Caroline,

I hope you are keeping well. It seems like a century has passed since we saw each other last winter. I was very saddened to hear the news of Lord Trowridge's passing. Please forgive me for the lateness of my condolences. I have been out of the country for some months, but you are never far from my thoughts.

How is young Rupert? I remember the week I spent with you in January with such fondness. He was such an adorable little baby and I'm sure he's bringing you even more joy as he grows.

I do not know if any gossip has reached your ears down in Dorset, but I am in a little bit of trouble. These last three months I've been exiled from London, sent to stay with my mother's family in northern Italy. I won't bore you with all the sordid details, but I have found myself with child, and you can imagine Mother's reaction to that little scandal.

Her plan was to tell the world I had gone to nurse my ailing grandmother—who is as strong as an ox and still shows up the young farmhands. I would reappear in society in a year and no one would be the wiser. My child was to be adopted by some Italian family and I would never set eyes on him or her again.

I know I should probably have been grateful, Caroline, but I couldn't bear the thought of my baby calling someone else Mama. Out of everyone I think you would understand the most.

Anyway, I escaped and now I've met an English gentleman who has offered to escort me back to England. He seems very capable and I feel safe in his company, even if he is rather forceful and confident in character.

Now I have the biggest favour to ask of you. I know if I return home my mother will send me back to her family in Italy and if that happens they will take my baby away from me. Caroline, can I come and stay with you whilst I wait out the rest of my pregnancy and work out exactly how to live my life as the mother of an illegitimate child? For I will not give up my baby for anyone, no matter what the future brings.

I remember you saying you have a certain freedom now Lord Trowridge has passed and I wonder if I can impose on you for a short while? I would be happy to be hidden away, or to live a simple life in one of the cottages on your estate.

I have no money and nowhere else to turn. Caroline, I'm sorry to ask so much of you, but I hope one day I will be able to repay you.

We will be leaving Italy any day now. Lord Hunter is just tying up a few loose ends from his life here and then we will be starting our journey back to England. I am not sure of the exact date we will arrive in Dorset, but perhaps I might call on you when we arrive to hear your answer.

I cannot wait to see you and young Rupert again.

All my love,
Rosa

Rosa sat back, folded the letter in half and slipped it into the envelope. She was asking a lot of her old friend, maybe too much, but she didn't have much choice. Caroline was kind and loyal and wasn't one to worry overly much about what others thought of her. Rosa knew her oldest friend wouldn't hesitate to take her in, but that didn't mean asking was any easier.

'Who are you writing to?' Thomas asked as he sauntered across the terrace, tossing a ripe orange up in the air and catching it with ease.

'Caroline, the Dowager Lady Trowridge,' Rosa corrected herself. 'She's my oldest and dearest friend.'

'She sounds severe.'

Rosa laughed. No one who had ever met Caroline would describe her as severe.

'She's twenty years old, no more than five feet tall and laughs at absolutely everything.'

'Not your average widow, then?'

Thomas was of course right, despite there being many young widows in society, the term often conjured up images of statuesque women in their later years presiding over a large family with an iron will.

'Not your average dowager,' Rosa agreed. 'She married at eighteen, had her son at nineteen and was a widow by the age of twenty.'

'Poor girl.' Then Thomas paused. 'Or maybe very astute.'

Rosa rather thought it was the latter. Caroline hadn't protested when the childless Lord Trowridge had started courting her, she'd actively encouraged it. He was kind, wealthy and willing to give her years of independence in exchange for a short time dedicated to making an old man happy. Rosa thought the union had been a success; Lord Trowridge had got a pretty young bride for the last months of his life and now Caroline was in charge of her son's upbringing and the entire Trowbridge estate until Rupert came of age.

'I've informed her of my plans to return to England and asked for her help when we arrive.' Rosa took a breath, then pressed on. 'I'm sure she would be happy to lend me the money to reimburse you for the travel expenses.'

Thomas shrugged. 'It doesn't cost that much for a passage from Italy to England, I'm sure I can afford it. We can find another way for you to repay me.'

Rosa's eyes widened and she felt the blush begin to creep into her cheeks.

Thomas threw his head back and laughed heartily at her expression. 'I meant you can cook me another one of those delicious meals.'

Rosa's blush deepened, but she resisted the urge to cover her face with her hands. Of course Thomas wasn't proposing she repaid his kindness with intimacy. Throughout the week she had stayed with him there hadn't been even a flicker of flirtation from him. He had meant it when he'd told her that her virtue was safe with him on the first evening of their acquaintance, he hadn't behaved improperly once. Rosa knew she should be thankful, especially after her awful experience with David, but she felt a tiny surge of disappointment every time Thomas didn't take an opportunity to get closer to her.

Gaining back control of herself, Rosa smiled. 'Next time I'll add less garlic.'

It wouldn't be quite so galling if Rosa didn't feel her heart start pounding in her chest every time Thomas stepped in close to her. He was an attractive man, his body toned and muscular from the early morning swims and his eyes full of mischief and laughter. Rosa knew she never wanted to get involved with a man again, but Thomas tested her resolve sometimes. At least when he wasn't ordering her around or teasing her.

'Signora Felcini is coming to cook tonight,' Rosa said. 'So I'm sure I can persuade her to give me one last lesson before we leave.'

The elderly Italian woman who came in to cook and clean for Thomas a few times a week had taken Rosa under her wing. She ordered Rosa around in rapid Italian and expected her to chop and help with the evening meal, but in return Rosa was treated to a lesson in rustic Italian cookery. In Rosa's mind it was a fair exchange.

'I have made arrangements for us to leave first thing tomorrow morning. Your family are causing a bit of a stir searching for you nearby, so I think it would be prudent to leave as soon as possible.'

'Thank you,' Rosa said quietly.

She still wasn't quite sure why Thomas was helping her, it wasn't as though he got much out of their arrangement, just trouble from the Di Mercurios and the expense of transporting her to England. Whatever his motivations Rosa was keen not to examine them too carefully; Thomas was her only hope now she was penniless and stuck so far from home.

Thomas wiped the sweat from his brow, adjusted the bandages on his hands and squared up to the punch-bag hanging from the branches of the sturdy olive tree. Quickly he hooked and jabbed, dancing lightly on his toes around the inanimate opponent.

He'd learned to box at school, along with all the other sons of the gentry, classes where their wiry games master instructed the small group on the basics of boxing. Of course that had been no use for the real world and nearly four years ago, when he'd first been beaten and robbed on his journey through Europe, he'd vowed to learn to defend himself better. The first year of his travels he'd been attacked five times. It was unsurprising really. He was a well-dressed young man who needed to carry money with him—a prime target for any ambitious criminal. After each attack Thomas had retreated for a while, licked his wounds, then restarted his training with renewed vigour. He picked up techniques from the countries he visited, practised his defensive and attacking modes every day, and soon he no longer had to hide his modest purse on his person or avoid the more unsavoury areas of the cities he visited.

Now training every evening had become part of his daily routine, just like the refreshing early morning swim in the lake.

With one last high kick Thomas began unwrapping the bandages from his hands. He loved this feeling just after he'd exercised, the heady mix of exhaustion and exhilaration. Over the years he'd developed a deep-seated respect for his body and worked hard to keep it in top physical shape. Too many people took their physical health for granted, but he'd seen how quickly a man could be robbed of his ability to control his limbs, to walk, to run, to jump. He was determined to enjoy every minute he had conscious control of his muscles so he would regret nothing if and when the Hunter family curse struck.

'Do you think...?' Rosa said as she rounded the corner of the villa and came into view. 'Oh.'

Thomas had to hide a smile. She became so flustered whenever she caught sight of his bare skin, a deep flush spread across her cheeks and she seemed to lose her ability to speak for a few seconds. He liked to watch her rally, to refuse to give in to her embarrassment and try to continue as if nothing was amiss.

Nonchalantly Thomas pulled on his shirt. No need to make the poor girl suffer any more than was necessary.

'Yes?' he asked.

Rosa wasn't an innocent, her growing bump attested to the fact that she'd been intimate with at least one man, but Thomas had the feeling that despite the fact she was soon to be a mother she wasn't actually well acquainted with the pleasures of the flesh. For a moment his body tensed at the idea of being the one to make her moan and sing out with pleasure, but quickly he pushed the thought away. They had a long journey ahead of them together, he needed to be in control of himself and banish these intriguing but unwelcome fantasies.

'Do you think we should eat outside?'

Thomas nodded. It was their last night at the villa and he wanted to watch the sunset over the lake one last time.

Together they set the table and, whilst Thomas poured the wine, Rosa brought out the dish she had prepared with Signora Felcini. As always it looked and smelled delicious; Thomas could detect hints of rosemary and garlic and a garnish of lemon sprinkled over lightly cooked fish.

As he sat down and watched her serve up the fish and accompanying vegetables he was struck by what an idyllic domestic scene this was. For many men this was all they desired: a good-looking woman as a companion, someone to run their household whilst they amused themselves with other pursuits. Even Thomas, with his deep-seated desire to travel, had to admit there was a certain appeal to the idea. Rosa would make an ideal companion. She was interesting to talk to, good-natured and kind. Of course he wasn't looking for someone to settle down with, but he wondered if she might be able to solve another problem for him.

He had just picked up his fork and tasted the first mouthful of the delicious dish in front of him when he heard a commotion coming from the front of his villa. At first, as he listened to the raised voices and clatter of feet on the road, Thomas assumed it was drunken travellers making the racket, but as the voices came nearer he felt his muscles tense and his senses heighten.

There was a hammering at the front door of the villa and Thomas just had time to see Rosa's knuckles turning white as she gripped the table before he was on his feet and moving inside.

'Stay out of sight,' he instructed quietly, in a tone that brooked no argument.

Rosa nodded and wobbled out of her chair before grasping the cane she was still having to rely on if walking more than a few paces.

'Englishman!' an angry voice called out in English with a thick accent. 'We know you're in there.'

Thomas suppressed the grin that was trying to break out on his face as he strode to the door. Already he could feel the energy coursing through his body, the anticipation of the confrontation making him feel alive. He never went looking for trouble, but Thomas couldn't deny he enjoyed the feeling he got when the odds were stacked against him in an encounter such as this.

Just as the hammering began again Thomas threw open the door with a flourish and flashed his most charming and infuriatingly calm smile.

'What can I help you fine gentlemen with this evening?' he asked, making sure he caught the eye of each man in turn. In total there were five; five small and wiry Italian men who looked as though they'd smelled blood and were eager for some more.

'We know you have her,' the man at the front of the group said.

'Who do I have the pleasure of talking to?' Thomas asked.

'Antonio Di Mercurio.'

'Ah, the lecherous one.' Rosa had told him much about her stay with the Di Mercurio family over the past week and Thomas was intrigued to match the characters to faces. 'That would make you two Piero and Michele.' He gestured to the other two young men roughly the same age as Antonio. 'And you must be Luca and Luigi, these fine gentlemen's fathers.'

'Where is my niece?' one of the older men snarled.

'Rosa? Oh, she left days ago. Decided to take a ship to India, I think, or was it the Caribbean?

I know it was somewhere far from here so she would never have to see the people who had kept her prisoner again.'

'Prisoner? We're her family. You're the one who's abducted her, stolen her from our care. Brought her to live in sin with you.' This was from Antonio again.

'Gentlemen,' Thomas said calmly, his thoughts returning to his dinner cooling on the terrace, 'tell me how you think this little expedition of yours is going to end?'

None of the men spoke and Thomas nodded in satisfaction. Although he'd led a private life here in Italy his reputation was still whispered about by the young men in the taverns. He was not a man to be trifled with, no doubt why the Di Mercurios had taken quite so long to approach his residence and demand Rosa back, and why there were five of them when ordinarily one would do.

'Turn around and return home and we will say nothing more on this matter.' Thomas even managed a friendly smile. One of the younger men recoiled, stepping back on to the foot of another family member.

'We will go to the magistrate,' Luca or Luigi threatened.

'That is not a good idea,' Thomas said slowly and quietly. He had learnt long ago that men responded to a low, quiet threat more than a shouted one and he saw the evidence again today as the Di Mercurio men huddled together for a few minutes, arguing fiercely in hushed voices.

'Rosa,' Antonio shouted eventually, craning to see over Thomas's shoulder. 'You are on your own. The family washes its hands of you. Go gallivanting about Italy with this scoundrel if you like, we no longer care. But just remember you will never again have the protection of the Di Mercurio name.'

Thomas watched as the Di Mercurio men each gave him a particularly dirty look, one of the older ones holding his eye and spitting on the ground by his feet.

'Good evening to you all,' Thomas called cheerily, before turning back into the house and closing the door behind him.

He almost laughed as he caught sight of Rosa in the corner of the room holding her cane aloft as if it were a weapon, but then saw the expression on her face. He crossed over to her with long, quick strides and instinctively took her into his arms, feeling her shudder with relief as he pulled her to him.

As he held her close, inhaling the sweet scent of her hair and feeling the pounding of her heart through both their chests, Thomas felt a momentary pang of desire. Not for Rosa—well, not exactly—but more for this lifestyle, this experience. Part of him longed to have a woman and maybe even a child to look after, someone to put above all else, someone to cherish and protect. He knew that was never in his future; he couldn't bear finding a woman he loved, marrying her and then having to watch her watch him suffer through the illness that might strike at any time. It wasn't fair and he wasn't that cruel.

Not everyone marries for love, the small voice in his head whispered.

It was something he had been contemplating for a while, but up until now it hadn't seemed possible. He could marry, find a kind and patient woman to give his family name to, someone he could take home to his mother and leave as a companion for the lonely older woman. It wasn't a great romance, but many of his contemporaries had married for far worse reasons.

As Rosa's head sunk to his shoulder the idea gripped hold of him and wouldn't let go. He could marry her, protect her and her unborn child, and rid himself of the guilt he felt at leaving his mother behind whilst he travelled the world in one swoop. It was madness, but maybe no more so than any other paths in life.

Chapter Seven

Rosa frowned as Thomas darted forward to take her hand and help her down from the carriage. He was being attentive, too attentive, and it was making her nervous. They had been travelling for three days, long dusty days spent in the carriage watching the scenery pass by, and for those three days Thomas had been the most perfect of travelling companions. He'd held doors for her, assisted her at every opportunity and organised their accommodation without her having to lift a finger.

'We'll rest here for the night,' he said, gesturing to the ramshackle coaching inn by the side of the road.

Rosa nodded, knowing she didn't have much choice in the matter. The whole journey had been taken out of her hands. Thomas had seen to it that she never lacked any possible comfort, but hadn't consulted with her on the details of their route across northern Italy to Venice. She knew she shouldn't complain, that was how things had to happen, but it was beginning to irk her to have all her decisions made for her.

'Have a rest before dinner,' Thomas instructed and Rosa felt herself stiffen.

'I think I'll go for a stroll,' she said, just to be perverse. Truly a lie down sounded heavenly and, despite being cooped up in the carriage for most of the afternoon, Rosa felt weary all the way down to her bones, but she refused to let anyone tell her what to do with her life ever again. For twenty years she had acquiesced to her mother's every wish, followed every rule, only to be thrown out and disowned after one single mistake. Never again would she allow Thomas or anyone else to make her decisions for her.

Thomas looked around sceptically. 'A walk? Here?'

Rosa followed his gaze and had to admit it maybe wasn't the most picturesque of spots. Their journey had taken them through rolling hills and towering mountains, past shimmering lakes and lush fields, but this little spot by the coaching inn was far from pretty. On the edge of a small town, the air was thick with the smell of manure and smoke and the buildings that lined the road were in various stages of disrepair. A stray dog wandered aimlessly down the middle of the road, sniffing at the heaped piles of rubbish and every so often letting out a mournful whimper.

'I need to stretch my legs,' Rosa lied, cursing her stubbornness. She could be heading towards a comfortable bed and a short rest before the evening meal, but instead she was going to have to pretend to want to explore the town.

Thomas regarded her for a moment through narrowed eyes and then shrugged. 'If that is what you desire. I will enquire about rooms for the night and then I will escort you.'

It was too much. Rosa wanted to scream, to grasp him by the shoulders and shake him until he told her why he was being quite so obliging. Before they had set out on their journey he had been kind, certainly, and extremely generous offering to escort her back to England, but he had teased her, joked with her. He would have wheedled out the real reason Rosa had refused to rest within a few minutes of light probing. She didn't know why he had changed, but it was making her feel uncomfortable, as if he wanted something from her.

As Thomas walked away Rosa stifled a sigh.

If only it were as simple as him wanting *her*, but there hadn't been any suggestion that he found her remotely attractive. She glanced down at her growing bump and had to smile; she supposed her days of attracting eligible young men were well and truly over. Despite pretending not to care Rosa knew this was more difficult to adjust to than she had initially thought. Sometimes it was nice to be wanted, to be desired. From now on she would be either a fallen woman or a mother, neither of which were thought of as conventionally attractive.

That still left her with the question of what it was exactly that Thomas wanted.

She watched him disappear into the coaching inn and waited for a few minutes, feeling her dissatisfaction grow. She wanted to kick something, vent her frustration, but with her ankle still paining her from time to time she knew it wasn't a very sensible idea.

When Thomas hadn't emerged after five minutes Rosa turned her back to the inn and started to wander away. He could easily catch her up and she was still in view of the inn, it wasn't as though anything untoward would happen to her just a few paces down the road.

'Pretty flower for a pretty lady,' an old woman croaked as Rosa walked past her.

'I'm sorry, I haven't any money,' Rosa replied, smiling kindly at the elderly woman, and started to turn away. She spoke slowly, testing out each word in her head before articulating it.

'Never mind, my dear, it pleases me to brighten up the day of a pretty young thing.'

The old woman levered herself up from the battered chair she'd been sitting in and approached Rosa, taking her firmly by the arm and looking up into her eyes.

Rosa struggled not to squirm under the piercing nature of the stare and gently tried to pull away.

'You're troubled, my dear, it doesn't do for a woman with child to be so worried.'

Rosa glanced down, wondering if her pregnancy had reached the stage where it was obvious to passers-by on the street.

'Come, let us see if we can't relieve you of some of those worries.'

Without really meaning to Rosa felt herself following the elderly lady in through a crooked wooden door and taking a seat on an upturned wooden crate. There was something mesmerising about her companion, almost hypnotic, and Rosa felt herself begin to relax as the woman bustled around preparing a pot of tea.

'I really should be getting back,' Rosa said

as the woman poured water into a battered old kettle.

The old woman didn't reply and Rosa wondered if she had even heard her. It would be extremely rude just to get up and leave, but she didn't really know what she was doing in this stranger's house.

'You worry about your future,' the old woman said. 'And the future of your unborn child.'

'Doesn't every woman worry about her future? Every mother worries about her child.'

The old woman pottered about the small room some more before setting a cup of tea in front of her. Rosa hadn't had a decent cup of tea since she'd left England many months ago and she longed to cradle the warm china in her hands, inhale the distinctive scent and take a sip.

'Go ahead,' the old woman said. 'Drink.'

With a backwards glance over her shoulder at the empty doorway Rosa picked up the cup and sipped. It was heavenly and reminded her of home, of long winter afternoons curled up on the window seat in the library reading book after book, watching the rain splatter against the glass, or warm summer afternoons sipping tea in the shade and her father declaring, *'Hot drinks do cool you down in warm weather.'*

'Mothers worry about their children,' the older woman said as Rosa took her first sip. 'But most do not have to worry about the scandal of birthing a bastard.'

Rosa choked on her mouthful of tea, the warm liquid spluttering out of her mouth as she looked up in shock.

'It is written on your face, my dear, but do not fret, I do not mean to announce your secret to the world. I only wish to help.'

'Help?' This was all becoming a little surreal.

'Do you not wish to know what the future holds, how you will live, what dreams for your baby will be realised?'

Suddenly all the pieces slotted into place. This woman was some sort of fortune teller, a wise woman who made her living out of luring weary travellers in from the street, then promising to reveal the mysteries of the future.

'I have to go,' Rosa said, standing up abruptly.

'Go, then.' The woman shrugged.

For some reason Rosa didn't move. She didn't believe in the supernatural, had never queued with the simpering, excited village girls at the fayres to have her palm read, to hear the lies about who she might marry or what she might achieve. She could understand the appeal, having a sliver of hope that the predictions might come true, but she had never wanted to listen to the same words as every girl in front and behind her.

'I have no money,' Rosa repeated.

'I don't ask for any.'

'Then what do you want?'

'To relieve some of your worries, my dear.'

Rosa sank back into her chair.

'Come, give me your hand.'

Rosa stretched out her hand, palm upwards, and felt herself stiffen momentarily as the old woman took hold of it and closed her eyes.

'You've had much suffering in your past. A loss of innocence, a betrayal of trust. You're hurting more than you care to admit.'

The words sliced into her and Rosa had to remind herself it wasn't anything that wasn't obvious from the way she carried herself and the fact she was pregnant and unescorted.

'You carry a broken heart, but don't want anyone else to know how badly you were hurt.'

Rosa squeezed her eyes closed as the memory of David's hot breath against her neck came crashing back. The memory she'd tried so hard to forget, the hot, sharp pain and the stone-cold dread.

'Hush, my dear. We all get hurt in this world, it is what you do afterwards that defines you as a woman.'

Rosa was just about to pull her hand away, to break the connection between her and this strange, observant old woman when the twig-like fingers tightened around hers.

'Now for the future.'

'Rosa.' Thomas's voice came low but insistent from the doorway and Rosa felt herself tensing with guilt. Slowly, with a great effort to remain calm and composed, she turned and faced him. She had nothing to feel ashamed about, no reason she could not go wherever she pleased, talk to whoever she wanted.

'What is going on here?' His voice was severe with a hint of concern and Rosa realised she was pleased to have jolted him from the polite persona he had been hiding behind these last few days.

'Just a cup of tea and a talk with a lonely old woman,' the fortune teller said with a secret smile towards Rosa.

'I was worried about you.'

She should have waited for him as she'd agreed, Rosa knew that, but she found she couldn't apologise for wandering off on her own.

'You're suffocating me,' she said quietly.

'Suffocating you?'

She nodded, not able to explain exactly what she meant, just wanting him to understand she'd noticed the difference in him these last few days.

'Come, we'll talk about this in private.'

Rosa was about to protest, but stopped herself. She didn't really want all the citizens of this small town hearing their argument. Thomas took her arm and just as he was about to lead her out Rosa looked back to thank the woman for her time.

'I don't think I need to tell you your future,' the old woman said, leaning in close so only Rosa could hear, a broad grin on her wrinkled face.

Before she could respond Thomas had guided her back into the street and started marching down the road. Rosa almost had to run to keep up, her body tilting to one side as she tried not to strain her injured ankle.

'Where are we going?' she asked, breathless.

'Somewhere private.'

'Back to the inn?'

'That's not private enough for what I have to say.'

His tone of voice told her all she needed to know. He was angry, although she couldn't quite make out why.

He didn't stop walking until they were well outside the town boundaries and then it was only to vault over a low wall. His hands were surprisingly gentle as he leaned back across the wall, gripped Rosa around the waist and lifted her over.

They were standing in a field of wheat, the green shoots just turning golden at the tips. For a moment Thomas's hands stayed in place, holding her above her hips, and Rosa felt her heart begin to flutter as his eyes met hers. There was something new in his gaze, something that hadn't been there before, and Rosa found she was unable to look away.

'Don't do anything like that again,' he said softly. 'I was worried about you.'

All the rebellion and the fire she had felt when he'd burst into the old woman's house and demanded she leave fizzled out with that one sentence. He was worried about her. He cared for her safety.

'I'm sorry,' Rosa murmured, still not able to look away.

'Why did you go off alone?'

Rosa tried to collate a sentence in her head, but found as soon as she thought of the words they were whisked away. Something strange was happening to her body, a heat was rising from deep inside her and she was unable to think of anything but the man in front of her.

'I wouldn't have been much longer in the coaching inn.'

'It wasn't that…' Rosa began, trying to make him understand it hadn't been impatience that had led her to wander the town unescorted. 'I felt stifled, constrained. I needed some time alone.'

Thomas dropped his hands from her waist and Rosa had to resist the urge to grip them and put them back.

This reaction to Thomas, this stirring inside her, was unnerving to say the least. He was an attractive man, both physically and in so many other ways, but Rosa hadn't expected to ever be attracted to another man again. Not after what David had done to her. It shouldn't matter that Thomas's eyes sparkled in the sunlight, that he had protected her at every opportunity and could make her laugh with a single sentence. Rosa knew she should be wary of all men, no matter their positive attributes, but with Thomas she seemed to want to throw all caution to the wind.

'Stifled?' Thomas repeated, turning half-away from her and looking out over the fields.

'When we were at the villa we laughed all the time. You teased me, challenged me.'

She glanced up at him, wondering if the silence meant he was offended.

Thomas sighed. 'And then suddenly I changed.'

Rosa nodded.

He remained still and quiet for a few minutes, but Rosa could see he was choosing his next words, his next explanation carefully. As she waited she felt her pulse quicken with anticipation. She wasn't sure what she wanted him to say, what reason she wanted him to give, but she did want him to touch her again, to take her hand and look into her eyes as he spoke.

Thomas's mind was reeling. It wasn't working, his policy of polite chivalry. A plan had begun to form in his mind on their last evening at the villa, as the Di Mercurios retreated and Rosa had looked at him with those big, worried eyes. A plan that would protect her from the worst the world had to offer whilst conferring certain advantages for his life as well.

He was considering asking Rosa to marry him, and soon. Of course he hadn't fallen in love with the girl, she was pretty, good company, and rather stoical given all the world had thrown at her, but he wasn't interested in love or romance. Despite this he did think they could be of use to one another.

Thomas kept repeating to himself the advantages Rosa would gain from the marriage: a stable home, a decent future, no fear of raising an illegitimate child, but he knew that was to try to assuage the guilt he would feel for deceiving her. He liked Rosa, respected her, but if he were to propose it would be surrounded with half-truths and lies.

He needed to make a decision. If he were to go ahead with his plan, then ideally they would need to wed before they set sail for England. That way the marriage would be a *fait accompli* when they arrived home, with no way of anyone interfering with the result.

'You look so serious,' Rosa said quietly. She raised her hand and hesitantly touched his forehead, trying to smooth out the frown lines between his eyes. It was an intimate gesture, one that he could see she had made on impulse, but her cool fingers felt soothing on his skin. She'd make a good wife, there was no doubt about it—not that he was planning on sticking around to take advantage of a traditional marriage.

'I'm sorry I've been behaving strangely,' Thomas said. 'I've had a lot on my mind.'

'I'm sorry I wandered off. I never meant to worry you.'

'I'm sorry I reacted so brusquely, I thought you might be in danger.'

'I'm sorry…' Rosa began, but was interrupted by Thomas's raised hands.

'Enough, enough. I think it is safe to say we're both sorry for our recent behaviours.'

Rosa smiled softly at him and Thomas felt something tightening inside him. Quickly he suppressed the feeling. That was the last thing he needed, an unwanted attraction to the woman he was considering marrying.

'Seeing as we're out here in the countryside, and seeing as you've been feeling stifled, why don't we take a walk?' Thomas suggested. He needed some time to think, to mull over his options, to wrestle with his conscience, but he also recognised he needed to keep Rosa agreeable.

He offered her his arm and felt a peculiar contentment as she slipped her hand into the crook of his elbow.

'So what did that old woman want with you?' he asked.

Out of the corner of his eye he saw Rosa blush, a pink glow blossoming on her cheeks. It made her look young and fresh, a healthy glow that he found strangely endearing.

'I think she was going to tell my fortune,' Rosa said eventually.

'You believe in all that?'

Rosa shook her head vehemently.

Thomas stepped quickly in front of her, took her hand and looked down at it, frowning and pretending to concentrate hard on the criss-crossing lines.

'I see a bright future for you, young lady,' he said, doing his best impression of an old crone.

'Stop it,' Rosa said, swatting his arm and pulling her hand away.

They walked on for a few more minutes, enjoying the late afternoon sunshine and revelling in the cool breeze that wafted across the fields.

'What's been on your mind?' Rosa asked eventually.

'Hmmm?'

'You said you'd had a lot on your mind. Are you worried about returning home?'

Thomas shook his head slowly. He couldn't tell her he had been contemplating asking her to marry him, she'd probably expire on the spot. He needed time to phrase the question correctly, show her it was to her advantage. It would be more like a business agreement than a traditional marriage, he would gain a companion for his mother, someone to keep his only living relation company whilst he was free to travel the world. And he'd gain an heir, not his own flesh and blood, but his mother could ensure the child was well brought up and it would stop the home of his ancestors leaving the family altogether.

'Have dinner with me tonight,' Thomas said, side-stepping the question.

'We always have dinner together.' Rosa laughed.

'I don't mean in the coaching inn. Be ready at eight and I'll collect you from your room.'

It was only a few hours away, but it would have to be enough time for him to make a final decision. Tonight he would either propose or discard the idea completely.

Chapter Eight

Thomas paced about the small room, struggling with the knot in his cravat. He hadn't had a valet for a long time, not since soon after he'd left England. The young man he'd employed to accompany him on his travels, to look after his possessions and keep him relatively smart, had wept throughout the crossing from England to France with homesickness and Thomas had promptly bought him a return fare as soon as they'd disembarked the ship. His wardrobe had suffered, but he had much preferred the freedom of travelling alone.

Forcing himself to stand still in front of the small looking glass hung from one of the solid beams, he concentrated on the delicate movements of his fingers. Normally he revelled in tasks such as this, tasks where he could enjoy still being able to complete fine movements with his hands, things that one day he might no longer be capable of doing. Tonight, however, he was distracted and preoccupied.

Still he hadn't made up his mind as to whether he was going to propose to Rosa. The past two hours he had swung from one decision to the other, talking himself round when he had thought his mind was made up.

A quiet tap on the door made him pause. He finished adjusting his cravat in the mirror and when he was satisfied he crossed over to the door and opened it.

'It is five minutes to eight, my lord,' a young maid said, looking down at the floor as she spoke. 'My master said to let you know the time.'

She had scurried off down the dimly lit corridor before Thomas even had the chance to thank her.

He pulled on his boots, straightened his jacket and left the bedroom, stepping across the hallway and knocking on Rosa's door.

As she opened the door Thomas felt his eyes widen a fraction at the sight before him. Before leaving Garda he had loaned her the money to buy some new dresses for the journey. One she had been wearing the past couple of days was practical, made of cotton and a dark shade of blue. This dress he had caught a glimpse of as she'd unpacked her packages, but it looked rather different on.

The dress was white with a bright red ribbon around the waist, but it was more the cut that made him linger over the sight of her. Cut to skim over her hips and pinch in just above her waist, it emphasised her curves and her naturally tanned skin. Rosa had let her dark hair cascade over one shoulder, pinning it loosely. She looked every inch an Italian beauty.

Throughout his years of self-imposed exile, and even during his time studying at university and running the family estate whilst his brother was unwell, Thomas had made a conscious effort to avoid female company. It wasn't that he disliked women, quite the opposite, in fact, but from a young age he had been aware of the disease he might possibly carry in his body, aware of the risk of passing it on to his own offspring. He would not inflict the suffering his family had endured on another generation, so he had avoided any situation where he might be tempted by a woman. Over the years it had been difficult, especially when his friends talked of their mistresses and the merry widows they were pursuing, but Thomas had held firm.

Right now, looking at Rosa as a woman for the first time and not just someone needing his help, Thomas felt his resolve falter a little. He had an unnerving urge to sweep her up into his arms, deposit her on the four-poster bed behind her in the bedroom and kiss every inch of her body. He wanted to peel the dress from her, revealing the silky soft skin underneath.

He had to suppress a groan. This was Rosa he was thinking about, the woman he was hoping to have an entirely platonic marriage with.

'Are you well, Thomas?' Rosa asked, reaching out and touching him on the arm.

The heat of her fingers seemed to burn through his layers of clothing and into his skin.

'Quite well,' he managed to croak.

'You look a little strange.'

Thomas rallied. It had been a long day and he'd made some momentous decisions, that was all there was to it. In five minutes he would be back to his normal self and completely under control.

Rosa stepped forward and turned her face up to his. Her breasts brushed lightly against his arm and her lips parted ever so slightly. Thomas could just imagine himself leaning down and covering her lips with his own, kissing her as she moaned underneath him, possessing her.

'I don't mind waiting a few minutes if you need to rest.'

Rest was the last thing on his mind as he reached out and placed a hand lightly on her back to guide her down the stairs. Thankfully the corridor was dark and allowed Thomas time to regain control of himself and by time his foot hit the bottom step of the staircase he felt much more like his normal self. Just as long as Rosa didn't turn to him with that concerned expression again, her lips pouting into a soft O-shape and her eyes wide with worry.

'Everything is ready for you, my lord, just as you asked,' the landlord said quietly as he sidled up to Thomas.

Leading Rosa out the back door of the inn and into the darkness beyond, Thomas felt the weight of responsibility as she trustingly laid a hand on his arm, allowing him to guide her. It was surprising she trusted him so much, out here alone in the darkness, but Thomas supposed he hadn't given her much choice these last few weeks. It was either trust him or try to forge her way in a foreign country all alone.

Nevertheless, the responsibility for another's well-being was unnerving. For years he'd only had to think of himself, to protect himself. Now there would be someone else to put first, at least until he could deliver her safely into his ancestral home with all the servants poised and ready to cater to her every whim.

'Where are we going?' Rosa asked. In the soft moonlight Thomas could just make out the gleam of her eyes looking up at him.

'Be patient,' he counselled. 'And the surprise will be even better.'

Two minutes later the first of the candles Thomas had ordered to light the way came into sight. From there on the landlord had placed a candle every few feet along the path, to guide them to their final destination.

Rosa gasped with pleasure as they followed the trail of candles to a small table in a clearing. It was surrounded by over fifty flickering candles, set up to make the whole area feel like an intimate grotto.

'Thomas, it's beautiful.'

He glanced at her, watching the pleasure on her face as she realised he'd done this all for her and felt a flash of guilt. He wasn't sure why he had insisted on such a spectacle for his proposal, it wasn't as though he was going to dress it up as a romantic gesture. Far from it—he was going to calmly and precisely set out all the reasons it would be advantageous for them to make a match, but still he had decided to make the evening special.

Deftly he pulled out Rosa's chair and waited for her to sit down before plucking the bottle of wine from the table and pouring out two glasses. He'd asked the landlord for dishes that could be eaten cold so they would have absolute privacy for the evening.

'What is all this in aid of?' Rosa asked, her big dark eyes seeking his own out in the candlelight. There were a hundred questions written on her face, mixed with just a little bit of hope. Thomas had seen how she'd looked at him from time to time, when she'd come across him topless whilst boxing or when he emerged from the lake after his morning swims. He might be sworn to a life of celibacy, but that didn't mean he didn't recognise when a woman's skin flushed and breathing became just that little bit more erratic. He wasn't sure if she just found him physically attractive or if it was the fact he'd swooped to her rescue when she was in need of help the most, but Thomas acknowledged Rosa was a little infatuated with him. What he found slightly worrying was his willingness to play on that attraction to get what he wanted.

'Eat,' Thomas said, gesturing at the plates piled high with brightly coloured salad in front of them.

As Rosa picked up her fork Thomas focused his mind for the task ahead.

'I have a proposition for you,' he said, choosing his words carefully. 'I would like you to listen to what I have to say and think about it very carefully before you give me an answer.'

Rosa smiled at him, but her expression turned serious as she studied him.

'I think we should marry.'

Rosa almost choked as he said the words.

'Don't jest, Thomas,' she said. 'I know I am unmarriageable, but please don't poke fun.'

'I'm completely serious.'

'Why would you want to marry me? You're not in love with me. You barely know me.'

All very good points, but he knew enough.

'You need to marry, and soon, or the child you carry will be illegitimate for ever.'

Rosa waved a hand, realised she was still brandishing her fork, placed it on the table and then resumed her gesticulating.

'That's not what I asked. I know why I'm in desperate need for a husband.' Rosa grimaced. 'But no man in his right mind would take me on.'

'Maybe I'm not in my right mind.' She regarded him in silence, almost warily, until he spoke again. 'Just listen and I will explain.

'You need a husband, a father in name at least to your child. Just imagine, your son or daughter growing up as my heir, with a good family name and no hint of shame or scandal.'

'It doesn't make sense…' Rosa started to say, but Thomas held up a hand imperiously so she would let him continue.

'We would return to England as husband and wife, at least in name, and I would take you to my home. You would have an income, somewhere safe to live, a good education for your child.'

He saw her eyes widen and her eyebrows raise as he continued talking. Rosa was an intelligent young woman and he was going to need all his guile to convince her it was a good idea without telling her all the sordid family secrets driving his proposition.

'It would be a marriage in name and law only. I am not talking about a romantic union, of course there would not be love between us, but I think we rub along well together and over time a certain companionship develops. You would be mistress of your own home, never having to bow to your mother's tyranny again. I would not interfere in how you led your life or how you raised your child.' He paused, watching Rosa carefully. He could see some of his arguments had appealed at least, but that he was far from convincing her at the moment.

'I don't see why you would do all of this.'

'I wish to continue travelling the world,' Thomas said slowly.

'Then surely it makes no sense to burden yourself with a wife and child.'

'I find myself worrying about leaving my mother with no companion, no one to share her old age with.'

'Then employ someone to be her companion.'

No, he needed someone who would be compelled to keep the family secrets, not someone who had no loyalty beyond the money they were paid. Of course he could tell her the truth, tell her of the awful Hunter family curse that had already claimed his father and his brother and might well claim him, too. One day he would, but right now the idea of reliving the awful years of slow decline was too painful.

'There is a certain expectation for a child to carry on the family name.'

'All the more reason not to marry me. My child would by law be your first born, despite not carrying your blood.'

Thomas shrugged and Rosa frowned at his assumed air of flippancy.

'No man wants that,' she said resolutely. 'Another man's child as their heir.'

'There are worse things.'

Rosa shook her head. 'You wouldn't think so when you decided to settle down and found yourself chained to me, with no hope of your own flesh and blood inheriting. No man wants that.'

'Do not presume to tell me what I would want,' Thomas said, hearing the icy tone to his voice and regretting it immediately. This was not the way to win over any woman.

'Then treat me with at least a modicum of respect and tell me the truth behind your proposition.'

'You are nearly five months pregnant and unmarried. My motivations should not matter.'

He regretted the words as soon as they left his mouth, but she was challenging him, provoking him more than he'd expected or prepared for.

Rosa drew herself up, straightening her back and lifting her chin, looking as though she were about to go into battle.

'I may be pregnant with an illegitimate child. I may have very few prospects and very little hope for a decent life, but that does not mean I will tolerate being lied to and deceived. I deserve more than that.'

He saw the tears in her eyes and the miniscule movements of the muscles in her throat as she swallowed again and again in an effort not to shed them. Up until now he hadn't fully appreciated the strength Rosa must possess to even think about raising an illegitimate child alone in a world that penalised even the most upstanding of women. He'd underestimated her in many ways and now the quick and easy marriage he had been hoping for was out of the question. She might have started the evening trusting him, but she certainly didn't trust him now.

'Rosa, I only meant to point out the advantages you would gain from the marriage.'

'And I ask again: what would you truly gain? You're a shrewd man, Lord Hunter, and you wouldn't be suggesting this match if there wasn't something substantial for you in it.'

'I told you…'

'You told me nothing.'

Rosa stood, the legs of her chair scraping along the ground.

'I may not have much in this world, Lord Hunter, but I do still have my dignity and a little self-respect. I think I will retire before anything further is damaged.'

He watched her go, cursing his brain for not being able to come up with the right words to convince her to stay, to convince her a marriage of convenience was the right thing for both of them, even if she didn't know his true motivations.He wondered if he were doing wrong by Rosa, asking her to marry him without telling her the whole truth, but quickly dismissed the idea. His proposal had made it clear it would be a marriage of convenience, nothing more. She would gain his name and his protection, and some day soon he would disappear from her life. What would it matter to her if he took ill in a few years' time? He had resolved never to be a burden on anyone, so he would suffer through the progression of the disease alone, without Rosa ever even needing to know.

Mumbling a profanity in Italian, Thomas stood and strode out into the darkness, letting out a primal growl of frustration once he was certain he was all alone. It should have been so straightforward, so easy. He'd imagined it a hundred times—outlining his proposition, the advantages for Rosa, her grateful acceptance. Never had he thought she might turn him down because he wasn't telling her the whole truth. His explanation should be enough.

He made to turn and follow Rosa, but his remaining self-control stopped him. He needed a new approach, a new line of reasoning, before he tried again. One thing was for sure, Rosa would marry him. There weren't many things in life Thomas didn't manage to make go his way, even if it took more work than he'd originally thought. Before the week was out Rosa would be his wife.

Chapter Nine

'What a strange night it has been,' Rosa murmured, looking down and placing her hand on the bump that was just visible through her dress. 'I wonder what you would make of Thomas's proposal.'

She should have headed straight back to her room when she'd left Thomas, but Rosa was restless and knew she wouldn't sleep. The last place she wanted to be was tossing and turning in bed on such a balmy night, so instead she had crept through the quiet courtyard, past the stables filled with sleeping horses and found a secluded spot a few hundred yards away from the inn. Her seat was an upturned log, but any discomfort she felt was more than made up for by the view in front of her. Away from the lights of the inn the sky was dark, but that darkness was studded by hundreds upon hundreds of sparkling stars. It made Rosa feel small, sitting here underneath such a sky.

'I'm sure I *should* have accepted his offer,' Rosa continued. It was strangely comforting to speak aloud to the tiny person growing inside her. It made her feel a little less alone, a little more grounded and sure of her place in the world. 'I just don't like being lied to.'

That was the crux of the matter. In truth Rosa could appreciate all the merits of Thomas's proposal from her point of view. How wonderful it would be to have the protection of a strong and powerful gentleman. Not to have to endure a hard life where she never knew where her next meal might be coming from or who might find out her terrible secret. Even just the fact that her child would not be born out of wedlock should have had her dragging Thomas to a church before he could change her mind.

'Maybe your grandmother is right. Maybe I am a foolish, reckless girl with only half a brain.'

Rosa fell silent. She should have given more thought to the offer before turning it down. What did it matter why he was proposing? He was a kind man, she doubted he would ever raise his voice to her, let alone a fist. He was courteous and entertaining, and when he looked at her with those sparkling blue eyes Rosa found the world around them merging into the background.

'Your mama is getting carried away,' she whispered. Thomas had never once mentioned romance. He liked her, Rosa was sure of that, just as people liked their spinster aunt or a younger sister, but he certainly hadn't proposed because he was overcome by love for her, he'd told her that theirs would be a marriage in name and in law only. The unnerving and unwanted attraction she felt towards him was most definitely one-sided.

Sitting back, Rosa considered the reasons Thomas had given for the proposal. He wanted a companion for his mother and an heir to his estate. None of it made sense. There was no guarantee his mother would like her, or vice versa. It would be much more sensible to hire a companion, someone who could be easily replaced if there was a clash of personalities. A wife was much harder to dispose of.

'And men want their own blood for their heirs,' Rosa said. 'As much as I would like you to inherit a grand estate, I cannot see a situation where Thomas would not want a child of his own. I will not have you put aside for another in a few years.'

This was a weaker argument. Even if Thomas

did change his mind completely after marriage Rosa's child would still be considered legitimate because it would be born in wedlock. It didn't seem to matter so much the circumstances around conception, as long as the mother was married when the child was born.

She tried to come up with a sensible reason for Thomas's proposal, but nothing came. None of it made sense and that was reason enough to turn down the offer. She would not trap herself and her child in a situation without fully understanding all the angles first.

'Am I making a mistake?' she whispered, more up to the stars now than to the child in her womb.

Of course there was no answer. It wasn't the first time in her life that Rosa wished for a confidant, a sister perhaps or a close friend to talk through the options and puzzle out the conundrums. She had never had anyone like that, her childhood had been lonely and grey, a strict upbringing in a solemn household ruled by her mother's iron will. When Rosa had come out in society she'd had friends for the first time, young women who weren't quite as sheltered as her, people to talk to in the noisy corners of the ballroom or over a hot, sweet cup of tea in the afternoon. She'd been close to Caroline, of course, but most of the other young women had been scared away by her mother's sharp tongue and dragon-like demeanour.

'Soon I'll have you, my little love,' Rosa said, feeling the warm glow she always did when she pictured the small baby she would soon hold in her arms. They would never be starved of love, never have to cower away from her as she had from her own mother. She might not be able to provide much, but she was determined her household would be filled with love and laughter, not dread and misery.

Standing, Rosa stretched and looked about her. She certainly hadn't found any answers to the many questions Thomas had left her with, but she knew even with another few hours of pondering she would not be any further forward. All of a sudden she felt weary, the events of the last few days catching up with her. She wanted her bed and she wanted a deep, dreamless sleep to restore her. Maybe in the morning, after a proper rest, things might be clearer.

Thomas paused outside Rosa's door, listening for any sign that she was awake. Everything was quiet inside, but still he lifted his fist to tap on the wood, only dropping it at the last moment. Now wasn't the right time. He might want to get the matter resolved as quickly as possible, but it wouldn't do to smother the girl. She might have even come round to the idea of marrying him by morning all by herself.

Instead of crossing the corridor to his own room Thomas padded silently back downstairs into the bar below. The landlord was still behind the wooden counter, stacking glasses and wiping surfaces, and gave a nod of acknowledgement to Thomas as he entered.

Without Thomas even having to ask, the landlord set a cup of wine on the counter between them before pouring one for himself.

'The evening did not go as you planned,' the landlord said, studying Thomas.

'How did you guess?' Thomas asked, then immediately regretted the hint of sarcasm in his voice. Signor Granese had been most obliging when Thomas had asked for his assistance in setting up the dinner arrangements that evening, and like landlords the world over had a genuine interest in the people sitting in his bar.

'No. It didn't go as planned.'

'I have four daughters. Good, strong, hard-working country girls. I could introduce you.'

'To all four? I think they'd eat me alive.'

Signor Granese gave out a hearty laugh, throwing his head back and allowing the rumbles of amusement to travel all the way from his expansive belly.

'Tomorrow is a new day,' Signor Granese said as Thomas took a mouthful of wine. 'Maybe your English lady will be more receptive to your advances after a night's sleep.' The Italian man regarded Thomas for a few more seconds. 'Or maybe you just need to try harder.'

'It's not like that,' Thomas said quietly. 'I'm not courting her, there is no need to win her heart over. It's her head I'm appealing to, her reason.'

Signor Granese guffawed with laughter again for a few seconds, his face only turning serious again when he saw Thomas's expression.

'You're serious? And here I was thinking you were an intelligent man. It seems I was mistaken.'

'I'm offering her security, safety, a good home and a future. She should be jumping at the offer.'

'And yet she turned you down,' Signor Granese said quietly. 'Why do you think that was?'

Thomas could still see her confused expression, the hope tinged with mistrust written all over her face. She had wanted to say yes, wanted to take the easy path and forget about all her worries, but she had been too wary, too mistrusting.

'She doesn't trust me.'

'Nonsense,' Signor Granese said. 'She travels with you alone, allows you to take her off into the deserted countryside. The lady trusts you.'

'I don't think she trusts anyone, not really.'

As he took another mouthful of wine he remembered the quizzical look on her face as he'd explained his reasons for proposing. In his head he'd expected her to be so grateful for the opportunity he was willing to give her she wouldn't question his motives too closely, but that had been the real sticking point. She hadn't believed him when he'd said he purely wanted a companion for his mother and a wife in name, to provide an heir and look after his estate.

He sighed. He shouldn't be too surprised—one of the things he liked most about Rosa was her shrewd intelligence, the way her dark eyes bored into you as if she were searching for your very soul. Well, today he'd certainly come up short in her estimation.

'Women are the same the world over. They want flattery, romance. They want to be chased, pursued, made to feel like the most important person in your life.'

'Rosa's not like that.'

Signor Granese shrugged. 'It's your choice, but try it and see. Show her the fantasy, the idea of the romantic life you could lead, and I guarantee she will say yes to you.'

The last thing he wanted was to seduce Rosa with romance. His reaction to her earlier that evening had been uncomfortable: the acute desire, the longing to touch her, to kiss her lips. He'd managed to get himself under control, to convince himself it was only natural for a man to have urges when he spent so long cooped up with an attractive young woman. Nevertheless, he couldn't guarantee he'd be able to keep his desire at bay if he started manufacturing intimate situations. Too long he'd spent celibate to ruin things now.

The landlord moved away, bidding Thomas goodnight and leaving a candle flickering on the counter to help guide him to bed.

Thomas finished the rest of his wine in one gulp and stood. He wasn't sure why he was quite so keen to have this matter resolved so quickly. Part of him wondered if it was the impending sense of something going wrong, the knowledge that he had outlived his older brother already and he was only a few months off the age his father had first noted symptoms of the disease that plagued their family. He had an urge to get things sorted, to tie up any loose ends and ensure everyone he cared for was provided for. Then he would be free to travel again, to set off into the world and pack as many different experiences into his life as possible.

'Romance,' he growled under his breath, as if the idea offended him. He pushed back the high stool he was sitting on and got to his feet. The irksome thing was the landlord was probably right. He'd seen how Rosa blushed when she looked at him, how she relaxed when it was just the two of them. A few days of courting and in all likelihood she would say yes to his proposal. The question was, could he be that ruthless?

Chapter Ten

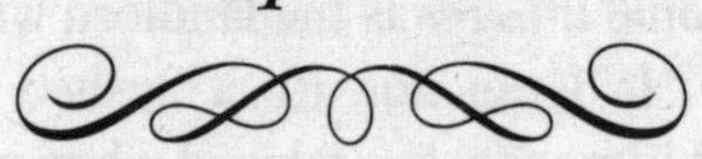

Rosa paced backwards and forward across the small bedroom, trying to prepare herself for the uncertainties of the morning. Part of her wondered if she had dreamed the surreal events of the evening before. The proposal had been unexpected to say the least and she wondered if in the cold light of day Thomas might want to just forget the idea.

Eventually she could delay her descent downstairs to breakfast no longer and cautiously opened the door leading out to the corridor. It was deserted. Rosa sighed in relief—she had half-expected Thomas to be waiting there ready to pounce on her as soon as she emerged. He was a man used to getting his own way, she didn't expect him to take her refusal without any protestation.

'Good morning, Rosa,' Thomas said in her ear

as she stepped outside. He must have been waiting just round the corner, out of view.

She jumped, darting her hand to her mouth to prevent a squeal of shock.

'I trust you slept well.'

She hadn't slept at all, but she felt a strange obstinacy blossoming. She would not let him see how much he'd unsettled her.

'Wonderfully, thank you. The bed was very comfortable.' She smiled as if she didn't have a care in the world, trying not to stiffen as Thomas took her elbow and guided her downstairs.

'I've asked the landlord to lay on a special breakfast. You ate so little last night.'

'There really was no need.'

'Nonsense.' Thomas waved a dismissive hand. 'You're eating for two. I wouldn't want the child you are carrying to go without sustenance because of me.'

Rosa's eyes narrowed.

'I'm sure one evening without food would not make too much of a difference.'

'I want only the best for you, both of you.'

Rosa looked at him with raised eyebrows, trying to convey that she knew what he was doing and she wouldn't fall for it. His concern for the baby she was carrying was genuine, that she knew. Throughout the time they had spent together he had taken the utmost care not to endanger Rosa's unborn child and to ensure she was well provided for at all times. That had been done discreetly and without any need for him to signpost what he was doing.

'I was thinking; we probably should ask a doctor to check you over before we commence our voyage back to England. Ensure you are fit to travel.'

'Is that really necessary?'

Thomas shrugged. 'We won't know until the doctor gives his verdict.'

'And if he says I'm not fit to travel?'

'I know of a wonderful villa on the edge of Lake Garda. Rumour has it the last tenant left quite abruptly so we may get it at a premium rate.' Thomas's eyes were sparkling as he grinned at her and Rosa couldn't hide her own smile.

Breakfast smelled divine as they entered the small dining room and Rosa felt her stomach gurgle in anticipation. She might have protested an evening without food did not matter, but reality was very different.

'Good morning,' a ruddy-faced young man said in English, rising as they entered. He was seated beside a pretty young woman of about Rosa's age. Both had breakfast laid out before them, but the man only had eyes for his wife.

'Fingers Peterson,' Thomas roared as he regarded the other man.

'Hunter. What on earth are you doing here?'

'Fingers?' the pretty young woman said in a soft, low voice.

'I beg your pardon, madam. Just a nickname from our schooling days.'

'This is Lord Hunter, my dear. Most decent chap at Eton.'

Thomas had been to Eton. Of course he had. Her mother would be fluttering her eyelashes and talking about pure bloodlines right about now.

'Hunter, this is my wife, Francesca. The most beautiful and sweetest woman in the world.'

They were newlyweds. No one who had spent more than a few months together could look that happy. Rosa thought of her parents. After twenty-five years of marriage they barely spoke to one another and when they did it was usually for her mother to admonish her father about something.

'A pleasure to meet you, Mrs Peterson,' Thomas said, taking the young woman's hand and bowing over it.

The Petersons turned expectantly to Rosa and she felt herself begin to fidget.

'I had no idea you were married, Hunter.

What a dark horse you are. No one's heard from you for years, travelling the globe, and it turns out you've got yourself hitched to a beautiful Italian mystery woman.'

Rosa opened her mouth to protest, but felt Thomas's hand slip around her waist and squeeze ever so gently.

'And you're expecting a child, how wonderful for you both,' Francesca Peterson chipped in.

The words of protest died in Rosa's throat. This was the first time that anyone had directly mentioned her pregnancy—that anyone had noticed solely from her appearance. She wouldn't be able to hide the growing bump any more. The dresses she had were already stretching over her lower abdomen and she knew her face and figure were filling out as happened to all pregnant women. Now her pregnancy would announce to the world she had lost her virtue and she would have to get used to being shunned by all the decent, godly members of society.

She'd expected to feel stronger, more defiant. She was unmarried and with child, but she'd hoped she would still want to shout it from the rooftops, to hold her head up high and withstand the withering looks and unkind remarks. Instead she wished no one would notice, that she could go back to carrying her child in secret. It was a sobering thought.

'My darling Rosa,' Thomas said, lifting and kissing her hand. 'Although not entirely Italian, she is with child.'

'Congratulations!' Peterson beamed.

Rosa smiled weakly.

'Sit down, my dear,' Thomas instructed, pushing her gently on to the long bench. 'You need to eat something.'

'I don't think I've seen you for, what? Four years. And then we bump into each other in the wilds of Italy,' Peterson was saying. Rosa felt as though the words were washing over her, but not quite penetrating her consciousness. 'The last time we were together must have been your dear brother's funeral.'

Rosa felt Thomas stiffen beside her and frowned. She hadn't known he'd once had a brother.

'Your brother?' Rosa murmured quietly. The look Thomas shot her would have silenced a lion.

'He was such a decent chap.'

'He's sorely missed,' Thomas murmured. 'So what brings you to Italy?' Changing the subject quickly.

'Honeymoon. I never managed to leave the Home Counties as we planned to at school. None of this travelling the world, but once we were married it seemed like the perfect opportunity to see a little of the foreign lands.'

'And how are you enjoying your honeymoon, Mrs Peterson?' Thomas asked.

It was the most innocent of questions, but Rosa would swear the new Mrs Peterson blushed a little under Thomas's gaze.

'It is most satisfactory, thank you, Lord Hunter.'

Not the most ringing endorsement of married life, but her husband didn't seem to notice.

'Are you honeymooning, too?' Peterson asked.

'No. We are travelling to Venice to find a passage home to England.'

Mrs Peterson beamed in delight. 'We are heading to Venice, too. We must join parties.'

'What a fabulous idea,' Mr Peterson agreed.

Rosa felt Thomas stiffen beside her. It would put a stop to any further marriage proposals on his part. She should be encouraging the coupling of their parties, but part of her wanted to push the Petersons away. She enjoyed the moments spent alone with Thomas, much more than an unmarried lady should. And if they travelled together they would have to keep up the charade of being married and of the child she was carrying being of Thomas's blood. It would be exhausting.

'We set out straight after breakfast,' Thomas said eventually.

'Brilliant. No need to dilly-dally in the provinces. We'll be in Venice in no time.' Peterson raised a glass of orange juice in a toast. 'To travelling companions.'

'Travelling companions,' Rosa and Thomas murmured, a little less enthusiastically than their new friends.

'Why on earth did you tell them we are married?' Rosa hissed as she ran across the yard, trying to keep up with Thomas.

'It seemed the most logical thing to do,' he said with a shrug. 'It was either that or explain why I'm travelling with a pregnant, unmarried, unescorted young woman.'

Thomas had to hide a smile at the Italian expletives that coursed from Rosa's mouth. She'd certainly learnt some of the native tongue during her time in the country, although hardly anything that could be used in polite conversation.

'And now we're stuck with this pretence for the rest of our journey.'

'Think of it as a rehearsal,' Thomas said.

'A rehearsal?'

'For when we are married.'

'We are not getting married.'

He turned quickly, causing Rosa to barrel into him, and caught her arms gently.

'We will be married, my sweet.'

He could see the defiance flicker in Rosa's eyes and wondered if this was why he liked her so much. She knew, in her heart, that the right thing to do was marry him, but still she protested. It was thrilling, if a little frustrating.

'I could just tell your friends we are not married. That this is not your child.'

'Go ahead.'

He saw her hesitate, then had to hide a smile as she huffed and stalked away.

It had been a shock to see Peterson as they walked in to breakfast, but now he had reconciled himself to the idea of sharing the journey with his old school friend he thought things had worked out to his advantage. He'd sensed Rosa stiffen besides him as her pregnancy had been noticed, heard her breathing accelerate and felt her agitation increase. For all her desire to not care what the world thought of her, Rosa had been brought up to be a respectable woman with good morals. Admitting to two near-strangers that you were unwed and were expecting an illegitimate child could not be easy.

So he'd given her an escape, a way to preserve her dignity with just a little lie. The timing could not have been better. Hopefully Rosa would realise her entire life would be a series of uncomfortable encounters if she insisted on raising her child alone.

Fifteen minutes later he was sitting across from her in the carriage, waving to the Petersons from the window. They had agreed to stop for lunch in one of the villages about three hours away, but until then he had Rosa to himself.

'Lady Rosa Hunter,' he murmured.

'What was that?'

'Just familiarising myself with your new name. Lady Rosa Hunter.'

'I like my current name, thank you very much.'

'How would you like me to address you in front of the Petersons?' he asked, watching her wriggle in her seat. 'Lady H.? Darling Rosa? Rosie-Posie? Sweetheart? Sugar plum?'

'Just my name will do very well,' Rosa said, trying hard not to rise to his baiting.

'We are meant to be in the first throes of love,' Thomas mused. 'Maybe we should endeavour to be closer to one another.'

Before Rosa could protest he slid in to sit beside her, looping an arm around her waist.

She regarded him with a haughty expression,

but through the thin fabric of her dress Thomas could feel the pounding of her heart.

'I'm sure the Petersons will expect us to kiss,' Thomas murmured. 'I'm assured all newlywed couples do.'

They were close, their faces mere inches apart, and as Thomas's gaze flickered down to Rosa's lips he realised he wanted this. Not because it would further his aim, but because he wanted to taste her lips, to run his fingers through her hair and pull her against him. He wanted her.

'I think ours was a more practical marriage, most assuredly not a love match.'

Thomas leaned in closer and could feel her breath dancing across his skin. He reached up and tucked a stray strand of hair behind her ear, letting his fingers linger for a few seconds. Rosa swallowed, her tongue darted out to wet her lips and Thomas felt something tighten deep inside him.

'Well we must have liked each other at least enough to consummate our marriage,' Thomas said, his voice low.

Rosa glanced down, then back up, her eyes meeting Thomas's. He saw confusion in them, tinged with desire, but there was something else as well. She was nervous, he realised, more nervous than she should be.

Slowly, against his better judgement, Thomas sat back, breaking off the intimate connection between them.

'What happened, Rosa?' he asked, the levity gone from his voice.

'Wh-what do you mean?' Rosa stuttered.

'How did you end up being alone and pregnant?' It was blunt, but he knew Rosa wouldn't tell him anything unless he asked directly.

'I'm sure I don't need to tell you what occurs between a man and a woman for a child to be made.'

Thomas levelled his best aristocratic stare at her.

Rosa sighed. 'It's not a particularly interesting story.'

'Like it or not, Rosa, our lives are tied together at least until we reach England. Help me to understand what happened to you.'

'What do you want to know?' Rosa asked, looking at him with large eyes imploring him to skim over the details.

'How did you meet him?'

'David? I've known him as long as I can remember.' Rosa stared off into the distance as if remembering a time far back in her childhood. 'My family had a country house in Kent and David's family owned the property next door.'

'You were of an age?'

Rosa shrugged. 'He was four years older than me, but he had a younger sister I spent my summers with.'

The allure of a friend's older brother. Thomas had known of a few young women seduced by someone who should have been looking out for their welfare, not exploiting it.

'So what happened?'

'I allowed myself to be seduced.' She paused, her eyes flitting about the carriage as if she weren't sure where to look. 'There wasn't any grand plot on his part, no excessive subterfuge.'

'Did you love him?'

Thomas realised the answer to her question actually mattered to him. He wasn't just asking because he wanted to work out the best way to proceed with her resistance to his proposal, he truly wanted to know if she had been in love with this man.

'I thought I did. I was infatuated, I suppose.'

'Did he love you?'

She snorted and Thomas could see the tears glistening in her defiant eyes.

'No.'

He waited, there was obviously a lot more to the story she wasn't letting on.

'Did he tell you that he loved you?'

'Not in so many words. There were gestures and tokens. But he never actually made me any promises, not explicitly.'

Thomas grimaced. He'd known plenty of his sort, the kind of man who seduces and entraps an innocent young woman, making her think he loved her only to pull away when he grew tired or someone new came along.

'You thought you would be married?' Thomas asked softly.

'The night…' Rosa trailed off, hugging her arms around her chest protectively. 'He gave me a ring, just a tarnished old thing. He didn't say a word when he placed it on my finger.'

'He let you believe it was a proposal.'

Rosa nodded. Reaching out, Thomas took one of Rosa's hands in his own, entwining their fingers before gently resting it down in her lap. 'And afterwards?'

'I didn't see him for a few days, but that wasn't unusual.'

Thomas could imagine Rosa waiting nervously for the man she thought she loved to come and make things right. To save her from scandal, from ruin. Rosa sighed and closed her eyes, and Thomas realised the effort it was taking for her to tell this story without breaking down and losing control of herself.

'Eventually I managed to sneak out one evening. I waited for hours for him to return home from some soirée he'd been attending.' She shivered as if remembering the chill that seeped under her skin as she waited for the father of her child. 'He was drunk when he returned and scornful. He dismissed me almost immediately, called me a harlot and denied the child was his.'

Thomas felt his muscles tense and his jaw clench. It was cowardly behaviour to condemn Rosa like that and completely unforgivable.

'I begged and pleaded with him, promised I had never been intimate with anyone else.' Rosa gave a wry smile, but Thomas could tell it pained her to remember the shame and embarrassment of having to beg the man she loved to acknowledge her. 'He told me never to contact him again.'

'That's when you told your parents.'

Rosa nodded. 'I knew I was with child as soon as I missed my monthly courses. I spoke to David about a week later and my parents as soon as he had rejected me.'

'What did they say?'

'My mother ranted and raved for about half an hour, told me I was a disgrace, a whore, no better than a common prostitute.'

'And your father?'

'He just looked at me, disappointed.'

Thomas could tell it was her father's reaction that had hurt her more. From the snippets of information he had gleaned about Rosa over the last few weeks, it sounded as though she'd had a difficult relationship with her mother at the best of times. It was her father who had read to her at night as a child, who had taken her for trips out into the countryside and discussed books and politics with her over dinner.

'Mother arranged for me to be sent away.'

'And your father didn't object.'

'It is hard to contradict my mother.' Despite Rosa's defence of her father Thomas wondered if she was a little disappointed not to have found someone to stand up for her on that front. 'So there you have it,' Rosa said with a grimace. 'All the sordid details.'

Not all the sordid details, Thomas thought. There was still more she was holding back, something deeper, more painful, that she wasn't quite ready to talk about yet.

'I think you have been very poorly treated,' Thomas said, shifting so he was facing her.

'I think I have been very foolish.'

'And I can see why you find it difficult to trust me,' he pressed on.

'I…' Rosa started to interrupt, but Thomas held up a silencing hand.

'You fear history may repeat itself, that I may promise you the world and then go back on my promise. You are fighting for your future, and the future of your child, and you are reluctant to put that future in anyone's hands but your own.'

He paused, but could see his speech was ringing true at least a little. He always had been eloquent, always won the debates at university and been able to talk round even the most hostile of hosts on his travels.

'I want to marry you, Rosa. And I want to do it here and now, or at least as soon as possible. Once we have said our vows there will be no backing out, no abandoning you.'

'Why?' It was barely more than a whisper, but the single word cut through Thomas and halted the flow of his speech.

'I told you why. I want to protect you and your child, give you a future. I want a companion for my mother, I want a family to enliven the estate.'

Rosa shook her head sadly. 'It still doesn't make sense, Thomas. You're not telling me something and I will not marry you unless you give me the whole truth.'

He felt his throat tighten, the uneasiness that

surrounded him whenever anyone got close to the truth about his family weigh down upon him.

'There is nothing else,' he said, trying to sound light and reassuring, but knowing the words came out stiff and untrue.

Rosa shook her head, disentangled her hand from his and waited for him to meet her eye.

'What about your brother?' Rosa asked.

Thomas felt every muscle in his body tense.

'What about him?'

'You never told me you had a brother, and by the way you reacted when Mr Peterson mentioned him he must have been very dear to you.'

'He was,' Thomas said stiffly. 'He died. It is difficult to talk about.'

Rosa waited, looking up at him with her big, inquisitive eyes.

'I'd rather not talk about it,' Thomas said.

Rosa sighed, leaving a long pause before continuing. 'I do find it hard to trust, after what I've experienced I think that is justifiable. I cannot tie my life to yours, to tie both of our lives to yours, when I know you are lying to me. Please do not ask me again unless you are ready to tell me whatever it is you are hiding.'

Chapter Eleven

Rosa flopped back on the bed and let out a weary groan. It was exhausting, pretending to be married to Thomas. Every time they sat down to eat he would put an arm around her, pull her in close and insist on feeding her morsels from his plate. Every time the carriages stopped to allow them to stretch their legs Thomas would lift her down, kiss her cheek and take her hand before Rosa could even think about making an escape. And every time they were alone together he would regale her of tales from his travels or escapades from his time at university.

It wasn't that she didn't like the attention, far from it. A day spent with Thomas courting her was thrilling and entertaining and pleasurable, but every moment they spent together she felt him chipping away at her resolve to resist him.

Rosa knew that was the point, he was a determined man, someone who wasn't used to being denied anything, and he was approaching her resistance to his proposal with an assault by charm. She was determined she would not falter.

She groaned as there was a soft knock on the door. After a day spent travelling all she wanted was five minutes to lie down before dinner.

She opened the door to find Thomas leaning in a relaxed manner on the doorpost.

'Is it time for dinner already?'

'Not quite. There is a small problem.'

Rosa heard movement in the corridor passage behind Thomas before she saw Mr and Mrs Peterson, followed closely by a worried-looking landlady.

'There aren't enough rooms.'

She frowned, watching Mr and Mrs Peterson open the door to the room across the corridor and enter, only to leave the door open behind them.

Rosa dropped her voice, aware they had an audience. 'Not enough rooms? What do you mean?'

'Very busy time of year… Lots of travellers heading for Venice… Last room available,' the landlady gushed in rapid Italian, but after a few weeks in the country Rosa was skilled enough to get her general meaning.

'It just means we will have to share a room, my dear,' Thomas said, his voice light and jovial.

'No.' Rosa shook her head adamantly. 'There must be another way.'

'No need to be shy, darling, we share a room at home after all.'

'No.' Rosa continued to shake her head.

'I know it is unpleasant when you are travelling,' Mrs Peterson said, her ringlets bobbing up and down earnestly as she spoke, 'You are weary to the bone and confined to such cramped quarters, but needs must, Lady Hunter.'

'I could share with Mrs Peterson,' Rosa whispered to Thomas. For some reason she hadn't really warmed to their female travelling companion, but she supposed she could endure one night in her company if it meant she wouldn't be sleeping in the same room as Thomas.

'I will be a complete gentleman,' Thomas said, his voice low. Quickly he grasped her hand and planted a kiss in the middle of her palm. Whilst Rosa was distracted by the feel of his soft lips on her skin Thomas turned to the landlady and the Petersons. 'The matter is resolved. My wife and I will share a chamber.'

Before Rosa could protest Thomas swept her into the room and closed the door behind them.

'No,' Rosa said emphatically.

'Many married couples share a bedroom.'

'We're not married.'

'Not yet.'

'My answer is still no.'

'To sharing a bedroom or to marrying me?'

'Sharing a bedroom. Marrying you. Everything.'

'Not everything, surely,' Thomas said, raising an eyebrow suggestively.

'Everything,' Rosa repeated firmly.

'I don't mean to ravish you and then force our marriage,' Thomas said, the smile lingering on his lips, but his voice becoming more serious. 'It wouldn't be appropriate.'

'Who is to know?'

'The Petersons.'

'They believe we are blissfully married. Rosa, you are travelling unchaperoned with a single man through a foreign country. And you are already pregnant. I don't believe spending one night, one *chaste* night, in the same room as me is going to make much difference to your reputation.'

She knew he was correct. Soon she would have to let go of her desire to keep up appearances. She would have to learn to show the world she was a ruined woman, disgraced and abandoned. It just went against everything she had been brought up to believe, although she knew ultimately any humiliation would be worth holding her baby in her arms, nurturing her son or daughter through their childhood. It still didn't make spending the night in the same room as Thomas any easier.

'There is no other option, Rosa. I will sleep in the chair; you may have the bed.'

She knew the matter was resolved in Thomas's eyes. When he spoke in that tone of voice, firm and unwavering, there was no swaying him. He began to unpack their small bags, shaking out the creases from the hastily packed clothes and hanging them in the small wardrobe. Rosa realised he did this out of habit, the movements so natural to him from his years spent travelling, moving on from place to place every few days.

As she watched his fingers danced over the knot of his cravat and for a second she thought he might start to undress right there in front of her. The memory of his taut body, the tanned skin pulled tight over the firm muscles, made her feel hot all over and Rosa felt her fingertips grip the edge of the bed just that little bit harder. After a second Thomas tugged at the cravat, pulling it from his neck and letting it fall to the chair.

'Damn uncomfortable thing,' he murmured.

Rosa already knew he was more comfortable

in simple shirtsleeves and trousers—the cravat and jacket were not only impractical in the scorching sun, but just other things to get dusty and dirty on the road. Once the cravat was dealt with he stripped off his jacket, turning quickly to catch Rosa watching him.

'I suppose I'd better stop there,' he said quietly, carefully folding his shirtsleeves over on themselves to reveal his bronzed forearms.

'I doubt they'll serve you dinner if you take any more off.'

'You'll want to get changed, I expect,' Thomas said, studying her intently.

Rosa nodded, waiting for him to take his leave, but he just stood watching her for a few more seconds.

'I can meet you downstairs,' she prompted.

Thomas nodded abruptly, spun on his heel and opened the door. He lingered, looking back over his shoulder as if he wanted to say something, but eventually shook his head and closed the door.

Thomas strode across the courtyard, avoiding the horse dung on the way, making straight for the barn. He needed to do something physical. For days on end he had sat in a coach all day long and barely moved even when they had stopped. He missed his early morning swims, his boxing training, even the exertion of vaulting on to the back of a horse and galloping through the countryside.

Inside the barn, once his eyes had adjusted to the dim light, Thomas saw exactly what he was looking for: somewhere to work up a sweat. The hay loft at one end of the barn was reached by a ladder, which had been fixed to the ground with large metal screws. The ladder was immovable and sturdy, and just the thing he could use to work out some of the tension he felt fighting to be released.

He walked round to the back of the ladder, reached above his head and gripped a rung. Slowly, his muscles protesting, he pulled himself up until his chin was level with the bar. His descent was controlled and steady, and Thomas found himself starting to relax.

No wonder he was tense, the situation with Rosa was enough to drive a man to despair. Still she was refusing him. He understood she was scared, he understood she'd been hurt and betrayed before, but he was offering her a way to save herself from complete ruin. Any other woman would be running to the altar before he could change his mind.

For a second he imagined her up in their

room, slipping out of the dress she was wearing, turning to look at him over her shoulder with those big, brown eyes. He'd wanted to stay. When he'd suggested she change for dinner he'd wanted to sit back and watch her as she slowly undressed.

Thomas grunted as he pulled himself up again, trying to focus on the burn of his muscles rather than the picture of Rosa letting her dress pool around her ankles.

Of course he'd been tempted by women before, he could appreciate a curvaceous body or bright smile as much as the next man, but he had always strived to keep women he found attractive at a distance. Ever since he had vowed as a young man the Hunter family curse would stop with him Thomas had known he would have to exercise tight self-control. Just one slip, one night where he gave in to his desires and there was the chance of a child being conceived, a child that might be damned to live their life in fear of the insidious disease that robbed them of control of their muscles. No, he wasn't going to risk that for a night of giving in to his desires.

So he had remained celibate. It had been harder at university, when all of his friends were off bedding women of the town, regaling each other with stories of their prowess in the bedchamber. Thomas had sat back on these occasions, affected a knowing smile, and infuriated his friends by not telling them anything. Of course that had earned him the reputation of being a consummate seducer, one who would keep a woman's secret, and there was all sorts of speculation on who he'd had affairs with.

Whilst he had been travelling things had been a lot easier. He'd avoided spending any amount of time with women he found attractive and thus avoided the problem.

But now there was Rosa. Rosa with her dark eyes that conveyed warmth and laughter. Rosa with her soft, caramel skin. Rosa with the body he wanted to sweep up into his arms and lay on the bed, exploring with his hands, his lips, until they both collapsed with pleasure.

Thomas lowered himself back to the floor and paused to wipe the sweat from his forehead. Rosa was pretty and good-natured and yet had a steely quality to her that he admired greatly. Maybe it was only natural he felt this desire for her as they spent more time together. It wouldn't be a problem if he was just delivering her back to England. He had managed to keep control of himself for many years, he could manage a few more weeks. No, the problem arose now he had decided to court her, to seduce her into marrying him. He wanted to kiss her, to run his hands over the curve of her waist, and it wasn't just so she went along with his plan and agreed to marry him.

With a sharp exhalation Thomas reached for the rung of the ladder and resumed his pull ups. He would just have to be strong, to stay focused on why he was doing this and what he wanted to achieve. Rosa was no seasoned seductress, he should be able to resist her.

'My, my, Lord Hunter, what a strong man you are.'

Thomas lowered himself to the floor before turning the quarter-circle to see who had entered the barn. Mrs Peterson smiled coyly as she walked towards him. There was something slightly predatory in her eyes and Thomas found himself moving a step to the left to keep the ladder between him and his friend's wife.

'I saw you enter the barn from my bedroom window and just had to come and find out what you were up to.'

'Exercising.'

'I can see that. So this is what it takes to maintain a physique like yours.'

Mrs Peterson had reached the ladder now and raised a hand, running her fingers over one of the wooden rungs. Thomas eyed her, trying hard to keep his expression neutral. She had been a quiet travelling companion, saying very little over the meals they had all shared, but nevertheless Thomas had felt her eyes burning into him on a number of occasions, noted the mischievous smile that flickered across her lips when she thought no one else was looking. Thomas knew exactly what sort of woman she was and he knew it would be wise to keep his distance.

'I should be getting back to my wife,' Thomas said, emphasising the last word.

'Surely there is no rush. In her condition Lady Hunter will be glad of a few moments' rest.'

Mrs Peterson took another step towards him, moving around the ladder like a snake slithering effortlessly round an obstacle. Thomas planted his feet firmly on the ground, he refused to retreat any further.

A flash of white caught his eye from the doorway of the barn and Thomas surreptitiously focused his gaze over Mrs Peterson's shoulder.

'We haven't had much chance to get to know each other, just the two of us,' the married woman said. Her hand darted out and brushed an invisible speck of dirt from Thomas's shirt, her fingers lingering on the soft material for far longer than was necessary.

Thomas glimpsed the figure outside the barn

freeze and knew immediately it was Rosa. She'd come to find him and now realised he was alone in the barn with Mrs Peterson. If she ran, the speculation on her part would completely ruin his chances of ever convincing her to marry him.

'I really should be getting back,' Thomas repeated, sufficiently loudly for Rosa to hear.

'Come now, don't tease a woman,' Mrs Peterson said.

Rosa hadn't moved from her spot just outside the barn doors. It dawned on him she didn't know he'd spotted her and had decided to see what unfolded between him and Mrs Peterson for herself.

Mrs Peterson raised her other hand and placed it on his upper arm, squeezing the muscle underneath her fingers. She'd taken a step closer to him and now there was only a couple of inches between their bodies. He smelled the sweet scent of lavender radiating from her skin. Despite her proximity, despite what she was offering him, there wasn't even the smallest flicker of desire on his part.

He glanced up again. Rosa was still outside, still watching, thinking she hadn't been spotted. There was the chance he could turn this encounter to his advantage. It would be underhanded and sly, but he hadn't exactly been truthful with Rosa so far, so why worry about it now?

'What are you suggesting, Mrs Peterson?' Thomas asked, his voice completely emotionless.

'I'm suggesting we enjoy each other's company a little more. That you put those big muscles of yours to good use.' Her body was pressed up against his now, her hips moving ever so slightly against his own.

Thomas grasped her by the arms and heard her moan at his touch, before the confusion blossomed in her eyes as he gently but firmly pushed her away from him.

'I am sorry if I have ever given you the wrong impression,' he said. 'But I care only for one woman.'

Hurt and rejection flashed across Mrs Peterson's face, but then she rallied and Thomas realised she hadn't been deterred yet.

'There is no suggestion that you don't love your wife, Lord Hunter. All I'm proposing is a little fun, indulging in a little mutual pleasure between two adults. I'm sure you do not wish to trouble your wife with your desires in her condition.'

'I do not wish to offend you, Mrs Peterson, but Rosa is everything I could ever want. She is beautiful and kind and *loyal*,' he stressed the last word, stepping back from his friend's wife at the same time. 'I would never do anything to jeopardise my relationship with her, whatever her condition and whatever anyone else offers.'

The speech was entirely for Rosa's benefit, listening outside the barn, and Thomas only felt a little guilt at being so underhand. If she would just see sense and agree to his proposal he wouldn't have to sink to these depths.

Mrs Peterson recoiled as if she'd been slapped, an unattractive grimace taking over her delicate features.

'I am sure this was just a momentary lapse in your dedication to your own husband and we will have no need to speak of it again,' Thomas said, brushing past Mrs Peterson and striding down the length of the barn. He had to hide a smile as he caught a glimpse of Rosa retreating back into the inn before she could be found eavesdropping.

Chapter Twelve

'Damn shame if you ask me—pardon my language, Lady Hunter.' Mr Peterson gesticulated wildly as he spoke, almost knocking over the bottle of wine that stood on the table.

Rosa wasn't sure what was a *damn shame*, she'd stopped following the conversation a few minutes earlier when it became clear Mr Peterson was completely drunk and not making any sense whatsoever.

'I think it's time we got you to bed,' Thomas said with a grimace.

'Oh, not yet, the night is young,' Mr Peterson protested.

'Your wife will be wondering where you are.'

Rosa thought she saw the inebriated man shrug his shoulders dejectedly.

'I doubt it,' he slurred. 'Has more headaches than a dog that's been kicked by a horse.'

Mrs Peterson had indeed sent her apologies she wouldn't be present at dinner, pleading an awful headache. More like embarrassment, Rosa thought, then chastised herself for being unkind. She wasn't sure exactly what she had witnessed in the barn when she had stepped out into the courtyard, but it had looked very much like Mrs Peterson propositioning Thomas and Thomas turning her down.

She watched as Thomas gripped Mr Peterson by the arms, manoeuvred him from his chair and took most of his weight before moving out of the room. Rosa followed behind, wondering if she should do anything to help, but not wanting to get too close to the stumbling feet and flailing arms.

Once Mr Peterson was safely deposited outside his room Thomas turned his attention to Rosa.

'Shall we retire for the evening?' he asked.

It was an entirely innocent question, asked with no guile or even a hint of ulterior motive, but Rosa felt a shiver run down the length of her spine all the same. This was the moment she had been anticipating and dreading in equal measure; the moment she and Thomas would step over the threshold of their shared room and decide exactly what the night held for them.

Rosa tried to stop the unbidden images that flashed before her eyes. Thomas emerging naked and glistening from the lake, Thomas pulling his shirt slowly over his head, his body slick with sweat after boxing. Thomas moving in closer to her in the carriage, his body flush against hers, his eyes heavy with desire and promise.

Rosa found herself nodding, not trusting herself to speak. Knowing her luck her voice would come out as a high-pitched squeak and Thomas would be fully aware of the trepidation she was feeling.

He held open the door for her, waiting for her to enter the small room before he followed behind her. There was a loud click as the door closed behind them and then silence.

'I can sleep in the barn if this makes you too uncomfortable.'

Damn him for being so chivalrous. She would have no qualms about sending a man to sleep in the barn if he didn't offer to do so with such good grace.

'Would you unlace my dress?' Rosa was gratified to see Thomas's eyes widen. At least she could still surprise him, even if she was probably ten times more nervous than he about their sleeping arrangements.

She turned slowly towards the window, glad the soft candlelight concealed the worst of her blushes. She sensed Thomas step in closer to her before she felt his fingers on her skin. Gently he unclasped the fastening at the top of her dress, before letting his fingers drop to the delicate ties beneath, pulling to loosen and unlace. Again and again Thomas's fingers brushed against her skin, each time sending tiny jolts through her body. His breath was warm against her neck and Rosa felt herself arch her back ever so slightly, letting her head roll back towards him. She swayed, knowing she should step away but not quite able to, and then as she felt his steadying palm against her lower back Rosa stiffened.

Even though her dress was loose and she wore only a cotton chemise underneath, it felt as though her chest was being held in a vice which was tightening second by second. A pain shot through her body and her breath came in short gasps.

'Rosa?' His voice sounded distant and faint in Rosa's ears. 'What's the matter?'

Not now. This couldn't be happening to her now. This wasn't David, pressing her up against the wall, forcing his lips on to hers. This wasn't David, lifting her skirts whilst she desperately tried to hold them down, silencing her protests with a rough hand over her mouth. This was Thomas, kind, patient Thomas. A man innocently unlacing her dress. A man who'd never once even tried to kiss her, not really.

She felt Thomas's strong hands encircling her arms and allowed him to lead her to the bed. Gently he sat her down and rested a hand on her shoulder. Even this platonic touch made Rosa tense and she could only breathe properly again when Thomas retreated to the other side of the room.

After a minute or two Rosa had gained control of herself enough to realise Thomas was watching her warily, but had not tried to approach again.

'I'm sorry,' she mumbled.

'Nothing to apologise for,' he said, giving her a smile that would reassure even the most anxious worrier.

She waited for the inevitable questions. A panic attack was not the usual way to react when a man placed a hand in the small of your back. Especially a man she had spent so much time with.

'I don't know why…' she started, but Thomas shook his head.

'You don't have to tell me anything.'

Rosa frowned. Normally Thomas wanted to

know every last detail about everything. He was a man who liked to be in control and for him to hold back from questioning her must mean she had worried him. Or he already thought he knew what had occurred.

'I wouldn't have suggested we share a room if I'd known,' he said after a few minutes.

'Known what?' Rosa was feeling more her normal self now and his understanding tone was beginning to grate on her.

'What you went through with David.'

'You don't know what I went through with David.'

'You're right, of course.'

He capitulated so easily that Rosa felt her entire face crease into a frown.

'My earlier offer still stands. I am happy to sleep in the barn.'

She was half-tempted to send him off to bed down with the horses just to wipe the understanding, commiserating look from his face.

She sighed. Thomas was being a complete gentleman, giving her space, not pressing to know why a man's hand on her back made her turn into a shuddering idiot, and she wanted to punish him for being so nice.

'No. We are adults and I am quite recovered now, thank you.'

He nodded, not moving from his position leaning against the wall next to the door.

'But perhaps you could step outside whilst I finish undressing,' she suggested.

He was out the door before Rosa had finished the sentence, closing it softly behind him and leaving Rosa to change in private.

As she slipped off her dress and brushed out her hair Rosa cautiously allowed herself to analyse her reaction to Thomas a few minutes earlier. David had done a terrible thing to her, that she knew. She'd known she would be skittish around men, had planned never really to get close to one ever again, but then her life had collided with Thomas's. Thomas with the startlingly blue eyes, Thomas with the taut muscles and the protective nature. Thomas who seemed intent on rescuing her from everyone and everything, including herself. The number of times she'd wanted him to kiss her, wanted him to take her in his arms and pull her to him. It had surprised her after what had happened with David, but she couldn't deny she was attracted to Thomas.

Then he'd laid a hand on the small of her back, the most innocuous of touches, and it was as though she'd been back in the kitchen of David's family home, petrified that someone would discover them, petrified someone wouldn't before it was too late. Maybe it was because David had always touched her there, his intimate little reminder when they were in public that they were bound together.

Rosa shook her head. She didn't want to think of David or the damage he'd inflicted on her. True, there would always be a reminder, the small life that was growing inside her every day, but Rosa knew that was a positive, something good that would come out of something bad.

She slipped into bed, propping herself up on the fluffy pillows, and waited for Thomas to reenter the room. She would have to give him some sort of explanation as to what had occurred, but she wasn't sure how much she wanted to tell him.

Thomas paced up and down the corridor outside their room, his fists balling and unballing as images of a faceless scoundrel accosting Rosa hurtled through his mind. He knew exactly what that little episode in the room had been about, exactly what had happened to her.

Over the last few weeks as she'd revealed parts of her story to him Thomas had managed to piece together much of what her life must have been like in England. The overbearing mother, the kind but downtrodden father, the dull existence of a well-bred young lady stagnating in the countryside when the London Season was over. Cue the entrance of a slightly older man. A man who should know better than to dally with a debutante. A man who should be interested in protecting a woman's reputation, not ruining it.

That was where Rosa had always skipped part of the story. He'd heard how she'd waited for a proposal that had never come, how even when presented with a pregnancy the so-called gentleman had not stepped up and married the woman he had ruined. But Rosa had never spoken about what had actually happened between her and this young man.

Now he was wondering if it had been entirely consensual. Given her reaction to his touch he rather thought not.

After ten minutes had passed Thomas knocked quietly on the door and waited for Rosa's command to enter. She was already in bed, the covers pulled up almost to her chin, and Thomas had to stifle a laugh.

'I can close my eyes whilst you undress,' Rosa suggested, her voice a little uncertain.

Thomas shook his head, kicking his boots off and then falling into the very upright and very firm chair that stood on one side of the bed. Rosa had placed a blanket and pillow to one side for him, but even with these he doubted he would sleep much. Maybe he would be better off in the hay with the animals.

'What did you think Mr Peterson meant by his comments at dinner?' Rosa asked, her voice unnaturally shrill. Thomas could sense her nervousness even from this distance and weighed up how best to put her at her ease.

'I get the sense Mrs Peterson isn't as attentive a wife as my good friend would hope for.'

He smiled at Rosa, seeing her weigh up his answer.

'Why do you think that?'

This was too easy. She was just giving him the opportunity to divulge the little meeting with Mrs Peterson in the barn, the meeting she had witnessed but didn't know he knew that. It was exactly the chance he'd been waiting for—the chance to show he was trustworthy, the sort of man she would want to marry.

Thomas opened his mouth to reply, but found the words catching in his throat. Now didn't seem like the right time to deceive Rosa. After what he'd found out about her relationship with David he couldn't quite palate his underhand plan to get her to agree to marry him.

'I saw you in the barn,' Rosa said softly.

Thomas remained quiet.

'I heard what you said.'

'It was the truth.'

'We're not married. It wouldn't have been a betrayal if you had taken up her offer. She's a very attractive woman.'

Thomas shook his head. 'It would have been a betrayal. Peterson is my friend. And we may not be married, but I hold you in much too high a regard to even contemplate any other woman.'

As the words left his mouth Thomas found he actually believed what he was saying. They weren't just the honeyed words to seduce her into marrying him, he actually did hold her in high regard not to want to hurt her in any way.

'And Mrs Peterson is not an attractive woman. Beauty comes from inside, cruelty and jealousy overshadow any skin-deep prettiness.' He looked at Rosa, took in her soft features and warm smile. 'You glow when you stand next to any other woman, Rosa, you outshine them all.'

He could see the now-familiar blush blossoming on Rosa's cheeks. He loved that blush...that signal that something he'd said or done had affected her in such a primitive way.

She shifted in bed, her hair falling around her shoulders and across the bedclothes, and Thomas found himself wishing he was sitting there next to her, close enough to touch her, to smell her. There was something so strong about Rosa, but tonight he had caught a glimpse of her vulnerable side and he wanted to wrap her in his arms and protect her from the Davids of this world.

Physically shaking himself, Thomas momentarily closed his eyes. This wasn't what all this was supposed to be about. He wasn't actually supposed to be seducing Rosa, for his entire adult life he had managed to resist the allure of attractive women, Rosa should be no different. Why then did his whole body thrum with excitement as he imagined slipping into bed next to her?

'What happened with David?' Thomas asked, surprising himself with the question. He was an inquisitive man, a man who always managed to make people tell him what he wanted to know, but the last thing he wanted was to hurt Rosa by making her retell a painful experience.

She sighed and for a moment Thomas thought that would be the end of the matter, but then she started speaking, her words quiet and measured.

'I suppose you deserve to know,' Rosa said.

He didn't, no one *needed* to know what had gone on between them, but Thomas didn't stop her. He wondered if that made him a bad person.

'We arranged a rendezvous one night. I thought David meant to propose. He hadn't approached my father, but I fooled myself into thinking we were far too modern, far too independent for that.'

Thomas could imagine Rosa creeping out, certain she was going to meet the man of her dreams, the Prince Charming young girls were conditioned to hope for.

'He let me in the kitchen door and kissed me immediately. I could tell there was something different about him, something that I hadn't sensed before.' She shifted in bed, letting the sheets fall a little, but Thomas could see she still clutched them tightly with her fingers. As she tried to speak again her voice caught in her throat and he realised he couldn't let her go on. He might want to hear it, might want to know what she had been through so he could better judge what advances she would respond to now, but he wouldn't be able to live with himself if he made her speak of something she didn't want to relive.

'Shhh,' he said, rising for his chair and taking the two short paces to the bed. He sat down beside her and took her hand in his own. 'You don't have to tell me anything, not if you don't want to.'

She looked at him, eyes wide and frightened, and her lips parted a little. In that instant Thomas knew he had to kiss her. He wanted to fold her in his arms and never let go, but more than that he wanted to kiss her soft lips, hear her moans as he trailed his fingers across her skin.

'Inappropriate,' he murmured. This was not the right moment to start acting on his lust for Rosa.

'What?'

'I can imagine what he did to you, Rosa. And I don't want you to have to think about it again, not for my benefit. If you wish to talk about it then please do, but if you don't then that is your choice as well.'

'He didn't force me. Not exactly.'

The *not exactly* almost broke his heart. The scoundrel had forced himself upon her and then made Rosa feel as though she was the one who'd done wrong.

'Rosa, you are a well-bred young woman, seduced by an older and trusted man. Even without anything else that is a wrongdoing on his part.'

'He gave me a ring,' Rosa said. 'But he never actually said the words, never asked me to marry him.' She closed her eyes and Thomas could see the blood draining slowly from her face at the memory. 'Somehow he manoeuvred me up against the wall and all of a sudden his hands were under my skirts.' She swallowed and Thomas realised he was holding his breath as she spoke. It was devastating to listen to Rosa's ordeal, to see how much she blamed herself for this scoundrel's actions. 'I said no, asked him to stop, but he just ignored me.'

Suppressing the rage he felt for this David, Thomas tried to concentrate on what Rosa was saying instead of the burning fury at how she had been treated.

'But I didn't scream,' Rosa said softly. 'I could have woken that whole household up, put a stop to what David was doing in that way, and I didn't.'

'That doesn't mean what he did was acceptable,' Thomas said. 'He forced you, even if you didn't shout out for help.'

'I thought he loved me.' She said it quietly, as if ashamed she had been fooled so easily.

'I'm sure that was his plan, to make you think he loved you.'

'I used to think girls who were seduced by men who had no intention of marrying them such fools.'

'Not fools. You see the good in people, Rosa. It is a wonderful attribute, but sometimes it means you get hurt.'

'Sometimes I still feel his hands on me, his breath on my neck.'

Thomas closed his eyes for just a second, trying to master the wave of anger that crashed over him. If he ever met this David it would take all of his substantial self-control not to beat the man to a pulp. No one should have to live in such fear.

He looked at Rosa, studying her features, the expressions that flitted across her face. Right now he had to put his own agenda aside. Tomorrow he could re-evaluate the best way to get her to agree to marry him, but tonight he would put her first.

'You're safe now, Rosa,' he said, squeezing her hand. 'And I promise to protect you all the time you remain with me.'

She looked at him, a half-smile playing on her lips.

'If I agree to be your wife?'

'Whether you agree to be my wife or not.'

They sat in silence for a few minutes, then slowly Rosa allowed her head to sink down to Thomas's shoulder. He listened to her breathing, watched the steady rise and fall of her chest. For a long while he could tell she wasn't asleep, but didn't want to shatter the peace by talking any more.

It was strangely comforting to feel the weight of her head on his shoulder. For so long he had made it an aim in life to push everyone else away, that way no one else would suffer if he became ill, but he was slowly realising that in doing so he was missing out on something important. The closeness that had blossomed between him and Rosa over the last few weeks was more than anything he'd experienced in years. Not since university had he encouraged friendships and never had he actually wanted to sit and talk to someone as he did with Rosa. Maybe he should just tell her the awful truth about his family, maybe it would be cathartic to be honest with someone he cared about.

As soon as the idea had occurred to him he dismissed it. Anyone in their right mind would run away screaming if they knew what possible fate would befall them if they tied themselves to him. Years of watching his mind and body decline, the worry about him fathering any children and their possible fate. No, it would be better to stick to his plan—to secure a companion for his mother, a healthy heir for the estate and then distance himself from everyone who cared about him to save them the pain later on.

Chapter Thirteen

'Venice is such a *smelly* city,' Mrs Peterson said, waving a dismissive hand out of the carriage window.

'You've been before?' Rosa asked, trying to keep the irritation from her voice.

'No, but everyone says so.'

Rosa managed to restrain herself from rolling her eyes and leaned forward further to try to catch all of the sights of the city they were entering.

'I think it sounds fascinating. A city built on water.'

'If you like that sort of thing.'

'I do,' Rosa said, a little more abruptly than she'd meant to. Six hours she'd been cooped up in the carriage with the annoying woman and her patience was starting to wear thin.

'So tell me,' Mrs Peterson said, a sly look crossing her face, 'what is the enigmatic Lord Hunter really like?'

Rosa sat back and regarded her companion warily. Over the last few days she'd noticed the sidelong looks, the fluttering of her eyelashes, the pouting lips and seductive smiles Mrs Peterson employed whenever Thomas was around. She didn't flirt overtly, not enough for poor Mr Peterson to complain, but Rosa had noticed how she changed when Thomas was close.

At first she'd felt some unexpected pangs of jealousy. Thomas wasn't hers to be jealous about, not really, but when Mrs Peterson stroked his arm or tilted her face up so the sun made her eyes sparkle Rosa had felt jealous all the same. As time had gone on and Thomas had not reacted even slightly to Mrs Peterson's flirtations Rosa had started to find the other woman's behaviour a little amusing.

'What do you mean?'

'Well is he a kind husband? Is he a bore? Is he wild in the bedroom? Come, Lady Hunter, we're friends and this is what friends talk about.'

The carriage was beginning to slow and Rosa wondered if she could delay enough to avoid having to answer any of Mrs Peterson's questions, but as the silence dragged out Rosa sighed and started talking.

'He is kind, the kindest man I've ever known. Generous, too, although he will not accept thanks for his generosity. He holds everyone to very exacting standards, most especially himself, and I don't think anyone could describe him as a bore.'

'You're ignoring one of my questions, Lady Hunter,' Mrs Peterson teased. 'Perhaps I am to assume therefore Lord Hunter is only mediocre in the bedroom.'

'Assume what you will, Mrs Peterson, but Lord Hunter is not mediocre at anything he turns his hand to.' Rosa said it without blushing, trying to hide her smile as Mrs Peterson's eyes widened.

'You mean...'

'Ladies,' Thomas said, throwing the carriage door open. 'Welcome to Venice.'

Rosa almost leapt into Thomas's arms she was so eager to escape the carriage. She regretted assuring Thomas she would be perfectly happy if he chose to ride into the city, he'd been such an attentive travelling companion sitting in the carriage with her day after day that he deserved one morning of freedom. What she hadn't been prepared for was Mrs Peterson's insistence she travel with her instead.

'Smelly,' Mrs Peterson said, nodding her head in satisfaction.

Rosa looked around her in awe. Although she had caught glimpses of the city on their journey through the outskirts, nothing had prepared her for this. Traders shouted in rapid Italian, enticing customers to buy their wares. Immaculately presented men strolled through the streets, calling words of greeting to the beautifully dressed women regarding the world below from their stone balconies. To one side the canal heaved with small boats, transporting passengers and goods, the men in charge of navigating the small waterways shouting and gesticulating as they bumped and scraped their way towards their destinations.

'Magnificent, isn't it?' Thomas whispered in her ear. 'I think Venice is my favourite city in the entire world.'

She could see why. Everywhere she looked there was life and vitality. Most people looked happy, and the ones that didn't were not afraid to show their emotions, gesticulating wildly and venting their anger or irritation.

'I'm sure our lodgings will have rooms available,' Mr Peterson said, dismounting his horse and taking his wife by the arm, guiding her out of the way of a young woman carrying a basket full of fresh fish.

Rosa held her breath. She wanted Thomas to refuse, for their party to split and to go back to it just being her and him. It wasn't that she didn't like the Petersons, or at least she liked Mr Peterson well enough, but she craved the private moments she'd shared with Thomas at his villa and on the first half of their journey.

'I'm afraid this is where we must say our goodbyes,' Thomas said, clasping his old friend by the hand. 'I have an apartment prepared for the night and tomorrow we seek passage to England.'

'Surely not, Lord Hunter. You must dine with us one last time at the very least.'

'It has been a pleasure, Mrs Peterson, but tonight I must insist my wife rests before we continue our arduous journey.'

Rosa watched the other woman pout and felt Thomas slip his arm around her waist, almost possessively.

'Can we not tempt you to join us, while Lady Hunter rests?'

'Hush, my dear, leave the poor chap alone. We have intruded on their company for far too long, Lord and Lady Hunter will be wanting some time together.' Mr Peterson smiled apologetically and for an instant Rosa felt sorry for this sweet man who knew all too well his wife was flirting with his old friend.

'Look after him,' Mr Peterson said as he kissed Rosa's hand.

She frowned, surprised by the comment. If

ever there was anyone who didn't need looking after it was Thomas. He was so strong, so capable.

They finished their goodbyes and watched the Petersons disappear into the crowd. Thomas spent a few minutes arranging for the groom they had hired to find a stable for the horses before he was back at her side.

'An apartment?' Rosa asked as he took her by the arm.

'Unless you'd rather spend the night with the Petersons?'

She swatted him lightly on the shoulder.

'It is the apartment of a friend. He is currently out of the country and has kindly offered me the use of it whenever I'm in town.'

'How very convenient.'

'Wait until you see it, my dear.'

Rosa felt herself almost skipping along she felt so light and happy. She had Thomas back to herself, they were in a city she had always dreamed about visiting and the Di Mercurios had been left far behind them.

Thomas led her through the maze of streets, over crumbling stone bridges, across quaint little squares. The entire city was moving and alive, and Rosa felt its vitality energising her as they walked.

* * *

After fifteen minutes they stopped outside a plain building with a thick wooden door. Thomas knocked and greeted the short, swarthy man who opened the door like a long-lost friend.

'The rooms we're staying in are upstairs.' Thomas grinned, indicating the sweeping staircase. Before Rosa could react he lifted her into his arms and took the stairs two at a time, following the Italian man up the three flights.

Thomas didn't set her down until they were over the threshold of the most beautiful room Rosa had ever been in. Light filtered in through shuttered windows, which when opened revealed a sumptuous sitting room. Silks and satins covered almost every surface and the floor was layered with thick rugs. A chandelier fit for the grandest ballroom hung from the ceiling and delicate glass lamps filled every recess.

'Do you like it?' Thomas asked.

'It's fit for royalty.'

Thomas grasped her hand and pulled her from room to room, showing her the beds laden with dozens of pillows, a room dedicated solely to bathing and finished with the highlight of the entire residence: the balcony. Out here they had a view over one of the canals. Far below them the boats skimmed across the water, the boatmen shouting at each other in rapid Italian as they passed. Over the rooftops Rosa could make out the tips of churches and bell towers, and far beyond the shimmering of the lagoon.

'Rosa,' Thomas said, his voice low and serious. 'Marry me.'

For an instant she almost agreed. It was a heady combination: a romantic spot and a man she adored asking to tie them together for eternity. She wavered. Still he would not tell her the true reason for his proposal, still she sensed he was holding something back, but as time went on and she found herself falling for the man asking her to marry him Rosa wondered how much that actually mattered. He was offering her a respectable future for her and her child. She knew he was a good man, a man who would never purposefully hurt her, so maybe it didn't matter if he couldn't open up to her fully just yet. There would be time for that when they were married.

'Marry me,' he repeated, looking deep into her eyes.

'Thomas…' she began, but before an answer could form on her lips his mouth was on hers. He kissed her hungrily, as if he'd been waiting for an eternity to kiss her, to taste her. Rosa felt all her protestations die in that moment as his lips met hers.

She stiffened slightly as his hands came up and encircled her back, but then as her body realised it was Thomas kissing her, Thomas holding her, she relaxed. Rosa felt his fingers stroking across her skin even through the cotton of her dress and moaned softly. For weeks she had been dreaming of this moment, craving Thomas's kiss, his touch. Now it was a reality and it was so much better than she'd ever imagined.

His lips danced across the angle of her jaw down on to her neck and Rosa shivered as his breath tickled her skin. A warm glow was building from deep inside her and Rosa felt pure joy as Thomas pulled her even closer to him, whispering her name. No matter what he was hiding from her, this couldn't be faked. He desired her, she'd seen it in his eyes before, just as she desired him.

'Marry me, Rosa,' he murmured into her ear, taking her lobe gently between his teeth as he waited for her answer.

'Yes,' she managed to utter, groaning in protest as Thomas pulled away to study her.

'Yes?'

'Yes, I'll marry you.'

Rosa saw the triumphant look for a second before his lips were back on hers, more frenzied, more passionate even than a few minutes ago. She felt his body press against hers, felt the evidence of his desire as he held her close to him.

'Say it again,' he whispered, as he ran his hands down her back, resting them tantalisingly just above her buttocks.

'I will marry you,' she repeated, loving the fire that was burning in his eyes for her. She'd never imagined wanting another man after David, but Thomas made her feel as though that was all just a bad dream.

He kissed her one more time, before reluctantly pulling away, holding on to the stone balustrade as if to steady himself.

'Then we have a wedding to organise.'

Rosa wanted to protest, to ask him what the hurry was. She wanted him to scoop her up in his arms and carry her through to one of the luxurious beds and kiss her until she begged for mercy, but something stopped her. She'd never been shy before, never doubted that men might find her attractive. She'd not been conceited enough to think herself the belle of the debutantes, but she knew she had a pretty enough face and no major flaws, but that had been before she was five months pregnant. Now she felt cumbersome and swollen, and wondered that

Thomas felt anything resembling desire for her at all. She didn't want to push him, only to be rejected, despite the fire she saw in his eyes.

'You rest, my dear. I will return later with everything organised.'

And without another word he left the room. Rosa remained where she was long after the door had closed behind him, uncertain of what had just occurred. She'd just agreed to marry him and then he'd as good as fled from her presence. Despite this being her first engagement Rosa was pretty sure that wasn't how things were meant to happen.

Slowly she sat down at the dainty writing desk and took a piece of paper, holding the pen for over a minute before beginning to write.

Dear Caroline,

I am to be married. Truly I do not quite know how this happened, but I am sure Lord Hunter is a good man who will provide for me and my child. I'm still in shock after accepting his proposal, but wanted to pen you this short note so you will not worry about me.

After our wedding we will return to England, to his family home. When we are back on English soil I will write again and hopefully it will not be too long until we are reunited.

I miss you and your sage wisdom.

All my love,

Rosa

Chapter Fourteen

Thomas strode up and down outside the bedroom, trying not to look down at his hands. Two minutes ago they had been shaking and he kept telling himself it was just from nerves. It was natural for a man to be a little tense on his wedding day, natural for there to be a minute tremor in his fingers.

He glanced down again, holding his hands out in front of him and frowning as he scrutinised them. Nothing. Not even a hint of movement. With a sigh of relief Thomas allowed himself to sink down into one of the plush chairs and close his eyes for a second.

Soon the wedding would be over and they would be on their way to England. True, they would be thrown in close proximity during the voyage, but once he had delivered Rosa safely into his mother's care he would be able to distance himself.

Again the memory of their kiss resurfaced, rekindling the desire that had been hiding just below the surface these past three days. He wanted Rosa, more than he'd ever wanted another woman in his entire life, and she was so tantalisingly close. Each day since she'd agreed to marry him he'd seen her hurt eyes as he had disappeared for hours on end, pretending there was much to prepare for the simple ceremony and their trip home. The truth was he couldn't bear to be close to her—every moment he could see her, touch her, smell her, he risked giving in to his desire and ruining everything.

'I will not desire her,' he murmured to himself. That was not the point of their marriage. Although in a few hours they would be husband and wife he had never planned for it to be a conventional union. He needed someone who would be grateful for the protection and status he could give them, and not be too upset when he declined to visit her bedchamber. If only he hadn't kissed Rosa. It hadn't been planned or calculated, hadn't been part of his ploy to get her to agree to marry him. He'd just seen her standing on the balcony, her lips pursed as she considered his proposal, and he'd just *had* to kiss her.

'Never again,' he promised himself, feeling

the stab of disappointment as he denied his body the one thing it really desired.

He stood abruptly as the door to Rosa's bedroom opened and she stepped out nervously. Immediately all his resolutions were forgotten as Thomas moved towards her and took her hand. He bent over it, kissing the soft skin gently, before raising his head and allowing his eyes to meet hers.

'Are you sure?' Rosa asked simply.

He almost laughed. She probably thought his absence the past few days was from doubting his decision to marry her now she had actually agreed. Little did she know he'd had to put physical distance between them, had to avoid any situation where he might accidentally touch her because one touch would be all it took to shatter his resolve.

'I'm sure.'

They walked in silence down the spirals of the staircase and out into the street below. Thomas could feel Rosa's hand clutching at his arm and for the first time he realised what a momentous day this was for her. All along he'd told himself she was gaining something from this arrangement, but he'd tried to deny all that she was giving up. Once they were married she would no longer be free to do as she desired, she would have a husband, someone else to consider, and whilst he was alive she would not be able to marry another man of her choosing. They would be tied together at least in name for the entirety of whatever future he had.

To make it worse Thomas felt uneasy about walking down the aisle with Rosa with the secret of the disease that ran in his family still unspoken between them. He knew Rosa had a right to know, soon she would be part of the Hunter family, too, but he kept telling himself she would never be directly affected. He would leave long before the disease had a chance to develop in him. Still, the guilt of his secret weighed him down as they crossed the cobbled street.

He led her down to the edge of one of the small canals, helping her down into one of the narrow gondolas awaiting them. He saw her eyes widen and a smile of delight appear on her face and part of him began to relax. This was Rosa he was marrying, not some stranger. He knew what she liked, what she disliked. Theirs might not be the most conventional of marriages, but they could rub along together well enough for the next few months until he set off on his travels again.

'Are you nervous?' he asked her as they settled back on the cushions lining the bench on the small vessel.

Rosa laughed. 'Of course. I'm about to marry a man I barely know. A man my mother would approve of.'

'I feel as though that's a bad thing.'

'It is. She would approve of your title, your family heritage. No doubt you have a large entry in *Debrett's*.'

'But would she approve of me?' Thomas asked, moving in closer so he could drop his voice and whisper in Rosa's ear. He was rewarded by one of her fabulous blushes and a stern, rather matronly look.

'No, probably not,' Rosa conceded. 'You are far too impulsive and spend too little time overseeing your estate.'

Thomas settled back on the cushions and watched the city float past as they skimmed over the water. He felt strangely content sitting here next to Rosa, for a while he could forget he was about to deceive her, trap her in marriage without telling her his awful family secret, instead just enjoying sitting with her by his side in his favourite city in the world.

Too soon the gondola bobbed to a halt and Thomas had to lift Rosa on to dry land. She fidgeted nervously whilst he paid the *gondo-*

liere, looking about her as if she couldn't decide whether to run whilst she still had the chance or cling to him until they'd said their vows.

He'd found a small chapel a few streets away from St Mark's Square with a priest who had agreed to marry them. For a hefty fee this man had overlooked the fact Thomas wasn't Catholic, their visitor status to the city and the need for an official ceremony quickly without all the usual rules and regulations. Thomas knew it would have been simpler to wait until they were back in England, but now he'd secured Rosa's agreement to marry him he didn't want to waste any time in making things official.

'Thomas,' Rosa said, her voice unusually quiet. 'I'm Catholic.'

He grinned at her, at the worried expression on her face and the momentary panic in her eyes.

'I know, my dear,' he said, patting her on the hand reassuringly.

'No, I mean I may not be a very good Catholic...' she grimaced, one hand floating to her abdomen '...but I cannot get married outside the Catholic faith. The ceremony has to be Catholic for it to be valid.'

'I know, my dear,' Thomas repeated. 'We're in Italy. All the priests are Catholic. All the churches are Catholic. The only thing that isn't

Catholic is me and I'm assured that as long as I'm baptised in a Christian faith, which I am, we can still marry in the Catholic Church.'

'Oh.' Rosa considered his words for a moment. 'You really have thought of everything, haven't you?'

'I aim to please.'

He led her through the narrow, winding streets, over a couple of stone bridges and to the Chapel of the Virgin Mother. As they neared the chapel Thomas sensed Rosa slow and her grip on his arm tightened a fraction.

'Is something wrong?'

Rosa shook her head, biting her lip at the same time.

'Rosa, look at me. Look at me.' He waited until she complied. 'You can still back out,' he said softly, hoping he wouldn't regret the words. 'We may not know each other well and it may seem like a rush to get married, but I promise you I will be a good husband to you. I will ensure you and your child want for nothing, that you are housed in comfort and cared for. I will never be cruel or demanding and you will be free to make your own decisions about your future.'

He watched her as she searched his eyes, as if looking for something more. He wondered if she wanted a declaration of love, but dismissed the idea immediately. Rosa was an intelligent and observant woman, she would know any such declaration was a lie. He was fond of her, he enjoyed her company and rather inconveniently he desired her in his bed, but he did not love her. He'd shut his heart off from the idea of love many years ago and even Rosa's plentiful charms could not change his mind on that front.

Eventually she nodded, even managing a weak smile.

'Shall we go in, my lady?'

Thomas pushed open the door to the small chapel and led Rosa down the narrow aisle. There were only five rows of pews, all of which were empty except the very front row.

'Who are they?' Rosa whispered as they walked towards the priest standing at the front of the church.

'Our witnesses.'

She gave them a sidelong look and then leaned her head in to Thomas again.

'But who are they?'

He shrugged. He'd paid the priest extra to provide the witnesses. They were probably devout churchgoers, or maybe the priest's drinking friends. It didn't matter to him, as long as the marriage was legal and witnessed by the correct number of people.

'Signorina Rosa Rothwell?' the priest asked.

Rosa nodded.

'Normally I would conduct a short interview in the weeks before a wedding to ensure both parties were entering into the union of marriage for the correct reasons,' the priest said quietly. 'I understand there are some time pressures at work which mean the usual formalities need to be dispensed with, but I must ask: is there any reason you would like to postpone the ceremony?'

Thomas found he was holding his breath as he waited for Rosa's response. Eventually she gave a small shake of her head and the priest smiled broadly at them both. Clapping his hands together, he arranged Thomas and Rosa in front of him and addressed the gathered witnesses.

Thirty seconds in to the ceremony and Thomas found himself wondering if the priest was drunk. A minute in he was quite certain of it and was contemplating whether there was a touch of madness about the elderly priest as well.

Rosa sent Thomas a worried glance and he responded with his most reassuring smile. It didn't matter if the old man was drunk or mad, he was an ordained priest, licensed to marry them and he seemed to be saying all the right words.

'Miss Rothwell, Lord Hunter, have you come

here freely and without impediment to give yourselves to each other in marriage?'

As Rosa said yes alongside him Thomas felt a swell of triumph. There were more questions to come, and the vows themselves, but he'd had a horrible feeling she might remember all of her reservations about marrying him and ask to postpone. Now she was committed. Only a few more minutes and they would be husband and wife.

'Will you honour each other as husband and wife for the rest of your lives?'

'Yes.'

'Will you accept children lovingly from God and raise them according to the law of Christ and his Church?'

All eyes in the chapel drifted to Rosa's bump as hurriedly he and Rosa agreed.

'Since it is your intention to enter into marriage, join your right hands and declare your consent before God and the Church.'

'I, Thomas William Hunter, take you, Rosa Rothwell, to be my wife. I promise to be true to you in good times and in bad, in sickness and in health. I will love you and honour you all the days of my life.'

He looked up at Rosa as he spoke, saw the nervousness and tentative hope in her eyes. She'd suffered so much, lost so much in such a short space of time. He knew she was trying to curb her hopes, to rein in any dreams of a normal life, but still her natural optimism and excitement were breaking through.

As she met his gaze he felt something stick in his throat. He knew he shouldn't be deceiving her like this, knew he did actually care for Rosa and this wasn't the way to treat someone that you cared about, but also knew there was no going back now. He'd deceived her, kept the illness that ran in his family from her, and consigned her to sharing the dreadful uncertainty of never knowing if or when the disease might strike.

'I, Rosa Rothwell, take you, Thomas William Hunter, to be my husband. I promise to be true to you in good times and in bad, in sickness and in health. I will love you and honour you all the days of my life.'

As she spoke a shiver ran down Thomas's spine and he felt as though his whole world had just altered. Quickly he dismissed the notion. Rosa was nearly his wife in name, but soon he would have escorted her safely to the family home and he would be back to travelling the world on his own. In reality, hardly anything had changed.

'What God has joined, no man must divide,'

the priest declared, grasping their joined hands and raising them up for the assembled witnesses to see.

A prayer followed, something long and rambling and spoken in Italian that even Thomas could barely understand, before they exchanged rings. This part of the ceremony passed in a blur for Thomas, he could barely remember a word that had been spoken after the priest's declaration.

What God has joined, no man must divide.

It was so final, so complete. He had a wife. The one thing he had always vowed not to have. Someone else who relied on him, someone else to be hurt by whatever cruelties the future had in store for him.

Quickly Thomas shook his head. This was just the shock talking. Rosa knew this wasn't going to be a conventional marriage, it wasn't as though it was a love match. She would be safe and cared for, along with her child, keeping his mother company and keeping an eye on the estate. He would be her husband by law, but in reality they would lead very separate lives. If he did become ill and die Rosa's life would hardly change.

As they exchanged rings he caught Rosa smiling at him. Her earlier nervousness had disappeared and she'd even warmed to the exuberant and gesticulating priest, the suppressed laughter visible in her eyes as she watched the official enthusiastically instruct Thomas how to place the ring on her finger.

He rallied. This was what he'd wanted. Rosa was his wife, they were legally bound together and he could ensure she was protected in the future.

'Now the bride and groom often kiss,' the priest whispered, leaning forward. 'I'm sure you two young lovebirds know what to do.'

He treated them to a salacious wink that made Thomas question how rigid the vows of celibacy were being followed in this little corner of Venice.

Rosa turned to him and Thomas knew he would have to kiss her. Part of him rejoiced, shouted and screamed with happiness that one more time it was acceptable to pull her in close to him and cover her lips with his own. The other part of him knew it would make the notion of never touching, never kissing, never even entertaining a single night of intimacy with Rosa even more difficult.

Slowly they came together, stepping closer as if it were part of a much practised and choreographed dance. Thomas's hands raised instinctively to brush away the hair from her eyes, to tilt her face up so she was gazing up at him, waiting for the moment they came together. Savouring every second, he dipped his head and brushed his lips against hers, kissing her gently at first, knowing all the things he wanted to do to her were inappropriate in this religious place, but not being able to stop his imagination anyway.

As he felt Rosa respond to him, rising up on her toes to get closer to him, one delicate hand grasping the back of his neck as though she were clinging on for her life, he groaned and deepened the kiss, almost devouring her before pulling away. Now was not the time or the place, but that didn't make it any easier to step away from his new wife, especially knowing this would be the last time they kissed.

Quickly they signed the register, thanked the witnesses, shook hands with the jubilant priest and made their escape back down the aisle of the chapel.

'Lady Hunter,' Thomas said, as they stepped out into the brilliant sunshine from the dark chapel, 'would you care to accompany me on a little trip?'

Rosa laughed. 'Where are you taking me now, Husband?' She said the last word tentatively, as if she couldn't quite believe it was true.

'Well, we leave for England tomorrow, so I thought we should explore a little more of Venice on our last day.'

'That sounds wonderful.' She paused. 'Although I'd be quite happy returning to our rooms for the rest of the afternoon.'

She blushed a wonderful deep shade of pink as she made the suggestion and Thomas was left in no doubt as to her true meaning. He felt a surge of desire, his body responding to his new wife's suggestion of retiring to bed together until the time they had to board the ship for England. He wanted nothing more than to hurry her back to his bedroom, lock the doors and spend twelve hours exploring every inch of her body.

Thomas clenched his fist, digging his nails into the palm of his hand. He was better at controlling himself than this. Better at doing what was right, not what he wanted. He hadn't spent all those years remaining celibate to cave just when all the aspects of his life were falling into place.

Chapter Fifteen

Rosa felt her heart begin to pound in her chest as they walked up the sweeping staircase hand in hand. The afternoon had been pleasant—a trip to the island of Murano in the Venice lagoon to watch the traditional glassblowers go about their work and then an hour spent being gently propelled along the canals and waterways—but the entire excursion had been overshadowed by her nerves about this evening.

She'd seen Thomas's reaction when she had suggested they return to their rooms immediately after the wedding, seen the desire overshadowed by something else. Throughout their short relationship he had acted warily around her and she rather supposed it was because of the small life growing inside her, and the manner in which it was conceived.

If she was truthful, Rosa was nervous. She

didn't know how she would react to another man's hands on her, but this wasn't any man. This was Thomas. Her husband. The man she wondered if she was falling in love with.

'I'm sure you're weary, my dear,' Thomas said as he unlocked the door and escorted her into the set of rooms.

'It has been a wonderful day,' Rosa said.

'You must rest before our journey to England begins tomorrow.'

Rosa nodded, wondering whether he would take his place in her bedroom immediately or leave her to change first before coming in.

Thomas stopped outside her bedroom door and kissed her gently on the forehead, his hands lingering on her arms as if reluctant to let go. Then all too soon he had turned around and disappeared into his own room.

Rosa darted into her bedroom, closed the door and rested her head on the painted wood. It was cool under her forehead and immediately she found herself calming. She wasn't being asked to do anything she didn't want to do, nothing more than what thousands of women around the world did on their wedding nights every single day.

Slowly she started to loosen her clothing, letting the layers drop to the floor one after another. Once only her chemise remained Rosa diligently tidied her clothes away and stood looking nervously at the door.

She had no nightclothes, nothing special to slip into on her wedding night. For the last few weeks she had slept in a simple chemise, not needing any further layers in the heat of the Italian nights. It hadn't bothered her until now, when she wondered what Thomas would think to his bride greeting him in her cotton undergarments.

Rosa grimaced and then climbed into bed. She felt a fluttering in her stomach, acknowledged the nerves that multiplied by the minute as she waited for her husband.

Ten minutes passed, and then fifteen. Despite reclining on the stack of plush pillows Rosa didn't feel in the least sleepy. There wasn't a chance she would doze off on her wedding night.

When forty minutes had passed without a peep from Thomas, Rosa got up from the bed and padded over to the door. Maybe he was waiting for her in his bedroom. She had never been married before, didn't know the etiquette. Her mother hadn't deemed it necessary to impart any feminine wisdom to her, so maybe it was usual for the bride to go and seek out her husband on the wedding night.

Feeling a little foolish and uncertain, Rosa

opened the door to her room and stepped out. There were no candles burning, suggesting Thomas had indeed retired to his bedroom. No doubt waiting for her and wondering what was taking his new wife so long.

Quietly Rosa tapped on the door and when she didn't receive an answer turned the handle and pushed it open. The room was in darkness, but a soft glow was cast across the bed by the moonlight shining in through the window. Rosa could see Thomas's hair on the pillow, his body beneath the sheets. Summoning up her courage, Rosa stepped into the room and walked over to the bed. Without listening to all the tiny doubts clamouring to be heard in her head, she lifted up the covers and slipped in beside Thomas.

As soon as her body touched his she felt him stiffen. For a few seconds she expected him to touch her, to murmur something to her and then to kiss her until she begged him to do more. That was what she'd been imagining ever since their first kiss on the balcony, what she'd pictured a thousand different ways each more pleasurable than the last.

He didn't move. Rosa lifted her hand, felt it tremble, but continued anyway. Gently she placed it on his chest and felt his heart thumping beneath his skin. With her own breathing becoming shallow Rosa let her fingers trail down Thomas's body, feeling his muscles tense.

'Rosa,' he groaned, sounding almost pained.

She moved in closer to him, aware that as yet he still hadn't touched her, hadn't done anything but accept her caresses. Something felt wrong, but she didn't know what. Maybe it was just her inexperience.

Angling her head upwards she moved in to kiss him, softly brushing her lips against his. For a short moment he kissed her back, went to grasp her and pull her close and Rosa felt herself relax. He wanted her.

Then his hands were on her, but pushing her away. She saw him leap out of bed, wondering how he moved quite so quickly.

'What are you doing?' he asked sharply.

Rosa felt her entire world crumble. She'd done something terribly wrong, broken some rule she didn't even know about. All she'd wanted was to be a good wife, to show Thomas she would not let her past stop her fulfilling any part of her new role.

'I thought…' she stuttered.

'You can't be in here, Rosa.'

'It's our wedding night.' She heard how pathetic and lost her voice sounded, hated the naivety there.

'Go back to bed, Rosa.'

Suddenly she rallied. This was not her fault, this was not normal. Throughout her short time as a debutante all the girls had whispered about what occurred once you were married. Everyone knew intimacy in the bedroom was saved for the wedding night, but then a husband would insist on consummating the union, and often.

They were married, there was absolutely no reason for them not to be intimate. Unless…

Rosa gasped, her hand flying to her mouth and then to her abdomen. He thought of her as sullied goods. She was carrying another man's child, she'd already given herself to someone else. He might care for her enough to marry her to protect her future, or whatever reason he insisted on keeping to himself, but he couldn't bring himself to be intimate with her.

She could feel her thoughts running away from her. A small voice of reason tried to protest, tried to tell her that Thomas did find her attractive, to remind her of the passion she'd felt when they'd kissed, but the horror and the embarrassment were way too much.

'We'll discuss this in the morning.'

Rosa climbed out of the bed, barely able to look Thomas in the eye. Wrapping her arms around her, she cursed her thin chemise, wishing she was wearing something more robust, more conservative.

Quickly she backed away from the bed, watching as Thomas kept as much distance between them as possible as if he was afraid she might attempt to rush at him again.

She'd almost reached the door by the time she'd recovered enough to meet his gaze.

'I don't understand,' she said, forcing her voice to remain firm and hating the slight quiver at the end of the sentence.

'We will talk about it in the morning,' Thomas repeated firmly.

Rosa felt the tears brimming in her eyes and knew she could not let him see her cry. She was confused, shaken by his rigid rejection of her, but she still had a modicum of pride.

Taking a deep breath, Rosa concentrated on holding her head high as she turned and walked from the room. She didn't look back, she couldn't, for as soon as she'd turned around the tears had started to fall down her cheeks and nothing on earth would entice her to let Thomas see how upset she was.

Thomas cursed and threw his boot across the room. It was difficult to get on at the best of times, but this morning, after tossing and turning all night long, the tough leather had got the better of him.

Forcing himself to calm down, Thomas retrieved the boot and tried again. Losing control would not help. He needed a clear head and a silken tongue. Rosa was a sensible woman, last night had just been a simple misunderstanding. Once he had explained things he was sure she would come round.

Thomas knew he was deluding himself. The look of hurt and confusion as he'd jumped out of bed, the sobs he'd heard through the walls despite her attempts to muffle them—all of it confirmed that he was a complete and utter bastard.

He could protest for hours that he hadn't led her on, hadn't let her believe their marriage was anything other than one of convenience, but Thomas knew it wasn't true. Yes, he had told her they were marrying so she would get the protection of his name and he would gain a companion for his mother and someone to oversee the minor estate business whilst he was away, but his actions hadn't backed up that cold reasoning. He'd seduced her, wooed her, courted her and then finally kissed her. Of course Rosa had been expecting a conventional wedding night.

Thomas knocked softly on her door. No response. He paced backwards and forwards for a few minutes before knocking harder. Still no response.

Letting out a low growl, he banged on the door with his fist before realising he was taking out his guilt on the ornately carved inanimate object.

Ten minutes later Rosa still hadn't emerged from the room and Thomas began to feel uneasy. She had every right to avoid him for as long as possible, but their ship left in less than three hours and he hadn't heard even the faintest hint of movement.

'Rosa, can I come in?'

He waited, listening for any sound that might reassure him.

'Rosa? Again nothing. 'Rosa, I'm coming in.'

He waited for another few seconds, half-expecting her to rush at the door to prevent him invading her private space, but there was still no sound. Gently he tried the door. It wasn't locked and opened smoothly.

Inside the room was filled with morning light. And completely empty.

'Rosa?' Thomas shouted, looking round in disbelief before going to search the rest of their rooms. It didn't take very long. With just two bedrooms, a sitting room, a bathroom and the large balcony there weren't many places to hide and Rosa wasn't in any of them.

'Rosa,' he shouted again, just in case he was being completely blind, but the reality of the situation was already sinking in. She'd left. Less than one day into their marriage and she'd left him.

A wave of concern washed over him. Rosa was young and pretty in a city she didn't know. Although in appearance she could pass for an Italian, as soon as she opened her mouth it was obvious she was foreign, which made her even more of a target. With no money of her own she wouldn't last more than a few hours.

Visions of all the awful fates that could befall her flashed across Thomas's mind and quickly he tried to suppress them. Imagining Rosa set upon by thieves or cornered by one of the many rowdy groups of sailors that tore through Venice as the ships docked made him curse out loud.

Quickly he dashed out of their rooms and down the stairs to the street, all the while trying to work out exactly where Rosa might seek solace in this city of strangers.

Chapter Sixteen

Rosa stared out over the rail at the shimmering water and frowned. It was getting late and soon the captain would want to weigh anchor and set sail, with or without his most influential passenger.

When Rosa had first fled their rented rooms not long after the first rays of sunshine had filtered in through the windows to signal a new day she had been so upset and angry that she'd planned on not informing Thomas of her plans at all. He hadn't given her the courtesy of telling her the truth about their marriage so why should she let him know of her plans. She'd boarded the ship, early, been shown to a small but perfectly comfortable cabin, and spent the morning pacing the deck and brooding.

Finally she'd relented and found a boy to take a message to Thomas to tell him of her whereabouts, but that had been well over an hour ago and there was still no sign of her odious husband.

Perhaps it would be better to sail for England alone. The passage had already been paid for and once back on English soil she could just pretend the whole embarrassing affair hadn't happened.

Just then Rosa caught sight of a familiar figure sauntering towards the ship as if he had all the time in the world. She heard herself growling and clamped a hand over her mouth. It was just like Thomas to expect the entire world to revolve around him, to be confident a ship wouldn't leave until he was aboard.

She wondered if she should retire to her cabin, but dismissed the idea almost immediately. Last night she had run from Thomas, but today she would not. With hours to analyse his behaviour, to revisit every little thing they'd said to each other, every little thing they'd done, Rosa knew he had been hiding something from her all along. He'd proposed, and then when she hadn't fallen into his arms, a twittering mass of gratitude, he'd courted her and seduced her. She'd even found herself thinking she might be falling in love with him. Today she knew he was in the wrong and she wouldn't leave to save him the embarrassment of having to face her, even if her actions hurt her as well.

'Rosa,' Thomas said in greeting, obviously aware of the audience they had on the ship.

'Lord Hunter.'

'I hope you are well.'

'As well as can be expected.'

Thomas stepped closer, his voice dropping low, his hand reaching out to touch her elbow.

'I was worried about you, Rosa. Don't do anything like that again.'

'Like what?' Rosa asked sweetly.

'Don't run off.'

'You noticed my absence?'

'Of course I noticed your absence. I was worried out of my mind.' He ran a hand through tousled hair and Rosa realised he was speaking the truth. 'I've spent the entire morning chasing around Venice, imagining you dead or robbed or worse.'

'Worse than dead?'

'Don't joke, Rosa. I was worried about you.'

'I sent a message.'

'An hour ago.'

'I didn't expect you to be up any earlier. Not after the exertions of your wedding day.'

'Our wedding day.'

'Of course.'

He was standing close to her and they both

spoke in low voices, conscious of the crew preparing the ship to leave around them.

'Rosa,' he said, having the common sense to break off first from their shared gaze. 'What happened last night...' He trailed off.

Rosa waited for the apology she knew would never come. Thomas was too used to getting his own way, too confident in his ability to win people over.

'I thought we had an understanding,' he said eventually.

'And what was that?'

'We both gained something from the marriage. You get the protection of my name for yourself and your child. I get a wife who will look after my family interests and be a companion for my mother.'

She regarded him without answering for over a minute. As the seconds ticked by he began fidgeting, something she'd never seen him do before.

'Lord Hunter, do you have any family interests on this ship?' Rosa asked, satisfied with Thomas's confused expression.

'No.'

'And is your mother currently in the vicinity requiring a companion?'

'No.'

'Then I suggest we talk again when we reach England.'

'Rosa...'

'Lady Hunter,' she corrected icily.

'Rosa...'

The rest of his protestation was lost to her as she spun on her heel and stalked off across the deck and down to her cabin below.

'Don't worry, little one,' Rosa whispered as she bent her neck and looked down at her now sizeable bump. 'Mama is here for you. We don't need anyone else.'

Four and a half weeks. It was ridiculous. Beyond ridiculous. Four and a half weeks they had been on this ship and she hadn't uttered a single word to him. When he greeted her she nodded politely in acknowledgement, but didn't speak. Whenever he approached she neatly extracted herself from whatever conversation she was engaged in with their few fellow passengers or the captain and glided away. He hadn't even had the chance to ask her a direct question and force an answer from her lips.

'Heave!' the first mate shouted from a few feet away.

Thomas watched as the sailors battled with the sail, trying to rein it in and secure it before the wind battered the ship even more. Four and a half weeks they'd enjoyed sunny skies and balmy temperatures and today, within sight of the English coastline, a storm was coming.

'Heave! Heave!'

The order was shouted again and again and Thomas could see the exertion on the sailors' faces. Suddenly one toppled, letting go of the rope which snaked through his arms, whipping backwards and forward like a wild animal. Quickly the other men braced themselves, but Thomas could see it wouldn't be enough. He jumped forward, caught hold of the rope, clenched his hands into fists and added his weight and strength to the line of men.

'Heave! Heave!'

Feeling his muscles bulge and burn, he heaved alongside the sailors, desperately trying to pull in the sail. Little by little they advanced and by the time it was safely tied down Thomas was sweating despite the bracing wind.

Just as he was rubbing his hands together to get rid of the rope burn Thomas felt the first of the fat raindrops on his face, and within seconds the rain was bouncing off the deck. In the distance the clouds looked ominous and dark and Thomas knew it wouldn't be long before the thunder and lightning hit.

'Lord Hunter,' the captain had to shout to be heard over the crashing of the waves. 'Your wife just headed below deck looking unwell. We're advising all passengers to stay in their cabins until the worst of the storm passes.'

'Will we reach the harbour today?'

They were heading for Portsmouth, the town almost visible on the horizon, but Thomas knew the ship battered by a storm might end up anywhere along the coast.

'It is in God's hands,' the captain said.

Thomas saw the concern on the older man's face and cursed inwardly. He'd sailed on many ships, weathered many storms, but he wasn't more than six months pregnant. Rosa would be uncomfortable and frightened and worried for her unborn child.

With quick strides he crossed the deck and swung himself down the narrow stairs. He wouldn't take no for an answer—today Rosa would let him into her room.

Thomas knocked firmly on the door, needing to hold his ear against it to listen for an answer over the whistling of the wind. Nothing, just silence. Cursing under his breath he rattled the door handle and to his surprise found the door swung inwards with no resistance. The sight that greeted his eyes made his blood chill.

Rosa was curled up on the bed, hugging her knees as best she could with the bump in the way. Her face was drained of blood, completely white surrounded by her tousled dark hair. Petrified eyes stared up at him without really seeing him.

'Rosa, what's wrong?' Thomas asked, rushing to her side. 'Is it the baby?'

He looked for the blood, for a sign that something was wrong with the small life inside her, and felt an immense relief when she shook her head.

He sat down next to her, grasping her hands in his own. They were icy cold and trembling and he could see the dents where her nails had dug into the skin of her hands.

'Rosa, what's wrong?'

Shuddering Rosa manoeuvred herself up into a sitting position and then flung her arms round Thomas's neck and buried her face in the space between his head and shoulder. He felt her warm breath on his skin, felt the fluttering of her heart in her chest and realised she was petrified.

'Is it the storm?'

A miniscule nod.

Slowly Thomas felt the icy dread begin to ebb away. He'd thought something was physically wrong with Rosa, something he wouldn't be able to fix. Fear of the storm was distressing for her, but with soothing words of comfort he could at least ease a little of her terror.

He raised a hand to her head and stroked her hair with long, slow movements.

'Hush,' he said softly. 'There's nothing to be afraid of. I'm here. I've got you.'

With a light touch he traced his fingers down her back, keeping her close to him and trying to draw away the pure fear he'd seen in her eyes.

The ship was rocking now, listing side to side as the waves no doubt battered it outside. The small pieces of furniture in the room were just beginning to slide backwards and forward with the movement and Thomas knew before long they would have to secure anything loose that might cause injury. Luckily Rosa did not have much in the way of belongings, just a small bundle of clothes and a couple of books borrowed from the captain. Apart from the bed there was a small chair and table, a shelf with a mirror above it that he supposed acted as a dressing table, and a ceramic washbowl.

'Rosa, I need to make this room safe for us,' Thomas said softly, eyeing the ceramic washbowl as it teetered precariously on its stand. 'I am going to let go for just a minute, remove the loose furniture from the room and then I will be straight back with you.'

She looked up at him, naked fear still in her eyes, but nodded nervously.

Quickly he stood, grabbed the washbowl and chair, dragged them out of the room and down the narrow corridor. He flung both into his own cabin before returning for the small table and the books and repeating the journey. No doubt things would break and get damaged in the storm, but all he cared about was keeping Rosa safe from flying debris.

Closing the door firmly behind him, Thomas took his place by Rosa's side again. She'd regained a little colour in her cheeks and this time instead of burying her head in his chest she managed to look up at him and give him a weak smile.

'I suppose you think I'm very foolish,' she murmured.

'There's nothing foolish about being scared of a storm,' Thomas replied. Many a good ship had been sunk in storms just like this one and many good men lost their lives. Living by the coast, so close to Portsmouth, had taught Thomas to respect the sea and acknowledge the power of the weather in determining the fate of ships and their sailors.

'I've always been scared of them,' Rosa said, giving a little self-deprecating laugh.

'You were scared as a child?'

'I remember when the storms would come I would hide under my bed, make a fortress with pillows and my favourite doll.' Rosa frowned at the memory. 'And then one day my mother came into the room and dragged me out, told me I was too old to be hiding from the storm. She pulled me all the way downstairs and out into the rain and made me stand there until the thunder was rumbling overhead.'

'That's cruel.'

'I know. I think she meant to cure me of my fear, but ever since then I've been even more afraid.'

'I'm not surprised.' He paused and then decided to go on. 'When I was a boy if there was a storm my brother would wake me and pull me from my bed. Together we would creep up to one of the attic windows and watch the lightning fork across the sky and try to guess when the thunder would rattle the window frames.'

'I often wished for a brother or sister to share those moments with,' Rosa said.

'I miss him.'

Rosa looked at him and Thomas realised he had not spoken to her about his brother before.

When she had questioned him on their journey across northern Italy he had answered abruptly and refused to talk any more of his family. He didn't talk often about his father or his brother, it was too painful to remember them as they had been in the prime of their lives before the illness had struck. Thomas felt an unfamiliar lump growing in his throat as he pictured Michael grinning as he led him into some mischief, laughing as they ran across the fields on the estate and looking after him when Thomas had first been sent to join his brother at school.

'You loved him very much, didn't you?'

He nodded. More than anyone else. He'd mourned his father when he'd died, felt the sadness descending on him and shed tears as he'd realised he would never get to talk to his father, hug his father, ever again, but it had been Michael's illness and death that had felt like a mortal blow. It was so unfair that someone so kind, so full of happiness and light, could be snatched away so cruelly.

'I'm sorry you lost him,' Rosa said, squeezing his hand.

'It was a long time ago.' It still felt like yesterday. Thomas could remember every detail from the day Michael had called him home and sat him down, how he'd tried to explain the disease that had claimed their father was now coming for him. Thomas had seen the naked fear in his brother's eyes and knew this was the worse fate; to know you were slowly going to lose the use of your body and mind and not be able to do a single thing about it.

'It doesn't matter how long ago it was, I don't think losing someone you love ever stops hurting.'

Thomas glanced up, saw Rosa's pale, anxious face and realised in that moment how much he had wronged her. She was kind and gentle and deserved so much more than the deceit and lies he'd built their relationship on.

'I'm sorry, Rosa,' he said.

Her eyes widened with surprise at his words. 'What for?'

'For everything. I've treated you badly.'

The ship lurched to one side, almost hurling them off the bed, and Rosa clutched at his arm so hard it hurt. Quickly Thomas gathered her to him, pulling her on to his lap whilst shuffling further back on the bed.

'I think I have some explaining to do.'

Chapter Seventeen

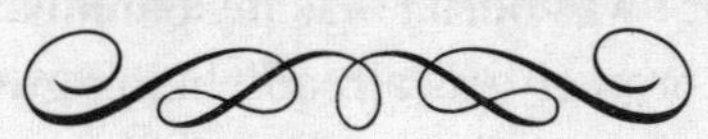

Rosa eyed Thomas warily. She felt strangely safe gathered up in his arms and sitting on his lap. The lurching of the ship seemed less worrisome with his arms around her, but that didn't mean she wasn't still angry with him.

'I'm not sure where to start,' Thomas said, smiling weakly at her.

'Why did you want to marry me?' Rosa asked.

He sighed, lifted his hand and ran it through his hair before pulling her a little closer to him.

'So many reasons. I like you, Rosa.'

'I like many people, our butler at home, the captain of this ship, the man who serves those wonderful iced buns in Hyde Park. Liking someone is not enough of a reason to marry.'

'I know. I think I need to tell you a little more about my family.'

Rosa saw him look down at her and realised

he was nervous. Thomas, the man who fought off armed bandits without breaking a sweat, Thomas, who had scaled the ship's rigging with the crew to help on particularly blustery days, was nervous about revealing the truth about himself.

'When I was born I was my parents' younger son. My brother was already being groomed to take over the running of the estate that he would inherit when he became the next Lord Hunter. I would perhaps go into the army or make myself useful to my brother.'

'Did your parents treat you differently?'

'Not really. We had the same education. The same love and care from our parents. It was more my perception of our roles. Michael had to be serious, to work hard. I could have a little more freedom.'

He paused and smiled softly, as if remembering the good times of his childhood. The smile faltered suddenly as he continued.

'When I was eight my father became unwell. It was gradual—first he started having twitches in his limbs, uncontrollable movements. Then he started forgetting things he would normally have had no trouble remembering. And then his personality, his whole being, changed.'

Rosa held back from asking the question that

was on the tip of her tongue. He would tell her if he desired what had caused the disease, whether it was syphilis or some other contagion.

'Over the years he declined, forgetting who we were, forgetting who he was. In the end it was a blessing when he died. At least he wasn't suffering any longer.' Thomas paused as the ship creaked after being buffeted by a particularly large wave. Rosa realised her anxiety over the storm had lessened since becoming so engrossed in Thomas's story.

'How awful,' she murmured, realising how devastated she would be to lose her father.

'It was then Mother sat us down and explained what our father never could.'

Rosa looked up at him as the silence stretched out, wondering what it was that was so awful, what secret their father had been hiding.

'You don't have to tell me,' she said, hating the anguish in his eyes.

'I do. You deserve to know. You're part of this now, part of the family.'

A clash of thunder sounded close by, reverberating around the ship, and making Rosa jump and cling on to Thomas. He waited for her to relax a little, for her breathing to become steady and her fingers to relax their grip, before continuing.

'There is a disease in my father's family, the Hunter family curse they call it,' he said, laughing without any trace of humour. 'It is handed down from generation to generation. Not everyone is affected, but there is no way of knowing why one person may suffer whilst another is spared.'

Rosa felt her eyes widen. Of course she had heard rumours of such things, whispered gossip about the families you didn't want to marry into, those that had an unnaturally high rate of madness or premature death, but she'd never actually met anyone who had confirmed these rumours before.

'My mother sobbed as she told us, knowing she was giving us something worse than a death sentence.'

Rosa felt all the blood drain from her face.

'You're afflicted?' He couldn't be, not Thomas. He was so vivacious, so alive. She couldn't imagine a world where he was struck down with the sort of illness he'd described.

Thomas shrugged. 'Who knows? That's the biggest cruelty. So far I have not exhibited any signs, but some people are affected at the age of twenty, some not until they are sixty. You have an entire lifetime to obsess about whether you will be affected.'

'And your brother?' Rosa asked, realising the truth behind his brother's death.

'He first showed symptoms at the age of twenty—he died nearly four years ago now.'

Rosa saw the pain on Thomas's face and felt the tears well up in her eyes. He'd suffered so much, lost so many close to him, and still he had to live with the uncertainty of never knowing if one day he would wake up with the signs of the disease.

'I can't imagine anything worse,' Rosa said, trying to digest everything. It now made sense why he had spent so long travelling the world, his burning desire to do as much as possible right now. Rosa knew anything could happen to anyone, people were struck down with particularly severe chest infections or were thrown from horses, but that was always an abstract threat to your life. She couldn't imagine having something like this hanging over her. She supposed he must feel chased, haunted even, as if he needed to keep moving, keep experiencing new things so he would have no regrets if he did become ill.

'So now you understand why I can never have children of my own.'

Rosa frowned.

'I will not risk passing this on to my own

offspring. This curse, this affliction, will stop with me.'

Suddenly a few more pieces of the puzzle fell into place. She'd thought it strange when Thomas had insisted he would not want any children, had dismissed her worries about him claiming her unborn child as his heir only to regret it when wanting a son of his own. Thomas had a very good reason never to want children, not any that might carry this awful affliction into the next generation.

'I never thought I would marry, Rosa,' Thomas said quietly. 'I'd resigned myself to a single life, but I did recognise my decisions had consequences for others. By marrying you I get an heir, one that I can be certain will not have to live his life in fear of this disease. I get a wife to take an interest in my estate whilst I am away and keep my mother company. And I get to protect you and a child who has done nothing wrong but will otherwise be stigmatised their entire life.'

Rosa felt a shiver run through her body. They were all very good reasons, very practical reasons. Everything he was saying made sense, but her brain couldn't help but replay one little phrase: *whilst I am away.* He was planning on delivering her back to England and setting off on his travels again. She would have a husband in name, but nothing more, not really. She would lose Thomas, the man she rather thought she would find it impossible to be without. These last few weeks of ignoring him had been pure hell for her. She'd missed his smile, his witty quips, his sharp observations about the other passengers. Every day she'd wished for his apology so she could go back to enjoying his company.

'When you turned up in my life it seemed like too good an opportunity to miss.'

The ship lurched suddenly and Rosa almost went tumbling off Thomas's lap and on to the floor. He caught her at the last minute, pressing her close to his body. Rosa placed one hand on his chest and looked up into his eyes.

Their faces were close, so close she could have tilted her chin just slightly and their lips would be touching.

'And of course you never wanted our wedding night,' Rosa said softly.

She saw Thomas swallow, saw his lips part and his pupils dilate just a fraction.

'It's not about what I want and what I don't want, Rosa,' he said, his voice low and gruff. 'I cannot risk passing this disease on, cannot risk siring offspring of my own. I will not do it.'

Rosa felt her heart squeeze in her chest. It

was admirable, really, his determination to stop anyone else suffering as he had. She couldn't imagine what it was like, losing first your father and then your brother, knowing all the time you might be next.

She sat cradled in Thomas's lap, her heart pounding every time the ship tilted, sending her few loose possessions over the room, and tried not to cry. Thomas's resolve was admirable, but it also meant they would never have a proper marriage. Not the marriage she had fantasised about on her wedding day.

Thomas felt drained. He'd never told anyone about the Hunter family curse before, never put into words his pledges and promises to himself, but Rosa was special. She was his wife. She would share the fear of the future now… she would be affected by the disease almost as much as he.

'If I do begin to exhibit symptoms, I will not ask you to look after me,' he said.

'You wouldn't have to ask. I'm your wife.'

He shook his head. 'I do not wish to burden anyone more than is necessary. In a few weeks I will set off for the Americas or perhaps China. If I become ill I have enough funds to pay for someone to look after me.'

'Of course it is your choice,' Rosa said, a little stiffly. 'But just remember when you care for someone it is no chore looking after them.'

She didn't understand, not really. Didn't grasp the trajectory of the illness, didn't grasp that it wasn't just like nursing someone through a bout of pneumonia, it was years of slow deterioration, with the sufferer slowly becoming more reliant on others to do everything for them.

'You care for me?' he asked, the question drowned out by the creaking of the wood surrounding them.

'What did you say?' Rosa asked, having to raise her voice to be heard.

A loud rumble of thunder made the ship vibrate and Thomas could feel the waves buffeting it from either side. Rosa was clinging on to him tightly again, her fingers pressing in to his neck. Part of him wanted to bend down and kiss her, to make her forget her fear and get lost instead in pleasure.

That thought was cut short as the ship keeled to one side violently, sending them both tumbling across the room. Thomas managed to catch Rosa before she hit anything and struggled back to the bed with her where he pinned her down.

'I may need to bind us to the bed,' he shouted over the creaking ship.

Panic blossomed in Rosa's eyes.

'No,' she said vehemently. 'I can't be trapped.'

'We can't have you thrown across the room again.' As he spoke the ship listed and gave an ear-splitting groan, as if the wood was protesting against the buffeting it was receiving.

Just as Thomas reached down to grab the bed sheet the door to the cabin was thrown open and a worried-looking sailor burst in.

'We're taking on water,' he shouted. 'Captain orders everyone up on deck.'

Thomas felt an icy chill travel down his back. There was only one reason the captain would order the passengers to the deck in a storm—the ship must have been seriously damaged.

Grasping Rosa firmly, he pulled her upright, steadying her as she stumbled before finding her balance. The whole cabin was definitely listing to the left now, even when the ship rocked from the impact of the battering waves.

Quickly he led her into the corridor, knowing their best chance was to get to the deck of the ship ahead of the other passengers so he could assess the situation before general panic endangered them all.

He had to haul Rosa up the narrow stairway and felt her slip almost immediately as they got to the deck.

'I can't swim, Thomas,' Rosa shouted, her eyes wide as they slid on the treacherous wood. Rain buffeted them from every direction and the wind was so strong it was a struggle to stand upright.

'Everything will be fine,' Thomas bellowed, keeping his voice as calm as possible, all the while cursing parents who didn't throw their children in a lake or pond and teach them the very basics of swimming.

They struggled over to the captain who was shouting orders to the crew.

'What's happening?' Thomas asked.

The captain's face was pinched and worried, his normally cheerful manner replaced with an overwhelming despair. He glanced at Rosa and lowered his voice.

'We're going down. It's only a matter of time. We're launching the longboats now.'

Thomas felt time slow as he digested the captain's words. Normally he would be asking what he could do to help, but right now he had one single priority: ensuring Rosa and her child reached land safely and unharmed.

'Captain,' a sailor shouted, his face a picture of alarm.

They all turned to see what he was pointing at. Approaching fast was a huge wall of blackness. A wave bigger than anything Thomas had ever seen. One glance at the captain's face said it all. There was no way the ship was going to survive an impact that big. As the crew noticed the growing wave one by one they fell still. A couple dropped to their knees, clasping their hands together, others stood and gawped at the monstrosity speeding towards them.

'Rosa, listen to me,' Thomas shouted, grabbing her by the arms. 'Hold your breath as we go in, kick for the surface and find something to grab hold of. I promise you I will come for you.'

The pure fear flashed across her face and Thomas wondered if she might freeze in the face of such a danger, but then the courage he knew was inside her broke through and she nodded.

'I promise I will come for you,' he repeated.

The wave was seconds away from them now, all other sound had been drowned out by the roaring of the wall of water. Thomas pulled Rosa to the rail of the ship, gripped her hand so tightly he wondered if he might crush her fingers and pulled her over.

They fell into the darkness. The impact of the water stung even through his clothes and immediately Thomas felt Rosa's hand wrenched out of his grip. For long seconds his body was tossed about in the water, limbs flailing this way and that. As he was buffeted Thomas felt the force of debris sailing through the water around him and knew the ship had been hit.

After what seemed like an eternity he allowed himself to kick, trusting his body's intuition to angle him towards the surface. He broke through, desperately gasping a breath of air, before immediately being thrust under by another wave. When he broke the surface again his eyes began searching for Rosa.

Behind him the ship was at an unnatural angle, half-submerged beneath the water and sinking fast. Broken slats of wood dotted the surface of the sea and to his left a ripped and battered sail flapped impotently. None of that concerned Thomas, he just needed to find Rosa.

Panic started to build and he had to force himself to suppress it. Panic was no use to him. He prized his clear head in a crisis and now was not the time to lose it.

Twice more he was dunked under the water by huge waves, coming up spluttering each time and trying to avoid thinking of Rosa's petrified expression as she'd told him she couldn't swim.

He couldn't lose her. He just couldn't.

Kicking hard, he propelled himself through the water, covering only tiny distances before being thrust this way and that by the sea. Just as the panic was about to seize him Thomas spun in the water. He'd heard something, a faint shout.

There, bobbing a few feet away, was Rosa.

She looked exhausted as he kicked his way over to her. She was half out of the water, clinging on desperately to a bobbing piece of debris.

As he reached her he gripped on to the wood and kissed her, tasting the salt on her lips and feeling an overwhelming relief that she was alive.

'My baby!' she shouted over the roaring of the wind.

Thomas nodded. He needed to get her out of the water and to safety.

'Can you stay afloat?' he asked.

Rosa looked as though she wanted to cling on to him and never let go, but bravely she nodded. Thomas knew she would do anything to save her child.

As he'd been searching for her he'd noticed one of the longboats bobbing on the waves. It was upside down, but looked more or less intact. If he could get to it and clamber in, he could pull Rosa to safety.

A fork of lightning lit up the sky, followed closely by a loud rumble of thunder. The storm was directly overhead now and for just a moment the wind seemed to drop a little. Thomas used the slight lull to thrash his way towards the longboat, wincing as another flash of lightning illuminated the crashing waves.

He risked a glance behind him, reassured himself that Rosa was still afloat, and pressed on. It seemed to take an eternity to reach the longboat. By the time he was clinging on the side he had to pause to suck in great gasps of breath and to allow his muscles to recover.

Quickly he ducked under the water, swimming just half a stroke and popping up underneath the upturned longboat. Without anything to brace against Thomas knew it was going to be near impossible to flip the boat over, but he had to try. He would not let Rosa drown, would not let her unborn child perish, he would use every reserve of strength to save them.

With his hands pressed against the wood, he waited as the sea swelled around him. Just as a big wave lifted him and the longboat up he pushed with all his strength. There was movement, but not enough. Again he waited, felt the swell of a wave and pushed again. This time he thought he'd done it, thought the boat was going to teeter over, but suddenly it crashed back down on him.

Gritting his teeth, Thomas braced himself again, waiting as some smaller waves buffeted him. As the sea started to draw away, a sure sign a large wave was coming, Thomas tensed and then pushed with every ounce of strength in his body. He roared as the boat lifted, caught the wave and flipped over, crashing into the water and sending a salty spray into his face.

Quickly he glanced towards Rosa. She was still clinging on to the wood, but by now she must be tiring, nearing the point where her strength would leave her.

Ignoring his own protesting muscles, Thomas gripped the side of the boat and hauled himself up, shouting in triumph as he saw the two oars still clipped in place. He gripped the two long poles, put them into position and began to heave the longboat over towards Rosa.

With the waves still crashing around them Thomas was certain the boat would capsize at any moment, but eventually he made it back to Rosa still afloat.

'Give me your hand,' he shouted.

She looked at him warily. 'You'll never be able to lift me.'

True Rosa was not as light as she once had been and Thomas's arms were tired from all the exertion, but he knew nothing would let him fail Rosa now.

'Do you trust me?' he asked.

He waited, realising he was holding his breath.

'Then give me your hand.'

Slowly, the fear etched on her face, Rosa let go of the wooden boards with one hand and reached for Thomas. He grabbed her by the wrist and pulled, knowing he would bruise her delicate skin, but aware it was the price he had to pay to get her out of the water.

Panting, they collapsed tangled together in the bottom of the boat. Immediately Rosa flung her arms around Thomas's neck and he pulled her to him, squeezing her and feeling his heart pounding in his chest.

'You're safe now,' he said, knowing it wasn't quite true, but saying it all the same. 'I've got you. You're safe.'

Chapter Eighteen

Rosa shivered and huddled in closer to Thomas. She could feel the chill from the water right down to her bones and her sodden dress clung to her body, emphasising the cold, but she was alive. The moments after they had jumped from the boat, hand in hand, Rosa had felt a blind panic take over her. There was no feeling like being plunged into the murky, roiling depths of the freezing sea when you couldn't swim more than a stroke or two. She'd been separated from Thomas immediately, but had followed his instructions, kicking for the surface, and luckily had broken through right next to the broken boards. There she had hung, clinging on with raw fingers, until Thomas had come for her, just as he promised he would.

'We need to get to the shore,' Thomas said,

raising his voice over the wind and crashing of the waves.

Rosa wasn't sure if the storm was moving on, or if they were just a little more sheltered, huddled in the longboat, but it felt as though the worst was passing over.

'Where is the shore?' she asked.

They both looked around them, searching the darkness for some clue to the direction of land. Rosa knew they had been mere hours away from the port when the storm had struck, but who knew how far they'd been blown off course in that time.

'This way,' Thomas said decisively. 'Keep alert for any signs of life—we may chance upon one of the sailors or other passengers.'

Rosa looked out to sea, her head twisting this way and that, looking for the slightest movement. She desperately wanted to catch sight of a bobbing head or a waving hand, anything that might tell them they weren't the only ones to survive this terrible storm, but the swell of the waves made it so difficult to see more than a few feet on either side of their small boat.

'We have to get you to dry land. Stay low in the boat, try not to move too much,' Thomas said as he picked up the oars again and started to propel them through the water. Rosa was suddenly very thankful for all the hours Thomas had spent building his physical strength. Although he was wet and dishevelled, he still seemed to have a reserve of energy.

They moved through the water, slowly at first, the small boat rocking violently from side to side as it was battered by the elements. Little by little the storm started to settle, the wind dropped, the sea calmed and the rain that had been pelting down became a fine drizzle until that, too, was gone.

Rosa kept still as the minutes ticked by, all the time letting her eyes roam across the surface of the water, ready to direct Thomas if she saw any signs of life. As they drew further away from the site of the shipwreck Rosa knew it was less likely that they would come across anyone, but still she looked, sometimes twisting to check behind her in the hope that she might detect some movement.

'Thomas, look,' she shouted after a few minutes.

She pointed in front of them to their left. It wasn't another survivor she had seen, but in the distance was a small, flickering light. Most likely from a lantern or a candle left in a window, but whatever it was it meant only one thing: they were heading the right way.

Rosa allowed herself to feel the first tentative stirrings of hope. Maybe they would get out of this, maybe they would survive. One day she might be sitting by the fire telling her child the story of how they had been shipwrecked off the coast of England.

'I see it,' Thomas said, and Rosa detected a new-found enthusiasm in his voice. He pulled at the oars just a little harder, propelled them through the water just a little faster.

It seemed to take for ever to get closer to the light, but as it began to burn brighter Rosa almost shouted in relief as another light joined it and then another. Closer to them she thought they were probably lanterns and where there were lanterns there had to be people.

'Hello, there!' a voice shouted from the shore.

'Hello!' Thomas bellowed back.

Three more pulls of the oars and the boat crunched into the stones of the beach and immediately two men waded into the water and grabbed hold of the side of the longboat to pull it further in. Thomas jumped to his feet, hopped out of the boat and without missing a step swept Rosa into his arms. He sloshed through the water, holding Rosa tight to his chest, and strode up on to the beach. Even when they were on dry land he didn't put her down and Rosa was glad.

She rather thought her legs might give way if she tried to stand.

'Lord Hunter?' a man asked, his voice tinged with disbelief.

Thomas turned and looked at one of the men who had pulled the boat up on to the beach.

'Todd Williams, what a sight for sore eyes you are.'

The other men standing round gawped at Thomas as they all recognised who he was. Rosa wondered if this was a surreal dream, some sort of hallucination. Surely Thomas didn't know everyone in England.

'Our ship sank,' Thomas said. 'It was hit by the storm. I would be most obliged if you could gather a rescue party and row out to the wreckage and search for survivors.'

The men on the beach nodded as if they had just been given a direct order.

'Yes, my lord,' Todd Williams said. 'We saw the storm hit, saw the ship listing, but couldn't risk launching our boats until the winds died down.'

'I also must ask for your assistance in getting my wife to safety.'

Rosa smiled weakly as all eyes turned to her. She felt as though she might fall asleep on her feet and her shivers had turned into full body shakes some minutes ago.

'I brought my horse down here, my lord. It would probably be quickest if you rode that home.'

'I'm much obliged,' Thomas said. 'I will see your horse is returned tomorrow.'

Giving a nod of thanks and wishing the men good luck with their rescue mission, Thomas clutched Rosa closer to him and began to stride up the beach. Rosa felt her body being lifted on to the horse and complied with Thomas's instructions to hold on tight. Immediately he was up behind her, cradling her between his arms and urging the horse on in the same breath.

Rosa thought she must have slept while they rode, despite the coldness and the wind that still whipped at her wet clothes, but it seemed only moments later that Thomas was pulling on the reins and stopping outside a grand doorway.

'Where are we?' Rosa asked. She'd only followed parts of the conversation on the beach, but realised they must be near Thomas's family home for him to know all of the men mounting a rescue party.

'Home, my dear.'

'Surely that's not possible.'

'The ship must have been blown west of Portsmouth,' Thomas said with a shrug. 'We're only ten miles outside the city.'

He helped her down and steadied her as she staggered forward, raising a hand to bang on the huge wooden door in front of them.

'Open up, for the love of God,' he shouted when thirty seconds had passed without an answer. Rosa saw him raise a hand to hammer again, but just as his fist hit the wood the door opened a crack. 'Took you long enough, Timkins,' Thomas said as a surprised butler in a dressing gown opened the door.

'My lord, we weren't expecting you for another few days.'

'Which room is the warmest?' Thomas asked.

'Thomas? Is that you?'

Rosa used the last of her strength to raise her head to look at the figure in white descending the staircase.

'I need to get Rosa warm, Mother. Now.' Rosa heard the panic in his voice, realised this was the most concerned she'd ever seen him and knew she should be worried, too, but everything seemed too surreal, too other-worldly, and as she felt Thomas slip an arm around her waist she felt her grip on consciousness loosen.

As she felt her body being swept upwards she caught a few odd words—*storm...shipwreck... longboat...chill*—before she slipped into darkness.

* * *

Thomas lifted his sodden clothes off his body and moved closer to the fire. He was tempted to throw on a nightshirt and dash back to Rosa, but he knew she was in capable hands, more capable than his own right now. He needed to get properly warm and dry so he could be there for her whatever the next few days would bring.

He thought about the baby inside her, thought about the stress and the cold it had been subjected to, and wondered if Rosa's body had been enough protection. He did know if anything happened to the baby Rosa would be devastated. She'd risked so much to protect her unborn child, it was cruel that fate had thrown so many obstacles in her way.

Rubbing his body dry, he slipped into one of his old nightshirts and wrapped his dressing gown around him. He took another mouthful of the whisky he'd found in his room and relished the burn as he swallowed, feeling the warmth inside his stomach seconds later.

With one last look at the fire that burned steadily in the grate he stepped away, dreading what he might find when he returned to Rosa, but knowing he could not keep away. Whatever she was suffering, whatever happened, he would be there for her. He just wished he could take some of her pain himself, he'd rather suffer than watch her hurt.

Quietly he tapped on the door to his mother's room. She'd insisted Rosa be taken there, it was the warmest room in the house and the bed was made up ready. As Rosa had slipped from consciousness his mother had taken over, summoning servants and ordering him to get changed and get warm before he returned. She hadn't asked a single question as to who Rosa was and all he'd told her was of the ship and the storm.

When there was no answer he opened the door a crack and stepped inside. It was wonderfully toasty in the bedroom and his mother must have ordered all the candles to be lit as the room was illuminated in a soft glow. Thomas looked at the bed. Rosa was lying there, tucked up under the covers, the top blanket pulled right up to her chin. She looked peaceful and innocent like that, as if she didn't have a care in the world.

'How is she?' Thomas asked as he walked over to the bed and looked down at his wife.

'She woke briefly, but the poor girl is exhausted. She asked for you. And about her child.'

Thomas's eyes flickered to the visible bump beneath the sheets.

'I've sent a groom to fetch the doctor, we'll

know more then,' his mother said, giving him a weak smile.

He perched on the edge of the bed, stroking the hair from Rosa's forehead and leaning in to place a kiss on the rapidly warming skin.

'Is the child yours?' his mother asked softly.

He went to shake his head but found he couldn't complete the movement. The baby might not be his true baby, his flesh and blood, but Thomas could not deny the growing bond he felt with Rosa's unborn child.

'It's complicated,' he said eventually.

'But you care for her?' his mother asked, glancing at Rosa.

'Rosa is my wife,' he said. 'I can't lose her, not like this.'

His mother nodded and Thomas was grateful she left the questions there. Soon he would tell her everything, but right now he didn't have the energy to explain the ins and outs of their relationship.

'Sit down. I'll have one of the maids bring you some food and then you must rest.'

'I can't leave her,' Thomas said.

'You can rest in the armchair,' his mother instructed. 'And I will stay with Rosa all night. I promise to wake you if anything changes.'

Thomas sank down into the soft armchair,

feeling his muscles finally relax after all the exertion during the night. For a few seconds he fought to keep his eyes open, but knew he was fighting a losing battle. Less than a minute later he had fallen into a deep, dreamless sleep.

Chapter Nineteen

Rosa awoke as the light started to filter through the curtains. She stretched, feeling every muscle in her body aching, and burrowed down under the sheets. As she became more aware of her surroundings the events of the last few days filtered back. Warily she opened one eye and then the other. She had absolutely no clue where she was. She remembered the ship sinking, Thomas rescuing her in a longboat and the long slog to shore, but after that her memory blurred.

'Good morning, sleepyhead,' Thomas said as she struggled to sit up.

He looked rested and refreshed and as if he'd spent the last few days relaxing at home, not battling to survive a storm and a shipwreck.

'Where are we?' Rosa asked.

'Home.'

'Home?'

He nodded, grinned, looked around him before flopping on to the bed beside her.

'How can we be home?'

'The storm blew up a little further along the coast, we washed up near my family home, so I brought you here.'

'How long have I been asleep?'

'Over twenty-four hours. We thought it best for you to rest.'

'We?'

Thomas grimaced. 'Dr Pewton. He's been four times to check you over. I'll summon him again in a minute to let him know you are awake.'

Rosa bit her lip. She didn't want to ask the question, but needed desperately to know.

'And the baby?' It came out as nothing more than a whisper.

Thomas's smile froze and Rosa felt her heart squeeze in her chest.

'The doctor said it's too early to say,' he said softly. 'But at the moment he seems to be unperturbed by your spell in the water.'

'Really?'

'Really.'

Rosa felt the tension that had been balling in her stomach ever since waking up start to dissipate and she allowed herself a tentative smile.

'I'm glad you are well, Rosa,' Thomas said, taking her hand. 'I have been worried about you.'

Rosa felt her pulse quicken as he brought his lips to the skin over her knuckles. She hadn't had time to process everything he'd told her in her cabin whilst the storm had raged outside, but she did know the hurt and the anger she'd felt on their wedding night had ebbed away and was being replaced by something new. Something warm and pleasant.

'I haven't thanked you for saving my life,' Rosa said, glad when Thomas didn't relinquish her hand.

'There's no need to thank me.'

'Thank you anyway. I know I would have died without you.'

He smiled at her, his eyes lingering on hers for just a second longer than was necessary.

'You're my wife. It's my duty to protect you, or have you forgotten our vows already?'

Rosa couldn't help but laugh. It felt good to have the old Thomas back, the man who teased her and laughed at every opportunity. She'd missed him on the long voyage back to England.

Resting her head back on the pile of pillows, Rosa closed her eyes momentarily and considered what Thomas had just said. It was his duty to protect her, although she doubted many other husbands would go to the lengths Thomas had to save her life. She wondered if duty was the only thing motivating him, or whether there was something else, some deeper feeling, hidden beneath his impenetrable exterior.

'Thomas,' Rosa said quietly. 'Were there any other survivors from the ship?'

He paused and Rosa knew he felt the same guilt at leaving people behind as she did, although she was certain her baby would have been at higher risk if they had.

'Some of the locals mounted a rescue once the worst of the storm died down. Thirty were saved, but twelve have not been found and assumed perished. The captain is amongst the missing.'

'He was such a kind man.'

Nodding, Thomas squeezed her hand. 'We should have a memorial service for all those that died once you have recovered,' he suggested.

'That's a lovely idea.'

'I should let you rest. I shall summon the doctor and ask him to check you over. And I must inform my mother you are awake. She's been beside herself with worry.'

Rosa's eyes shot wide open and she felt her breath catch in her throat.

'Your mother?' she asked.

'Yes—middle-aged woman, lives here, raised me from childhood.'

'Yes, yes, yes,' Rosa said with a dismissive wave of the hand—she was too agitated to pay much attention to his words. 'Have you told her we're married?'

'Of course.'

'And what about…?' Rosa trailed off, placing a hand on her abdomen.

'I've told her it is complicated. It is up to you what more you say.'

Thomas bent over and kissed her lightly on the forehead, his lips only just brushing her skin before they were gone all too soon.

'You are a very lucky woman, Lady Hunter,' Dr Pewton said, snapping his doctor's bag closed with one hand before straightening up.

'You truly cannot find anything wrong with the baby?'

'It is difficult to tell, but the movements are usually a good indicator things are progressing as they should. If you do not feel any movements for a long while then please have your husband fetch me.'

'I cannot believe there is no damage after such a lengthy submersion.'

'The female body was built to nurture and

protect the unborn child, it would appear your body did just that. I will return to see you tomorrow. Please rest until then, we can talk about getting you out of bed tomorrow.'

'Thank you, Doctor.'

Rosa watched as the elderly man left the room and allowed herself a small smile of relief. She had been convinced the time she'd spent underwater and bobbing around in the cold sea must have damaged the baby, despite feeling the strong kicks she knew so well. It was reassuring to know the doctor was not overly concerned for her baby.

She was just about to close her eyes and rest as the doctor had ordered when there was a quiet knock on the door. A few seconds later it opened and a petite, pretty, middle-aged woman slipped into the room.

'Rosa, my dear, I wanted to pop in and check on you.'

Rosa felt a flutter of nerves in her stomach. This was her mother-in-law, the woman Thomas held in such high regard, the woman she was destined to spend the rest of her life living with. On first glance you couldn't have imagined a more different woman to Rosa's own mother. She was smiling where Rosa's mother was haughty, welcoming where Rosa's mother was stand-offish. Physically, too, the two women were opposites. Thomas's mother was small, with delicate features and blonde hair streaked with a few strands of silver. Rosa's mother was statuesque in her bearing, with dark hair and olive skin.

'I am the Dowager Lady Hunter, but you must call me Sarah.'

'Thank you for taking me into your home,' Rosa said, having to clutch her hands together to stop them from shaking.

'Nonsense, my dear, it is your home too now. My son tells me you two were married a month ago.'

Rosa searched for the reproach, the disapproval, in her mother-in-law's tone, but could find none. There was just genuine interest and happiness.

'I must confide in you, Rosa, I never thought I would have a daughter-in-law, I never dared to hope these last few years. And now to be blessed with a daughter-in-law and a grandchild on the way, I cannot tell you how happy I am.'

Rosa shifted under the bedcovers and immediately Sarah was by her side, adjusting the pillows behind her.

'Thomas tells me I must not wear you out,' she said with a tender smile. 'But I had to come in and meet you properly. We will have plenty of time to get to know one another over the coming weeks.'

Sarah stood, squeezed Rosa's hand and turned to head for the door. Rosa felt a wave of turmoil crash over her. This lovely woman had welcomed her into the family home, provided for her every comfort and was doing her utmost to make Rosa feel comfortable, all the while probably believing Rosa was carrying her flesh and blood. She should say something, explain the truth.

'Lady Hunter…' Rosa started. 'Sarah…' But she could not find the words.

'We can talk more later, my dear. You rest now.'

'If I don't get out of this room I will scream,' Rosa said, plastering her most determined expression across her face.

'I can't see anything wrong with this room,' Thomas said cheerily. 'Beautiful wallpaper, nice airy feel, good view over the lawns.'

Rosa growled. Since returning home, and especially since the doctor had given her the all clear, her husband had regained much of his old carefree nature and sense of humour. Rosa was glad, but sometimes he could be infuriating.

'There's nothing wrong with the room,' Rosa

said through gritted teeth. 'That is not what I meant, as you very well know. If I do not move from this bed soon I fear I will become stuck to it for eternity.'

Thomas raised an eyebrow as if he was considering the merits of having her stuck in bed. Rosa thought she saw a flash of desire as he eyed her, but quickly he covered it. Interesting.

'Either you help me to get up and go downstairs or I will do it all by myself.'

'Shall I find you a big old branch to use as a crutch?'

Rosa reached out to swat his arm, but Thomas dodged her efficiently. She struggled upright, swung her legs over the edge of the bed and started to push up. Her bump had become more cumbersome over the course of their voyage to England, and now she had to take a second whenever she changed positions to regain her balance.

Once she was steady on her feet she looked up. Thomas was just staring at her, he'd made no move to take her arm or come to her side as he normally would.

'Rosa,' he said, his voice barely more than a whisper. 'I just saw a movement.'

She glanced down and placed a hand on her belly. It was mid-afternoon, the time the baby was at its most active and she loved it when she could feel the kicks and movements inside her.

'Come here.' Rosa took Thomas's hand and sat back down on the bed, pulling him to sit beside her.

Gently she placed his hand on her belly, feeling his warm fingers through the thin cotton covering. They sat, completely still and completely silent, for thirty seconds until another strong kick came from the baby inside her.

'I felt it,' Thomas exclaimed. 'I felt the baby kick.'

Rosa watched his face as he gazed at her belly, his hand still in place. She saw amazement and awe as well as something else in his eyes, something that looked a little like love.

'Does it do this a lot?' Thomas asked.

'All the time, especially mid-afternoon. Normally in the morning he's quiet.'

'Are you going to be a late riser like your mother?' Thomas asked, directing his question down towards her belly. 'Your mother does like to waste the morning lounging in bed.'

'It's not a waste,' Rosa said with a smile. 'It makes sense to wake up slowly rather than to jump into the day.'

'I think on that matter we will have to agree to disagree.'

Still he hadn't removed his hand from her belly and Rosa felt a peculiar warmth spreading through her. It felt wonderful to be touched like this, to have Thomas's hands on her slowly stroking her skin. For a second she allowed her eyes to close and her head to drop back.

'Mmm…' she moaned involuntarily.

'I think your mama likes being stroked,' Thomas said, bending his neck and speaking softly.

Gently he raised his other hand to join the first, moving both in sweeping circles around her belly, scrunching up the material of her nightgown before smoothing it out again.

She watched him stroke her, watched the rhythmic movements of his hands across her skin, and realised she was happy. True, she'd only just survived the storm and the shipwreck, was married to a man who planned on running away abroad at the first opportunity and would have to make a life for herself in someone else's home, but still she felt happy. She was alive and her baby was well. She was safe, and would be safe for the rest of her life. Although Thomas's mother might not know all the details about their marriage, she seemed lovely and accommodating, and Rosa knew she could make the best of living here.

Glancing at Thomas, Rosa realised she had forgiven him. Forgiven him for deceiving her, forgiven him for his reaction to her on their wedding night. He should have told her before about the illness that ran in his family, but she could understand why he hadn't. Just as she could understand why he had sworn himself to a life of celibacy to stop any future generations from suffering from the disease.

'Thomas,' Rosa said, closing her eyes and letting her head fall back. 'Whilst I am pregnant there is no chance of you fathering a child with me.'

She felt his hands freeze on her belly, but couldn't bring herself to open her eyes to gauge his reaction.

He cleared his throat, made a noise as if he were about to say something and then cleared his throat again.

'It was just a thought,' Rosa said, opening her eyes and pushing herself upright.

She had to take Thomas's arm and tug on it to get him moving, and as she glanced at his face she could see he was still lost in her words.

'Come,' she said. 'I really would like to get some air.'

Chapter Twenty

'Whilst I am pregnant there is no chance of you fathering a child with me.'

How many times in the last two weeks had he repeated that phrase in his head? Rosa's voice, so soft and calm, giving him an invitation to do what he most desired.

He glanced over at his wife as she walked arm in arm with his mother through the gardens. They were fast becoming good friends, as he knew they would. Often he would find them laughing together, walking arm in arm or with their heads bent over a book. Thomas knew he should be pleased, it was just what he'd planned. A safe haven for Rosa to raise her child in and a companion for his mother. Now there should be nothing to stop him from packing his bags and picking a new destination for his adventures.

Except there was. Thomas looked again at

Rosa. She still seemed graceful despite being over seven months pregnant. Her feet glided across the ground, her back was straight and the folds of her dress hung flatteringly around her figure.

He wanted her. He wanted to sweep her up into his arms, carry her to the bedroom and spend the next three months making love to her. He wanted to hold her close to him, stroke her skin and run his fingers through her hair.

Thomas groaned. It would be simpler if it was just pure desire that consumed him, but as the days went by he found he was actually happy, he was content to stroll through the gardens with Rosa, to show her the familiar sights from his childhood. He wanted to spend every waking minute with her, listen to her insights and tease her so her cheeks turned pink.

Last night he'd found himself making bargains in his head. He would just stay until the baby was born and then he would go; he would just stay until Rosa was recovered from the birth and then he would go; he would just stay until the baby had smiled or crawled or walked.

'Thomas darling, will you be joining us for tea?' his mother called over.

He started to walk across the lawn, reaching the wrought-iron table just as Rosa did and pulling out her chair for her. She smiled up at him with affection in her eyes.

Thomas felt his heart squeeze. This was all any man could want. A lovely wife, a child on the way, a family who loved him and a comfortable home. Maybe he should allow himself to be content, to enjoy his unexpected good fortune. Surely after the years of uncertainty, after all the people he had lost, he deserved a little slice of happiness.

He shook his head. It would be too selfish. Giving Rosa that hope, that glimpse of a normal life, only to burden her with a rapidly declining husband if and when the disease struck. His aim had always been to protect his loved ones from the illness, he couldn't falter now.

Rosa had just poured the tea and was digging into a large slice of sponge cake when one of the footmen came hurrying across the lawn.

'My lord, a gentleman is here to see Lady Hunter.'

Rosa looked up expectantly, but Thomas could hear the hesitation in the footman's voice.

'Who is it?'

'He wouldn't give his name, my lord, but he insisted Lady Hunter see him. He is a little out of sorts. Indisposed.'

'Drunk?'

'Quite, my lord.'

He saw the colour drain from Rosa's face, just as it had when the Di Mercurios had turned up at his villa demanding she be returned all those months ago.

'I will deal with him.'

'No.' Rosa caught his arm. 'I wish to come with you. I won't hide away in my own home.'

Out of the corner of his eye Thomas saw his mother smile as Rosa described the place as home.

Thomas was about to protest, about to insist she stay safely hidden whilst he dealt with whoever this drunkard turned out to be, but then he saw the determination on her face and knew she would not be deterred. She'd come so far from the scared girl he'd met climbing over the Di Mercurios' wall. He wouldn't deny her the chance at saying her piece to whoever this was from her past.

Hand in hand they followed the footman across the lawn and into the house.

'I have put the gentleman in the green room, my lord. Do you wish for me to come in with you?'

Thomas waved a dismissive hand. There weren't many men he'd met that he couldn't best in a one-on-one fight. Not that this would come to that, hopefully.

'David,' Rosa said, her voice flat and devoid of emotion. 'What are you doing here?'

The man standing by the window staggered as he took a few steps towards them, but then stopped as he caught sight of Rosa's figure.

'It's true,' he slurred. 'You are pregnant. I didn't believe it when you told me.'

Thomas felt Rosa bristle beside him, but allowed her to remain in control. Any sign of violence and he would step in.

'There were rumours you'd been sent to Italy in disgrace.'

Rosa said nothing, just laid a hand protectively on her bump.

'And now you've married this…' he seemed to search for the right word '…libertine.'

As insults went it was rather weak.

'I can't see that is any of your concern, David.'

'Of course it's my concern. You are carrying my child.'

'No, she isn't,' Thomas said calmly.

David spluttered and held up an accusing finger. 'That is my child. I know it is.'

Thomas put a protective arm around Rosa and gave her a little squeeze.

'Rosa is my wife. The child she is carrying is my child. Now please state your business and then leave.'

'Do you know what a whore you married?' David spat, hatred in his eyes.

Thomas dropped a kiss on the top of Rosa's head in a way he knew would just infuriate the man.

'I know exactly the kind of woman I married.'

'She begged me to take her. Couldn't keep her hands off me. Squealed like a whore, too.'

'We both know that isn't true,' Thomas said with a shrug. 'But if you need to tell yourself that to sleep at night then so be it.'

'I bet she said I raped her, forced myself upon her. She was willing, looked up at me with those big eyes and pleaded for me to take her.'

'I thought you loved me, David,' Rosa said sadly. 'I was young and naïve and stupid, but I never asked you to ruin me. I begged you to stop.'

'What do you want?' Thomas asked.

'I could tell the world,' David said, a malicious grin spreading across his face. 'I could tell the world the baby is mine—that you have married a fallen woman and the child is a bastard.'

Thomas took a step closer to David, drawing himself up to his full height. The other man took an involuntary step backwards as he approached and Thomas had to suppress a smile.

'You could tell everyone that, but what would be the point?'

'I want money. Five hundred pounds and I won't say a word.'

'No.'

'No?'

Thomas shrugged. 'There's no scandal here. Rosa is a married woman. She's pregnant with my child. My heir. The baby will be a Hunter.'

'Rumours can cause a lot of damage.'

'I'm sure they can. But you won't be the one spreading them.'

'I will.'

Thomas placed a hand on the other man's shoulder and felt him flinch.

'Your name is David Greenway, is that correct? Son of Mr Peter Greenway.'

David nodded, obviously nonplussed at the change of direction the conversation had taken.

'Your family home is a lovely old Tudor house with seven bedrooms and your father employs four servants. Unfortunately the Greenway family fortunes have taken a turn for the worse in the last few years—do correct me if I'm wrong.'

David mumbled something under his breath.

'As I understand it your father has borrowed a substantial amount of money against the family home. Money that he is struggling to pay back.'

'How…?'

'How do I know? Well, I had a long chat with a new friend who was moaning about a debt that will never be paid. He was loathe to turn the family out of their home, seeing as there are four women in residence to consider, but really couldn't continue as it was. I offered to buy the debt from him and he almost bit off my hand in his eagerness.'

Thomas watched as the blood drained from David's face and smiled in a businesslike manner.

'So I could call in your father's debt at any time. Or not. Tell me, you are the eldest son, are you not? You stand to inherit the house once your father dies.'

There was a minute nod from David.

'Stay away from my wife, stay away from our child. If I ever hear even a hint of a rumour about the legitimacy of our child then I will call in the debt so fast your mother and sisters won't even have time to pack their bags before they become homeless. Do you understand?'

David nodded.

'Good. Thank you for your visit. This has been most helpful. I hope we never see each other again.'

Thomas stepped back to let David past, watching as he stumbled towards the doorway.

'You were magnificent,' Rosa said. 'And you didn't even hit him.'

'I'm not all about the violence.'

'How did you know about the debt? I didn't even tell you his full name.'

Thomas smiled at her, placed a finger on her chin and tilted it up towards him. He was feeling reckless and a little out of control. Without thinking of the consequences he dipped his head and brushed his lips against hers, lacing his fingers through her hair and pulling her body closer to him.

Rosa melted in his arms and as he deepened the kiss Thomas knew he could lose himself in her for ever.

'I thought he might make trouble for us, so I sent a man to find out who he was, where he lived and any dirty family secrets. When my man uncovered the debt it seemed too good an opportunity to miss.'

'You did all that for me? For us?'

He kissed her again.

'Of course. You are my wife, I will do anything to protect you.'

Including keeping his distance, a voice screamed inside his head, but for once Thomas shut it down and gave in to his desire.

He ran his hands down Rosa's back, caressing her through the thin cotton of her dress, and cupped her buttocks. As he caressed her he felt Rosa stiffen in his arms, and then as if giving in to her own desires she relaxed.

'I've been thinking about what you said,' Thomas whispered in her ear. 'Constantly.'

'I say a lot of things.'

'You know what I mean.'

'I do.'

'I'd like to take you up on that offer.'

Rosa pulled away just a little and smiled up at him. Thomas felt his whole body tighten with desire and knew their whole relationship had been leading up to this moment.

'Come.' Rosa took his hand and pulled him from the room, giggling as they ran up the stairs.

Thomas knew he should say something to dampen her expectations. This didn't change his plans in the long term; he would still have to leave in a few months. Theirs would not be a normal marriage. He knew he should say something but he couldn't, he wanted this too much, couldn't bear the thought of Rosa pulling away from him now.

Upstairs, in Rosa's bedroom, they paused for a second and just looked at one another.

'You're sure?' Thomas asked.

'Can I tell you a secret?' Rosa whispered. 'I've been dreaming of this for a very long time.'

With a groan Thomas kissed her again, pouring all his passion and desire into the meeting of their lips. His tongue flicked out and tasted her, and he knew at that moment one taste would never be enough.

Gently he spun her round and with dextrous fingers unlaced her dress, pushing it down hastily to reveal the chemise underneath. The thin cotton was almost see-through, and Thomas felt his desire swell and grow as he saw the outline of her body beneath it.

Pulling her in close to him, Thomas peppered kisses all the way down her neck to her collar bone, loving the way her body responded to his caresses.

'I want to see you,' he whispered in her ear, then grasped the hem of her chemise and lifted it up over her head.

Thomas took a step back, but as his eyes slid over her body Rosa raised her arms to cover her belly. He caught them and gently pressed them back to her side.

'You're beautiful,' he said. 'All of you.'

Raising one hand, he trailed his fingers down in between her breasts, over the bump of her belly and down to her most private place below.

Rosa gasped as he touched her there and he felt her legs wobble underneath her.

Quickly he gripped his shirt and pulled it off over his head, his trousers following closely behind. Then he led Rosa to the bed and laid her down, sliding in beside her.

Through all his years of celibacy Thomas had imagined how this moment would feel, but never had he imagined anything quite so perfect. He realised he was glad he had waited, glad Rosa was his first, his only. No one else would ever make him feel this good.

He kissed her again, a long, sensuous kiss, and let his hands caress her body. He felt her fingertips on his back, pulling him closer to her. Dipping his head, hearing her moan of protest as he broke the kiss, he captured one of her nipples between his teeth. Rosa groaned, arching her back.

'I need you, Thomas,' she whispered.

And he needed her. Carefully he rolled her on to her side, facing away from him, and pressed his body up against hers. With one arm around her waist, pulling her tighter to him, he pushed forward, entering her and hearing her moan of pleasure as he did so.

Thomas had never felt so alive, so stimulated and slowly he began to rock his hips backwards and forward. He was gentle at first, conscious that he didn't want to hurt Rosa, but as she pressed back into him again and again he picked up speed.

He dropped his hand that had been around her waist down lower and began to stroke, guided by her moans of pleasure as his fingers grazed her.

Thomas felt the climax build inside him, knowing he would not be able to last much longer, but determined to give Rosa her pleasure before he took his. He kissed her neck, thrusting inside her at the same time, and after a few more strokes felt Rosa's body grow taut around him as she let out a low moan. Immediately Thomas felt his own release, pushing into Rosa one last time and hearing his own moan of pleasure.

They lay there, bodies pressed together, skin against skin, for a long time without speaking. Thomas felt a peculiar contentment wash over him. For months he had wanted to take Rosa to his bed and it had been even better than he had imagined. He knew, no matter what he told himself, this could not be a one-off. Their intimacy had just fuelled his desire for his wife rather than slaked it.

Chapter Twenty-One

Rosa beamed as she watched Thomas galloping over the fields in the distance. She loved to watch him in action, appreciated the effort that went into keeping his body in prime physical condition. Now, after he'd confided in her about his family secret, she could understand completely why he worked so hard to maintain peak physical fitness. The threat of losing control of his movements and his body made him look after himself more than the average man.

Rosa could appreciate the result as well. For two weeks now Thomas had slipped into her bed, pulled her close to him and worshipped her body every night, and Rosa could picture every groove of muscle, every firm contour of his body.

Each night he whispered it would be their last, that he would not succumb again, but it was as though he were drawn back to her bed as the sun went down.

Rosa didn't complain, she was dreading the day he did stay away, knowing that once he had broken away from her she might never get him back. She cherished the closeness between them, loved those sleepy moments when he held her in his arms before they both drifted into unconsciousness. One day soon the doctor would tell her to cease anything even remotely physical and then Thomas would not dare to touch her until the baby had been born. After that…well, Rosa knew how adamant he was that no future generation should be afflicted with the Hunter family curse.

'Is my son showing off again?' Sarah asked as she joined Rosa on the bench that looked out over the estate.

'He is a very fine horseman.'

The older woman smiled, a hint of pride in her eyes. 'Thomas does many things very well. The trouble is he knows it, too.'

They watched him in silence for a few minutes, enjoying the late morning sun.

'How are you settling in, my dear?' Sarah asked as Thomas disappeared over the brow of a hill.

'I feel so at home,' Rosa said quietly. 'More at home than I ever did in my own house.'

'This is your house now and your home.'

Rosa felt a lump form in her throat. They'd been living at Thomas's family home for a little over a month and she felt more at ease here than she ever had before. Her days were spent reading, strolling through the gardens and taking tea with her mother-in-law. Her nights were even more enjoyable and Rosa felt her cheeks flush at the thought.

'I'm very happy here,' Rosa said and knew it was the truth. For all her hurt and upset when Thomas had revealed his intention to escort her back to England and then leave her to live as mistress of his estate, Rosa now knew it was an enjoyable life.

'I haven't seen Thomas this happy in years. You're good for him. And this baby will be good for him, too.'

Biting her lip, Rosa suppressed a nervous laugh. She did think she was good for Thomas. The last few weeks he'd been happy and relaxed. The haunted look on his face, had disappeared, and the sense of urgency he'd had ever since she'd first met him had mellowed. For once he seemed to be enjoying living a normal, simple life and Rosa knew she'd played a big part in that.

'I wish…' Rosa started, but found herself unable to complete the sentence.

Sarah looked at her with the same dazzling blue eyes as her son and smiled encouragingly.

'I wish I could make Thomas want to stay.'

'He's planning on leaving?'

Rosa immediately regretted voicing her thoughts. The last thing she wanted to do was cause Sarah any unnecessary distress. She was about to open her mouth to try to rescue the situation when the older woman spoke.

'Of course he is. I don't know why I'm surprised. Silly boy.'

An unbidden smile flitted across Rosa's lips and she quickly tried to suppress it.

'Well, he is a silly boy. Look at what he's got: a lovely wife, a child on the way, a beautiful home. Men would kill to have half of what he does and he's determined to run away from it all.'

'I think he doesn't wish to be a burden if he does become unwell.'

Sarah sighed. 'I know. He saw how it hurt me when his father became ill and again with his brother. Thomas lived through the agony of watching someone he loved be slowly stripped away until just a husk was left. He wishes to protect us both from that.'

'But he doesn't even know if he will develop the disease.'

'After his brother died I told him to travel,' Sarah said quietly. 'I saw the fear and the sadness in his eyes and knew he needed something else to focus on, something positive. And I wanted him to have something to remember, something to be proud of, if he did develop the disease.' She stared out into the distance for a few minutes in silence. 'But he's too focused on gaining those new experiences to realise exactly what it is that would make him happy now.'

Rosa felt tears threaten to spill on to her cheeks.

'He could be so happy being a husband and a father, if he just let himself,' Sarah said. Taking Rosa's hand, she patted it softly. 'I'm sure he'll come round with time, realise what he would be giving up if he left.'

Rosa watched as Thomas re-emerged over the brow of the hill, allowing his horse to trot happily back towards them. Maybe he would realise how perfect the life they could have together would be, but she wasn't sure. He was so determined, so stubborn, that she knew once he'd set his mind to a particular course of action not much could sway him away from it.

'Well whatever happens I am thrilled to have

you here with me. And I never expected to be a grandmother. I feel doubly blessed.'

Rosa cleared her throat, knowing she had to confess the child was not Thomas's. She couldn't bear to deceive the kindly older woman any longer.

'I'm not sure how much Thomas has told you about how we met and the circumstances of my being in Italy,' Rosa began nervously.

Sarah looked at her with interest. Rosa felt her mouth go dry and stuttered the next few words. The older woman held up a hand to stop her.

'If you are trying to tell me this child is not of Thomas's blood, I am well aware of that fact,' Sarah said, squeezing Rosa's hand. 'Thomas told me far from everything, but I could fill in the gaps with educated guesses.'

Holding her breath, Rosa waited for her mother-in-law's reaction.

'In a way I'm glad,' Sarah said with a small smile. 'Thomas would never risk passing on the disease to the next generation of Hunters and I have to respect his decision. But this way he gets an heir without having to spend his life worrying about what future the child might have to endure because of his cursed blood.'

'That's exactly what Thomas said.'

'And of course I get a grandchild. I do love children.'

Rosa could tell from the warmth in Sarah's voice that she would shower this child with love and affection, even though it was not her flesh and blood.

'You two look awfully serious,' Thomas said as he reined in his horse and swung down from its back.

'We're discussing you,' his mother said with a smile.

'Surely I don't have so many flaws to warrant such concerned expressions.'

Both Rosa and Sarah remained silent for a few moments and then burst out laughing.

'May I deprive you of Rosa's company for a while?' Thomas asked his mother, holding his hand out to Rosa and helping her from the bench.

He loved watching her move, loved seeing the slow, careful way she manoeuvred herself into a standing position, how she had to steady herself for a few seconds to find her balance and the slight waddle to her gait as she walked.

'Of course. You two go and enjoy yourselves.'

Slowing his pace so Rosa didn't become overtired, Thomas led her away from the house across the lawn.

'Where are we going?'

'Have a little patience and you will see. It's somewhere new. Somewhere secret.'

'Thomas, I've strolled through all the gardens ten times over this past month. I think I would have noticed somewhere secret.'

'That's the beauty of a secret place, you can walk past ten times without even noticing it's there. You need someone to show you the way.'

'I told your mother about the baby,' Rosa said, her eyes fixed to the ground.

He knew she felt awkward discussing the child, awkward talking of the baby from another man she was carrying.

'What did she say?'

'She had guessed that you were not…' Rosa trailed off. Even though the child was not of his blood he would still be its father.

Thomas stopped abruptly and turned to face Rosa. He saw the worry in her eyes and the little pucker between her eyebrows.

'Rosa, I know this child is not of my flesh and blood, and until it is born I suspect I won't truly know how I feel about him or her. But I can promise you I will nurture and cherish this baby as if it were my own.'

He saw the flicker of hope in Rosa's eyes and knew it was the right thing to say, even if he wasn't sure it was the truth. If he was completely honest he had mixed feelings about this child that was about to burst into their lives. He wanted to love the little boy or girl Rosa was carrying, and he thought he might do so already, but he just wasn't sure. Could a man love another man's child as he would his own? Thomas didn't know the answer to that and he rather suspected he wouldn't know until he looked down into the child's eyes and held the little bundle in his arms.

Not that Rosa needed to know all of that. She had enough to worry about with the impending arrival, she didn't need to dwell on whether her husband would love her baby.

'I know it is an impossible situation.'

'I was well aware of your condition and the consequences of that when I married you,' Thomas said with a smile.

'But then you were planning on bringing me back to England and then bidding me farewell.'

Thomas felt his whole body stiffen. These last few weeks had been marvellous. He'd been cocooned in happiness, surrounded by love and joy, but he knew it had to come to an end. He thought Rosa had known that, too.

'Rosa, I want to be here when you give birth,' Thomas said slowly. 'And of course for a few weeks afterwards.'

He watched as she tried to hide the pain as she understood the true meaning of his words. He was still going to leave her, still planning on abandoning her in his country estate whilst he went to travel the world.

'I wish to see you settled with the baby, of course.'

'But then you will leave.' Rosa's voice was completely flat and devoid of emotion, but her eyes betrayed the true pain she was feeling.

'That was always the plan,' Thomas said.

He'd never deceived her, never lied to her and told her he would stay, but he'd seen the hope blossoming in her as they'd grown closer these last few weeks. Every time he slipped into bed beside her Thomas had known it would make the eventual farewell so much harder, but he just hadn't been able to keep away.

'I know. You will return to travelling the world and I shall be a companion to your mother.'

'Do you not get on well with my mother?'

'That's not the point,' Rosa said, her voice low and overflowing with emotion.

He went to reach out and touch her arm, but Rosa pulled away.

'I can't stay here, Rosa.'

'Why not?'

'You know why.'

'Tell me again. Make me understand.'

'Come with me.' Thomas didn't try to touch her again and was acutely aware of the space between them as reluctantly she followed him. He led her through the formal gardens and off to one side, out into a wooded area. They walked for about ten minutes in silence before Thomas stopped and motioned to the monument in front of them.

It was his brother's grave. Situated in a clearing in the woodland his brother had loved so much as a child, the grave was neat and lovingly tended.

'I wanted to show you this. I come here to talk to my brother sometimes. To ask his advice.'

Rosa carefully knelt in front of the grave and bent her head for a few moments. Thomas could see her lips moving, but didn't recognise the words.

'I understand you lost two people very dear to you,' Rosa said softly. 'And I understand you live in fear of one day succumbing to the same disease. What I don't understand is why you feel you must push everyone away and face this on your own.'

Thomas stepped forward and placed a hand on the smooth headstone, running his fingers over the inscription.

'I saw the pain my mother had to live through every single day watching my father lose first his physical abilities and then his mental. By the end there wasn't even a trace of the man she had married left.'

'She must have been devastated by the loss,' Rosa said. 'But I know she was glad to be there for your father through those years of decline. To share the good days along with the bad.'

'I don't ever want to be a burden like that.'

Rosa stepped towards him and cupped his face in her hands. Thomas felt her soft skin against his rough stubble.

'If you love someone it isn't a burden. It's just what you do.'

Thomas looked into her eyes and saw the raw emotion and felt his throat begin to constrict. He knew she cared for him, had known it ever since they'd travelled across Italy together, but now he could see pure love in her eyes.

Before he could answer, before he could even begin to formulate a single word, Rosa dropped her hands and turned away. Without looking behind her she walked back through the trees and into the garden and Thomas wondered if he'd lost her for good.

Chapter Twenty-Two

Dear Caroline,
I must apologise for leaving it so long in between my letters. So much has happened since I last penned you that short note from Venice, letting you know of my pending marriage.

We are now back in England and have been for some weeks, but much of that time I have been recuperating from a shipwreck on our voyage home. It was terrible, Caroline. I've never experienced such fear. Not for myself, as you must understand better than many, but for my child.

The doctor is as confident as he can be that the baby sustained no injury or damage during my time in the water, but I find myself fretting still. The only thing that can reassure me is feeling my little baby's determined kicks and somersaults inside me.

I am now residing at Longcroft Hall, my husband's family home in Hampshire. At present there is me, my husband and his mother in residence, but I fear that soon Thomas might leave England again and set off on his travels around the world. He is determined to go, even though I know he is happy here with me.

The situation is perhaps too complicated to go into in a letter, but suffice it to say Thomas thinks he would be protecting me in the long term if he left now. What he does not seem to understand is that my heart will break if he leaves me. Every day I hope he might change his mind, and when I catch him looking at the child growing inside me I can see him waver.

Is it completely pathetic that I don't care if it is me he stays for or the baby? As long as he stays close.

Enough about my woes. I know I am very lucky to have a safe and stable home and a legal father for my child.

Caroline, I yearn for news of you and your darling son. It will not be long before I give birth myself, but I wish I could see you and confide all of my hopes and fears. You always did have a level head and a way of making everything work out for the best.

You are most welcome to come and visit here at Longcroft Hall, or once I am recovered from childbirth I could make the trip to you.

With all my love,
Rosa

Rosa waited for the ink to dry and then folded the sheet of paper in half, slipping it into an envelope and penning the address on the front. She wished dearly for her old friend, Caroline always knew what to do in a difficult situation and Rosa wanted someone she could tell about every aspect of her life, good and bad.

Rosa looked up as the door opened and Thomas strolled inside.

'I've received a note,' he said and, although his voice was light and untroubled, Rosa could see the concern on his face.

'Who from?'

He cleared his throat. 'Your father.'

'Papa?'

Rosa stood a little too quickly, had to hold out her arms to try to catch her balance and then gave up and fell back on to the sofa.

'It seems he arrived in the village yesterday evening and is currently staying in the inn.'

Rosa felt her heart leap and then sink again immediately.

'And my mother?' she asked.

'He doesn't mention her in his note.'

Rosa had a flashback to the hatred and disgust on her mother's face when she had sent her on her way to Italy.

'Your father has asked if he may call on us, at our convenience.'

Hope and doubt mingled in Rosa's mind. She wanted to see her kind, gentle father so much, but she didn't think she could stomach the upset of listening to her mother rant and rave. She felt Thomas's eyes on her, watching her closely.

'I was planning on taking my horse out for a ride this afternoon,' he said slowly. 'Perhaps I could travel to the village and see whether he came alone. If he has, then I will extend an invitation to dinner tonight.'

'Thank you,' Rosa said softly. He always seemed to know exactly what she needed, sometimes even before she knew it herself. Except when it came to his plans to abandon her in England, of course.

'Our child should know at least one more

grandparent,' Thomas said, taking her hand and placing a kiss on her wrist.

Rosa glanced surreptitiously at his face, wondering if he'd realise what he had just said. *Our child.* Up until this moment Thomas had always referred to the baby growing inside her as *her* child. She wondered if it was just a slip of the tongue or if he was coming to think of the baby as theirs.

Stepping closer, Thomas tilted her face up and kissed her gently on the lips. These last couple of days he'd started being more careful as he touched and kissed her. The caresses were no less in number, but it was as though he was subconsciously aware that soon Rosa would be going through a great ordeal and wanted her to save her strength for that.

She looped her arms up around his neck and pulled him closer to her, giggling as he brushed against her bump. Hearing him whisper her name as he peppered kisses along her jawbone and down her neck made her shudder with delight and Rosa allowed herself to be swept away by the moment.

They were both all too aware that soon they would not be able to share the ultimate act of intimacy, but Rosa was keen to persuade Thomas that they could still have a close and physically loving relationship without risking her getting pregnant with his child.

Running her hands down his body, she grazed her fingers over the toned muscles of his chest and abdomen, smiling as he let out a faint moan as she tucked a finger into his waistband.

'You don't know what you do to me, Rosa,' Thomas whispered.

Deftly she unbuttoned his trousers and sunk to her knees in front of him. She felt his eyes on her, watching with a mixture of disbelief and pleasure as she took him into her mouth. Slowly she began to move backwards and forward, watching his reaction to every flick of her tongue or stroke of her hand. Soon she knew exactly what made him groan in pleasure and what made him clutch at her shoulders in delight.

Rosa looked up at him, saw him looking lovingly down at her, his eyes a little glazed as he stiffened and climaxed.

Dropping lower, Rosa watched as Thomas recovered, stroking her hair and cupping her face until he was composed enough to help her to her feet.

'Where on earth did you learn that?' he asked.

Rosa blushed. It had been a very awkward but very enlightening conversation with one of the housemaids. A couple of days ago Rosa had decided she would fight for Thomas. She loved him, that much she knew, and she wasn't going to let him leave without doing her utmost to persuade him to stay. That included showing him the sort of relationship they could have over the coming years.

'We women discuss these things all the time,' she said, hiding a smile as he looked momentarily alarmed. It wasn't often she was able to ruffle her husband and she appreciated her small victory even if it was short lived.

'We men talk, too,' Thomas said, a mischievous glint in his eyes.

For a second Rosa didn't grasp his meaning, but gentle hands guiding her to the armchair were enough to make her eyes widen.

'Men can't do that to women,' she said, feeling foolish as soon as the words left her mouth. Patricia the housemaid hadn't told her anything about this.

'Oh, yes, we can.'

Deftly Thomas lifted Rosa's skirts and she felt his hand on her thighs. He caressed the smooth skin for a second before grasping hold of the top of one stocking and rolling it down. Quickly he repeated the movement on the other leg. Even though her dress was still covering most of her upper legs she felt exposed and a thrill of excitement ran through her.

'Anyone could come in.'

'Then they should know better than to disturb a man alone with his wife.'

Rosa felt any further protestations die on her lips as he kissed one ankle, moving up her leg ever so slowly, making her enjoy every caress.

Rosa gasped as his lips reached the very top of her thigh and then let out a disappointed sigh as he pulled away and returned to the bottom of her other leg.

'Patience, my dear,' he said with a wicked grin.

Trailing his lips up her leg, he paused again at her thighs and for one frustrating second Rosa thought he would pull away again, but then his mouth was on her and Rosa groaned in pleasure.

Letting her head drop backwards, she closed her eyes as he kissed and caressed her, his touch making her want to scream in delight. Clutching at Thomas's hair, Rosa felt her hips buck up to meet him again and again until something exploded inside her.

It was a full two minutes before she felt ready to open her eyes and look up at her husband, who was now standing over her looking very pleased with himself.

* * *

Thomas pulled at his cravat and sighed. Despite being back in his family home surrounded by servants who were at his beck and call he still didn't have a valet. He didn't want one, didn't want to share his daily rituals with a stranger, but he couldn't deny a valet would come in handy when faced with a cravat.

'Tell me again how he seemed,' Rosa said, slipping up behind him and looping her arms around his waist. Thomas felt a strange contentment as he allowed Rosa to spin him round and felt her dexterous fingers deftly pulling the cravat into shape.

'Nervous,' Thomas said, thinking back to the unassuming, quiet man he had met briefly at the inn.

'Did he look well?'

Thomas hesitated, recalling the dark circles around Rosa's father's eyes and the clothes that didn't seem to fit properly.

'You'll be able to judge for yourself in a few minutes,' he said, inspecting his neatly tied cravat in the mirror in front of him.

He watched as Rosa paced nervously backwards and forward across the room, halting only to peer out of the window every so often.

'And you're sure my mother wasn't with him?'

'Completely sure.'

Thomas could see the anxiety in Rosa's eyes and realised how important this evening was for her. When she'd talked of her parents she'd always recalled her father with love and fondness. He knew she was still hurting from being sent away by her mother and her father not stepping in to put a stop to the plan.

'He's here,' Rosa said, leaning into the window to catch a glimpse of her father.

'Are you ready?' Thomas asked.

She nodded, but didn't look in the least bit ready.

'Remember I am here, no matter what happens this evening.'

Rosa looked up at him with silent gratitude and Thomas felt his heart squeeze in his chest. He hadn't realised quite how much Rosa had burrowed into his heart these last few months. They had gone from unlikely companions to so much more. He knew he couldn't have made a better choice for his wife, although he did worry he was beginning to care for her maybe too much. On occasions like tonight he felt every inch of her anxiety and worry as if it were his own and he wanted to protect her from anything that threatened to hurt her.

They walked down the stairs and heard soft

voices coming from the drawing room. Thomas's mother had agreed to take on the official role of hostess for their small dinner party, leaving Rosa free to try to mend the rift between her and her father.

Pushing open the door, Thomas led Rosa inside, noting the increased pressure on his arm as she gripped him a little harder. The conversation between Rosa's father and Thomas's mother petered out as father and daughter laid eyes on each other. For a moment it was as if the whole room was frozen in time and then Rosa slipped from his side and threw herself into her father's arms.

'Papa,' she said as he embraced her, his entire face lighting up with delight.

'My little Rosa. I have missed you terribly.'

He drew back from her, held her at arm's length and regarded her. 'How you've changed these last few months.'

Thomas stiffened, ready to jump to Rosa's defence if her father even thought about uttering a harsh word.

'You look so healthy, and so happy.' There were tears in the old man's eyes as Rosa took both of his hands in her own and squeezed them.

'I am happy, Papa,' Rosa said quietly.

Thomas felt the stab of guilt in his gut. She was happy—they both were. There was no denying it. However much he tried to pretend he wasn't thoroughly enjoying domestic life, he knew it was a lie. He loved being married to Rosa, loved how she offered sage words of wisdom over the running of the estate he was just re-familiarising himself with, loved how they laughed together all day long, and loved the closeness when they fell into bed side by side at night.

He often found himself wishing that this part of their lives could stretch on for ever—that they could continue to live this carefree existence without the ever-present worry of his family illness.

'This is my husband, Papa. Lord Hunter.'

'We had the pleasure of meeting earlier today,' Thomas said, stepping forward to shake his father-in-law's hand.

'Rosa, my dear, before we say anything further there is something I must talk to you about.'

Thomas saw Rosa's face drop and stepped closer, wondering how he might shield her from any potential bad news.

'I have been an awful father to you,' Mr Rothwell said, his face a picture of misery and regret. 'I should never have let your mother send you to Italy to stay with that wretched family of hers. I failed you when you needed me the most.'

'Papa, there's no need…'

'There's every need. I am not a strong man, not forceful in my personality, but I knew you needed me to stand up for you and I cowered away, taking the easy path. I have regretted it for every moment since.'

'I forgive you, Papa,' Rosa said quickly, looking pained by her father's distress.

Thomas saw the tears slip out of the older man's eyes as Rosa embraced him and heard Rosa sniff some back of her own.

'Come,' Thomas's mother said quietly, 'dinner is served. Please take your time and follow when you are ready.'

Thomas waited for Rosa to enter the room on her father's arm, pulled out her chair and ensured she was comfortable before taking his own seat.

'Papa, where is Mother?' Rosa asked softly as the first course was placed in front of them.

Reaching for Rosa's hand under the table, Thomas gave it a quick squeeze.

Mr Rothwell grimaced. 'We have been leading separate lives since you were sent to Italy,' he said. 'Your mother resides in London, I spend most of my time in our country house. I haven't seen her for many weeks now.' He paused as if considering whether to say more. 'And I must say we're both much happier for it. But enough about me and your mother—that is an ongoing saga no one wishes to hear about. Tell me how you two met.'

Thomas sat back and listened as Rosa recounted their early relationship, laughing as she recalled how she'd flattened him on the road outside the Di Mercurios' villa and been lured into the wise woman's house on their journey to Venice. So much had happened in the four months since he'd first met Rosa, so much in his life had changed, yet one thing, this disease he might or might not have, was still hanging over him.

'I hope I can be a good grandfather to your child, my dear,' Mr Rothwell said as the conversation turned to the baby.

'You should come to stay once Rosa has recovered from the birth. If that is what you wish, Rosa?' Thomas's mother suggested.

'I would love that, Papa.'

Mr Rothwell beamed, pure joy in his eyes, and Thomas realised that whatever the older man's faults he loved his daughter and her unborn child unconditionally.

'Come, Rosa,' Thomas's mother said as they finished their dessert. 'Take a stroll with me along the patio.'

Standing, Thomas watched his wife exit

through the doors on to the veranda that they'd thrown open part way through the meal due to the balminess of the evening.

'Whisky?' Thomas offered as he crossed to the side board, picking up two glasses.

'Yes, please.'

Thomas poured two glasses of whisky and led his father-in-law through to his study. In Thomas's mind it was the most comfortable room in the house, with two soft leather armchairs positioned by the fire, which thankfully today did not need to be lit.

'I need to thank you as well, Lord Hunter,' Mr Rothwell said as they both settled back into the armchairs.

He waited for the older man to go on, regarding him with curiosity.

'I know how much you have done for my daughter over the last few months. I dread to think what would have happened to her if you hadn't found her when you did.'

The myriad dangers for a woman travelling alone played out quickly in Thomas's mind. Rosa had been so desperate to escape from the Di Mercurios that she hadn't properly considered the consequences of her running away.

'Any gentleman would have done the same.'

Mr Rothwell shook his head. 'Many gentlemen are scoundrels, or just not interested in anything other than themselves.'

He couldn't argue with that. Thomas had come across many so-called gentlemen in his time. Often the ones with the loftier titles were the most selfish and uninterested in others.

'I also want to thank you for marrying Rosa, you've saved her from a lifetime of hurt and pain. I am well aware I do not know the full circumstances around your marriage, but I thank you for the benefits it confers on my daughter. She has suffered enough.'

Thomas nodded. From the very beginning he had repeated all the advantages their union held for Rosa, it had been his way of convincing himself he was doing it all for her and not himself. He felt strangely comfortable with this kindly older man, as if he could tell him anything, unburden all his secrets and regrets.

'When I first proposed to your daughter I told myself it was to save her from ruin. To protect her from the heartache of being shunned by everyone she had ever known, to protect her child from growing up under the cloud of illegitimacy.'

'That is a very selfless reason to propose.'

'I also wanted a wife to protect my interests at home and a companion for my mother. Someone who I could bring back to England and leave here to oversee the parts of my life I wanted to run away from,' he confessed, swirling his whisky around his glass.

'You weren't planning on staying with her?'

Thomas heard the shock in Mr Rothwell's voice and knew Rosa's father probably wasn't the best man to confide in when it came to his marital dilemmas, despite his kindly demeanour.

Mr Rothwell sighed. 'Do you know I was madly in love with Rosa's mother when we first met? She was so beautiful, so exotic, so different from all the debutantes my parents pushed in front of me. I even thought her disdain for me was exciting, a challenge to be overcome.'

Thomas couldn't imagine pursuing a woman who actively disliked him, but everyone was different.

'When she agreed to marry me I thought the disdain had all been an act, part of her ploy to keep me interested. I thought once we were married things would be different between us.'

From the snippets Rosa had told him Thomas knew this hadn't been the case. It sounded as though Rosa's mother had disliked her father every day they'd been together.

'It wasn't different. She never loved me, never

even liked me. At the time her family were in a dire financial situation so she was sent out to marry well. She'd always dreamed of a title, to be Lady Elena, but no one with a title was foolish enough to take her on, so she had to settle for me.'

'Does Rosa know all this?'

'Mostly. Elena has a terrible temper. She says the most hurtful things when in a rage.'

Thomas regarded the man sitting across from him sipping at his whisky. Rosa was certainly not like her mother, her disposition was sweet and kind, but she wasn't entirely like her father either.

'Perhaps our lives would have been better if we'd resided in separate countries,' he mused, smiling softly. 'Anyway, I suppose the point I was trying to make, is that all marriages are complicated.'

They sat in silence for a few minutes, staring at the empty fireplace in the dwindling evening light.

'She loves you, did you know that?' Mr Rothwell said eventually.

Thomas nodded. He did know it. He'd known it ever since she'd been so hurt when he'd rejected her in the bedchamber in Venice. Only a woman in love would be quite so pained by the rejection. And every day since their return to England he'd seen that love blossom and grow, thrilled to be the recipient of that love and petrified that he would break her heart.

'Whatever the reason for wanting to lead a separate life to Rosa, just remember that she loves you. And I'm told the love of a good woman is nothing to be sneered at.'

'I don't want to hurt her.'

'Then don't leave her.'

Thomas shook his head. 'I'm worried I will hurt her more if I stay. If we build a life together, raise our child and allow ourselves to be happy, then it will be all that much worse when something bad happens.'

'What will happen?'

Thomas remained silent. He wasn't quite ready to tell anyone else of the family curse just yet, especially the man whose daughter had just married into the family.

When no reply was forthcoming Mr Rothwell pressed on. 'How certain are you that this awful event is going to happen?' he asked.

'There is no way of knowing.'

'So you are giving up a future of happiness for something that may never occur.'

'But it may do.'

'If it were me,' Mr Rothwell said slowly, as

if still pondering his words, 'I would want to do everything in my power to be sure one way or the other before condemning myself to a life of misery.' The older man stood, crossed to his chair and placed a fatherly hand on his shoulder. 'Both you and Rosa deserve that.'

Half an hour later the room was becoming so dark it was getting difficult to see, but still Thomas hadn't moved. He felt paralysed with indecision and it was as uncomfortable as it was unfamiliar.

He didn't want to condemn Rosa to a life of misery, of course he didn't, and he knew after a few months without him she would settle into a comfortable routine, especially with the baby to keep her company. He, on the other hand, would be miserable for ever without her. No matter where he went, which exotic countries he travelled to and which wonders he immersed himself in, he would know what his life could be like with Rosa. Nothing could compare to the simple pleasures of the last few weeks.

Decisively he stood. He still couldn't make the final commitment to stay here with Rosa just yet, but he would take Mr Rothwell's advice, he would consult a doctor about his family's disease, get a better idea of what might face him and the odds that he would develop it, and then work out if he could follow his heart and stay.

Chapter Twenty-Three

'He's left?' Rosa asked, hating the tremor in her voice.

'He didn't tell you?' Sarah asked, eyes wide with surprise. 'He didn't tell me either.'

'He came and kissed my cheek this morning, but I was half-asleep. I don't *think* he said anything.'

Rosa's mother-in-law took her hand and squeezed it softly. 'I'm sure he isn't gone for good.'

'Last night, after my father left, he was very quiet, very pensive. I asked him what was troubling him, but he didn't really give me an answer.'

Instead he'd pulled her into bed with him, told her not to waste her energy worrying about him and tenderly made love to her. Rosa had fallen into a deep, dreamless sleep afterwards and barely remembered her husband rising and bidding her farewell early in the morning.

'He doesn't seem to have taken much with him,' Rosa added, hopefully.

Surely he wouldn't abandon her like this, without saying goodbye. She knew he was still planning on leaving one day, but he'd given no indication that day was drawing near.

Rosa spent the rest of the morning curled up on one of the armchairs in Thomas's study with a book. She had less than a month to go in her pregnancy now and even the exertion of getting up and getting dressed each morning took its toll. Each time the baby inside her kicked Rosa smiled, loving the little signs of life.

After a couple of hours in the study Rosa felt much more relaxed, but sitting in one position had made her back ache more than normal. Hauling herself to her feet, Rosa started to stroll through the hallways, taking time to admire the paintings on the walls. She laughed at the stern visages of Thomas's ancestors and delighted in the beautiful landscapes, all the time, using one hand to massage her lower back.

A sharp pain made her stop and hang on to the back of a conveniently positioned chair just as Thomas's mother emerged from the drawing room.

Immediately the older woman was at her side,

guiding her down into the chair and calling for one of the maids.

'What is wrong my dear?' Sarah asked, her face clouded with concern.

'I'm sure I've just twisted awkwardly,' Rosa said, sure of no such thing. 'I've got an aching pain in my back and sharper pains coming round the front.'

'Betty, go and fetch two of the footmen and ask Mr Timkins to come here, too.'

The young maid scurried off to find the footmen and the butler as Rosa felt Sarah's hands rest softly on her bump.

A few seconds later the pain started again, a faint tightening sensation accompanying it.

'I am no doctor, but I think it may be time.'

Rosa shook her head. The baby couldn't be coming yet—she wasn't ready.

Two footmen emerged into the hallway and quickly Sarah instructed them to carry Rosa upstairs.

'I'm sure I can walk,' Rosa protested, trying to stand.

Another pain gripped her as she moved and Rosa fell back into the chair, closing her eyes as if trying to block out the discomfort.

'Upstairs,' Sarah ordered.

Rosa felt the chair being lifted slowly and then

the soft rocking as the two footmen carried her through the hall and up the stairs. Clutching the seat with both hands, Rosa gripped so hard her knuckles turned white, only letting go as the chair was placed gently on the floor in her bedroom.

'I want Thomas,' Rosa whispered. It was all she wanted right now, her husband's reassuring voice telling her everything would be fine, his arms wrapped around her giving her strength and his lips pressed against her skin.

'Fetch the doctor,' Sarah ordered. 'And send for Emma.' Emma was the young housemaid currently acting as Rosa's lady's maid.

Rosa heaved herself up from the chair, ignoring the ache in her back and the taut muscles in her stomach. She suddenly felt constricted, as if all her clothes were shrinking as she stood up in them, and she grappled with the ties on the back of her dress.

'I need to get out of this,' Rosa panted, pulling at the material when it wouldn't come loose.

Immediately Sarah was by her side, quickly unlacing the fabric and lifting it up over Rosa's head. By the time Rosa's maid Emma had entered the room Rosa was clad only in her long chemise.

'Let's get you to the bed,' Sarah instructed.

'No, I need to move. It feels better when I move.'

Rosa clutched at her bump, holding it gently as she waddled across the room. She paused at the window, looking longingly out to see if Thomas happened to be galloping down the driveway.

No one appeared, and Rosa felt the tears threatening to spill out of her eyes. He couldn't have left her, not like this, not when she needed him the most. Over the last few weeks she'd really felt as though she were getting through to him, really believed that he had started to see the benefits of them enjoying a conventional married life. She'd noticed the affection in his eyes when he looked at her. It wasn't love, he'd never mentioned love, but it was affection, and for now that would have to be enough.

She didn't want to cope with this on her own.

Rosa swung her legs on to the bed and grimaced as the doctor placed his cold hands on her belly.

'Do you feel a tightening now?' he asked, frowning as he concentrated.

'Yes,' Rosa panted, breathing hard as the pain built to a crescendo.

'Good. Your body is getting ready to deliver this baby. It shouldn't be too long now.'

'How long?' Rosa asked, her grip on the bed-sheets relaxing as the pain began to subside.

'Difficult to say, but I should think you will have your son or daughter by tomorrow morning at the latest.'

Tomorrow morning was a long time away, especially when she was in so much pain. Every hour the pains worsened, so much so that each time she told herself this must be as bad as they got, knowing full well it was a lie.

'I will come and check on your progress in a few hours' time,' the doctor said. 'In the meantime you know where I am if there are any problems.'

'He's leaving?' Rosa asked, her voice laced with panic.

'Hush, my dear,' Sarah said. 'It's better that way. Men, even medical men, get in the way during childbirth. We women have been doing this on our own for generations.'

'You won't leave me?'

'I won't leave you.'

Rosa looked up into her mother-in-law's eyes. 'I wish Thomas was here.'

'I do, too, Rosa.'

'I think I love him.'

Sarah squeezed her hand and Rosa closed her eyes, letting out a loud, guttural groan as the pain began to build again.

Chapter Twenty-Four

Thomas looked down, wondering how many pages of the newspaper he'd flicked through without taking any of it in.

'Dr Jones will see you now,' a young and eager assistant said as he emerged from the consulting room.

'Lord Hunter, it is a pleasure to see you.'

'Have we met before?' Thomas asked. He didn't recall the man, but over the years his father and brother had consulted many doctors.

'I knew your father well, but I think you were always away at school when I visited. How is your mother?'

'Still grieving, but she has found a way to start living her life again.'

The doctor smiled, leaned back in his chair and adjusted his glasses.

'So tell me, Lord Hunter, what brings you to see me today?'

Thomas hesitated. The questions he'd come to ask were difficult to formulate.

'I wish to know more about the disease that afflicted my father and brother. And my risk of developing it.'

Dr Jones steepled his fingers together, contemplating Thomas's request before he started speaking.

'Your father and brother suffered from an inherited condition that affected both their movement and their memory. We know it was of gradual onset and it was progressive. They both became worse with each passing month.'

Thomas nodded, remembering coming home from school at the end of term and not knowing what state his father would be in, dreading what he would find.

'When I first met your father we spent quite some time tracing this disease back through the family. Your father had known many of his relatives had died an unnaturally early death, but there was a lot of secrecy surrounding the illness and those who suffered from it.'

Thomas realised he was holding his breath as he waited for the doctor to continue.

'Not everyone in the family was afflicted. Both men and women suffered from the disease, but only about half of the family members developed it. It was difficult to be sure as in some generations people had died young of other causes.'

'So there is a chance…' Thomas trailed off, unable to complete the sentence.

'There is a good chance you are not affected.'

'How can I be sure, one way or the other?'

Dr Jones shook his head. 'Unfortunately it is impossible to be sure. The disease seems to develop at different ages in different people. Do you have any symptoms?'

'Sometimes I think I have a tremor in my hands.'

'Let me examine you.'

Thomas obligingly removed his jacket, feeling the tremor in his hands as he did so.

'You are nervous,' Dr Jones stated. 'Understandably.'

'My hands are shaking.'

Slowly, as if he had all the time in the world, the doctor inspected Thomas's hands, turning them over and watching the minute movements.

'Make a fist,' he instructed. 'Now relax. Pick up the pen on my desk and write your name. Good.'

Thomas complied with all the instructions, writing his name, turning the key in the lock on the door and untying a knot the doctor presented to him.

'I now need to see you walk.'

Trying to walk normally, Thomas paced backwards and forward across the consulting room, changing his gait as the doctor asked him to walk first on his toes and then as if on a tightrope.

'Good.' The doctor's face was serious and his tone of voice didn't give anything away. 'Come and stand in front of me. Now, I need you to follow my finger with your eyes, keeping your head still.'

Half an hour later, once Thomas had been prodded and poked and undergone a rigorous examination, the doctor sat back in his chair and motioned for Thomas to have a seat.

'You're as healthy as an ox,' he declared.

'And the tremor?'

'Anxiety. You believe you will one day develop a movement disorder, so you are more aware of the smallest movements in your hands than the general population.'

'You can find no sign of the disease?'

'None.'

'But you can't tell me I will not ever develop it?'

'Lord Hunter,' Dr Jones said with a heartfelt sigh, 'I could be trampled by a horse on my walk home tonight. Does that mean I should hide away in my house and never leave it again?'

Thomas shook his head. He knew exactly the point the doctor was making, but his situation was different.

'The likelihood of you being trampled by a horse is much less than me developing my father's disease.'

'Very true,' the doctor said, but didn't appear as though he thought he had lost the argument. 'And it is entirely your choice if you wish to squander your life worrying about something that may or may not ever happen.'

The illness had been a black cloud following him around for so many years the idea of trying not to worry about it was almost inconceivable.

'It is not an active choice I make.'

'And I do understand that, Lord Hunter. Just as I acknowledge I have no real idea how it must feel to have this disease, the very disease that killed your father and brother, hanging over you. But you came to me for advice and my advice to you would be to live your life, whether you have five years or fifty. Cherish every single moment *because* you may have less time than the average man. Find what makes you happy and keep on doing it again and again.'

Rosa. The thought flew unbidden into his mind. *Rosa made him happy.*

'Stop letting this disease ruin your life before you have developed a single symptom.'

Thomas stood abruptly, the doctor's words hitting him and making him feel as though he were seeing the world for the first time.

'Thank you, Doctor.'

'One more thing, Lord Hunter,' the doctor said as Thomas shook his hand vigorously. 'You may consider whether you wish to father any children.'

Thomas smiled. 'This disease stops with me, Dr Jones.'

Leaving the doctor's office Thomas felt lighter than he had for years. He knew he had been consumed by grief after his brother's death, and that had clouded his judgement in many matters. He'd fled the country, telling himself he had to squeeze as many experiences into his life as possible as he didn't know when it would end. Thomas didn't regret that, he'd seen so much, experienced so many different cultures these last few years. What he did regret was his insistence that he must face the future on his own. He'd pushed away the people who loved him, first his mother and then Rosa.

Still, the idea of subjecting Rosa to the pain of watching him suffer through the terrible disease made him uncomfortable, but he knew if he abandoned her now, fled the country and continued his travels around the world, that would hurt her even more. He would be choosing to leave her.

Quickly he pushed his way through the crowds towards the inn he had left his horse at earlier that morning. It would take him nearly two hours to ride home from Portsmouth even if he pushed his horse hard. Suddenly he just needed to be home, needed to hold Rosa in her arms, kiss her lips and tell her what a fool he'd been.

A cold shiver shot down his spine as he wondered if she would forgive him his folly. Ever since he'd proposed he'd treated her badly. He'd seen her growing affection for him and tried to ignore it. He'd allowed the love between them to blossom, but at the same time told Rosa it could not last. He had treated her appallingly.

With a shake of his head he dismissed the notion. Rosa loved him, any fool could see that. She would forgive him and if she didn't he had a whole lifetime to make it up to her.

Two hours later Thomas pushed open the front door, wondering where all the servants were. Normally a footman would be positioned in the entrance hall, ready to receive any visitors, but today there was no one to be seen.

A bloodcurdling scream shot down the stairs and stopped Thomas in his tracks for a second. Then he was running, taking the stairs three at a time. He reached Rosa's bedroom door in less than ten seconds and threw himself inside.

Another scream nearly deafened him before he could take in exactly what he was seeing.

'Rosa…' he whispered, trying to make sense of the scene in the room.

Rosa was half-sitting, half-lying on the blood-soaked sheets covering the bed. His mother was standing by her side, squeezing Rosa's hand and murmuring words of encouragement, whilst two maids hovered nervously in the background. A motherly-looking older woman stood at the foot of the bed, waiting with outstretched arms and a frown of concentration.

Thomas heard Rosa panting, then came another scream that seemed to last for eternity, followed by total silence.

A small cry pierced the silence, more of a gurgle than anything else.

For two seconds no one moved, then Thomas dashed forward. Rosa smiled up at him weakly and then looked hopefully at the bundle the older woman was scooping up.

'Your son,' she pronounced and Thomas felt as though the ground had shifted beneath him.

He leaned in, pausing to kiss Rosa on the forehead, and look down at the pink little face wrapped tightly in a blanket.

Thomas had been both waiting for and dreading this moment. This was the moment when he would know if he could truly love another man's child as his own.

The baby opened his eyes and looked up at him.

'Our son,' Thomas whispered.

There was no doubt, no second guessing. Thomas felt an overwhelming surge of love and happiness looking down into the innocent child's face.

'Our son,' Rosa repeated, tears spilling from her eyes.

Chapter Twenty-Five

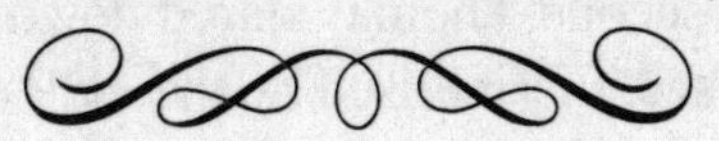

Thomas stroked the silky soft hair on his son's head and wondered if Rosa would be offended if he compared it to moleskin. It wasn't that he thought their son looked like a mole…although sometimes when he first woke up from one of his numerous naps…

'Edward?' Rosa suggested.

'I knew an Edward with a squint once,' Thomas said, shuddering.

'Lionel?'

'Scrawny child in the year below me at Eton. Think he wet his trousers during games once.'

'Oliver?'

'Had a dog called Oliver when I was young.'

Rosa took a deep breath. 'Are there *any* names you consider acceptable?'

'Thomas is a good strong name.'

Rosa laughed. 'You would never know who I was referring to.'

'There's another benefit I hadn't thought of.'

Rosa leant out of bed and swiped at him, missing and almost falling in the process.

'Your mama didn't mean to hit us,' Thomas whispered.

'I wasn't aiming at our son.'

For a second Thomas stared down into the child's face, mesmerised by the dark eyes and tiny features.

'Michael,' Rosa said quietly.

Thomas looked up, saw Rosa biting her lip, waiting for his response.

'Michael,' he repeated. 'It suits him.'

Leaning in over the bed, Thomas kissed Rosa, smiling as he felt her arms clutching at his neck as if willing him never to leave her. In the excitement of the birth he hadn't had time to tell her about his trip to the doctor's office in Portsmouth or of the decisions he'd made whilst he was there. Now didn't seem to be the right time. He had treated Rosa so badly, toyed with her heart, he felt as though he needed a big declaration, something that would make Rosa realise he meant what he said and he was here to stay.

'Are you sure you don't wish me to find a wet nurse?' Thomas asked as baby Michael looked up at him and started smacking his little lips.

'Quite sure. Did you know the children of the nobility are more likely to be undernourished than the children of the common people in the first six months?'

'That can't be true.'

'Many wet nurses will feed their own infants first, meaning the children they take in often go hungry.'

'Well, we wouldn't want you to go hungry,' Thomas said, bending down to kiss his son on the tip of his nose. 'Your mother turns into a wild beast when she needs her food.'

'I do not,' Rosa said indignantly.

He looked at her with a raised eyebrow until she glanced down, muttering under her breath.

'Anyway, Michael is my child and I will feed him.'

Thomas stood and passed her the baby, helping her to position him against her breast.

'I will be back soon, my love,' Thomas said as he leant down and kissed her forehead. 'Get some rest once Michael has finished feeding.'

Quickly he made his way downstairs to his study. He was loathe to leave Rosa and their baby, but mother and child needed to sleep and he had an important event to organise. With a steady hand he penned three letters, summoning a footman to take them once he was finished.

Rosa would likely be back on her feet in a few days and mostly recovered in a couple of weeks. He would plan his surprise for two weeks' time, to ensure she could enjoy it properly.

'We are very lucky,' Rosa said softly, looking down at her lovely son cradled in her arms. His nose was pressed against her breast and he was suckling loudly, a dreamy, faraway look in his eyes. 'We have your father to look after us.'

Even in the midst of childbirth Rosa had noticed when Thomas had entered the room. She'd felt pure relief, his presence was the one thing that could reassure her through the haze of the pain and the ordeal of giving birth.

She'd watched warily as Thomas had approached their son, seen the uncertainty on his face as he stepped forward to see the child who would bear his name, but not his blood. There was no doubt in Rosa's mind that Thomas had felt instantaneous love for the small child, the love of a parent for their baby, that indescribable rush you felt when you held your little bundle for the first time.

'I think he cares about us both very much,' Rosa continued. 'And I think you've made it much harder for him to leave us both behind.'

'Am I disturbing you?' Sarah asked as she

poked her head through the gap between the door and the doorframe.

'Not at all. Thomas has given me strict instructions to rest, but I feel so happy I don't think I could sleep now anyway.'

'I won't stay long. I just wanted to see my grandchild again.'

'We have decided on a name,' Rosa said softly. 'But if you don't like it then we would be quite happy to come up with something different.'

'Your child's name is your decision, my dear.'

'We would like to call him Michael.'

Rosa saw the tears fill the older woman's eyes and run down over her cheeks.

'If it is too painful…'

'No,' Sarah said firmly. 'It is one of the loveliest things anyone has ever done.'

They sat side by side for a few minutes, staring down at Michael's angelic face and drooping eyelids.

'A child unites people like nothing else.'

'I was so scared when I first found out I was pregnant,' Rosa said quietly. 'This pregnancy threatened to tear my whole life apart, and in a way it did, but something much better was built from the wreckage. I feel very lucky.'

'Do you think you will attempt a reconciliation with your mother?' Sarah asked.

Rosa shrugged. She had suffered through so many years of her mother's harsh judgements and cold demeanours that she wasn't sure how much more she could take.

'I think I will focus on my life here for a while. If she wishes to reconcile then I would welcome her, but I don't think my heart could take another rejection from her.'

Sarah stood, leaned over and kissed first baby Michael and then Rosa on the forehead. 'This is your home now and you will always be welcome here.'

Chapter Twenty-Six

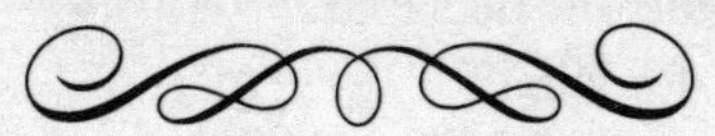

Rosa opened the door a crack and heard the furious whispering outside. Straining to catch the words in between the giggles of the excited maids, Rosa grimaced as the door creaked and gave her away.

'It's not time yet, my lady,' the older of the two maids said, her voice uncertain.

'Lord Hunter said you must stay put until he comes to fetch you.'

Rosa sighed and closed the door again. There was no point arguing, the poor maids were only following orders, but she wished Thomas would hurry up. Twenty minutes ago Sarah had come to take Michael downstairs, and it was the longest time Rosa had spent apart from her baby since giving birth.

She wasn't entirely sure what Thomas had planned, but her sharp ears had picked up the sounds of doors opening and closing multiple times and hushed voices whispering in the hall down below.

Flopping back on the bed, Rosa was startled by a knock on the door and was still reclining when Thomas flung it open and strode in.

'It's time,' he declared.

'Time for what?'

'Your surprise.'

'What is my surprise?'

He grinned. 'Just a little something I've organised. Come downstairs and you will see.'

Rosa smoothed her dress—a new gown Thomas had ordered for her especially for this occasion—and slipped her hand into the crook of her husband's elbow.

'Is that music I can hear?'

Soft notes were beginning to float up the stairs as they left the bedroom and walked along the landing.

'Yes. It's your favourite piece.'

He was right, it *was* her favourite piece, but she had never told him that.

Thomas grinned again at her expression. 'Your father told me.'

'Father is here?' Rosa asked, looking around as if expecting him to spring out from behind one of the paintings.

'Enough questions. You'll spoil the surprise.'

Rosa found herself smiling. These past couple of weeks Thomas had seemed lighter in mood, more carefree. He thrived as a father, responding to Michael's needs as if he had been trained for the role, and he and Rosa had been closer than ever before. Not physically, not yet, Rosa was still recuperating from the birth, but he'd hinted that he wanted to be when she was ready.

Time and time again Rosa had to tell herself not to read too much into his words, not to get carried away with the dreams of a perfect life with her perfect family. Thomas still hadn't confirmed whether he was planning on staying or going, although every morning when she woke in his arms she allowed herself to hope just a little bit more.

They reached the closed doors into the drawing room and Thomas squeezed her hand before flinging them open. The music became louder all of a sudden and Rosa saw a dozen heads turn to look at them.

'Thomas, what is happening?' Rosa whispered.

She could see her father, sitting in the front row next to Thomas's mother, head bent over his grandchild. Behind them sat her dear friend Caroline and her son Rupert. On the other side of the room were a couple of elderly women that Rosa took to be Thomas's relatives and two young men accompanied by their wives.

He didn't answer for a few seconds, first leading her to the front of the room down the aisle in between the chairs. A smartly dressed man smiled indulgently at them both before taking a step back.

'Thank you for coming today,' Thomas said, turning to face their intimate audience. 'As you may know, Rosa and I wed in a hurried ceremony whilst we were still in Venice. None of our family or friends were present and I did not mark the occasion with the celebration it deserves.' He paused, turning to Rosa. 'Fortunately my beautiful wife has forgiven me for that, and many more omissions, and has given me the chance to improve upon that behaviour.'

Rosa saw their gathered guests smile as Thomas spoke. For her part she felt as though she were in a dream. She could hear the words coming from Thomas's mouth, but seemed unable to process them.

'Rosa, my darling, my love. I know I have wronged you in so many ways both before and after our wedding. Can you forgive me?'

'What is all this?' Rosa whispered so only her husband could hear.

'A fresh start.'

'Do we need a fresh start?'

'Most decidedly. Rosa, I know I badgered you into marrying me, but I honestly feel it was the best decision of my life. You've made me realise what is important.'

Rosa felt her heart soar and struggled to listen to Thomas's next words.

'Before I met you I thought the most important thing was seeing and experiencing as much of the world as possible, just in case I became unwell and couldn't do the things I wanted to. I was restless, but largely directionless. These last few months you've made me see what really makes me happy.' He turned and smiled at Michael who was cooing and gurgling softly. 'You and our son. That is what makes me happy.'

'And the disease?' Rosa whispered.

She'd seen something change in Thomas around the time of the birth of their son, but she hadn't been able to work out exactly what. He'd become more positive, as if he'd decided not to let the terrible disease that one day might affect him spoil the here and now.

He shrugged. 'Maybe one day I will develop symptoms, maybe I won't, but I realise I cannot let the possibility of what might happen in the future ruin my life now. I'm a lucky man, I have a beautiful wife, a lovely home and a perfect son. I need to start appreciating my blessing rather than worrying about the future.'

Rosa beamed. It was all she had ever wanted for him. She knew the shadow of his brother's and father's deaths would always hang over him, as would the disease that might one day claim his body and mind, too, but he really was trying to appreciate all the good in his life right now.

'I love you, Rosa,' Thomas said softly. 'I've loved you for a long time, I was just too caught up in my worries to realise it.'

'You love me?'

'Do you doubt it?'

Rosa realised she was shaking her head. She didn't doubt it. Their married life might have been far from ideal initially, but once Thomas had allowed himself to enjoy her company she had seen the pleasure and happiness bloom.

'I love you, too.'

'I know,' he said with a mischievous grin.

Rolling her eyes at his confidence, she allowed him to pull her in closer to his side.

'Marry me?'

'We're already married, Thomas.'

'I know, but it was such a rushed affair, so impersonal, I thought we could have the marriage blessed.'

'Is that possible?'

'Father Young, here, assures me it is allowed.' Thomas dropped his voice. 'And he was particularly keen to bless the marriage seeing as the initial ceremony was not in his beloved Church of England.'

Rosa glanced up at the vicar and saw him smiling benevolently at her.

'Shall we begin?' Father Young asked.

After a short prayer Rosa and Thomas repeated their marriage vows and then Father Young uttered a blessing over their union.

'Congratulations,' he said quietly once he was finished with the blessing.

The assembled guests stood and clapped as Thomas led Rosa down the short aisle, before turning back and retracing their steps so Rosa could take baby Michael from her mother-in-law's arms.

'Where would you like to go for our honeymoon?' Thomas asked as they led their guests through to the dining room where a mouth-watering selection of food had been laid out.

'I know of a beautiful villa on the edge of Lake Garda that might be available,' Rosa said.

'You little minx,' Thomas whispered. 'You just want to see me swimming naked again.'

'The thought had crossed my mind. It would almost be worth braving the voyage again.'

'Only almost?'

'Well, it's not as though you need much of an excuse to take your clothes off, is it?'

Thomas threw his head back and laughed, before slipping a hand around Rosa's waist and making her shudder with anticipation by trailing his fingers over her lower back.

'Do you know, I never imagined I could be this happy?' Thomas said as he pulled out her seat, watched her as she cradled Michael into a more upright position in her arms and then pushed her chair in towards the table. 'I never dared to hope.'

Quickly, before their guests entered the room, Thomas bent his neck and kissed Rosa softly on the lips, pulling away only to drop a kiss on Michael's forehead.

'My perfect little family,' he murmured.

Epilogue

Rosa glanced impatiently to where Thomas was talking quietly with his solicitor, Mr Biggins. She knew the words of advice the elderly man was bestowing on her husband were important, but she wouldn't be able to contain her excitement and anticipation much longer.

'This institution holds over a hundred children at any one time,' Mr Pitt, the governor of the orphanage droned in her direction. 'Over a hundred children to house, feed and clothe.' He shook his head as if he couldn't believe the expense was justifiable.

'The children provide an income too, though,' Rosa said sweetly. 'They work.'

Mr Pitt scoffed and shook his head. 'Barely enough to provide one meal a day. The rest of the money comes from charitable donations.'

'Shall we go upstairs?' Thomas said, stepping away from the solicitor and taking Rosa's hand.

Rosa watched with a smile as Thomas scooped their son on to his shoulders and dashed up the stairs, making Michael scream with delight. Mr Pitt grimaced at this outward display of merriment, but held his tongue.

'Tell your mama to hurry up,' Thomas said as Rosa approached the top of the sweeping staircase.

'You're too slow, Mama,' Michael giggled, squirming as Rosa bent and placed a kiss on the top of his head.

'The girls have a dormitory to your left, the boys on the right. The nursery is at the end of the corridor.'

Rosa and Thomas had visited the orphanage before, but never had they ventured upstairs to the nursery.

'Tell us more about the child,' Thomas said, his face suddenly serious.

'Elizabeth is two months old and came to us two weeks ago,' Mr Pitt informed them. 'Her father was a sailor, he perished at sea before Elizabeth was born. Her mother died of a bad chest. She has no other relatives to take her in and look after her, hence she came to us.'

As he spoke Mr Pitt led them through the nursery, past row after row of cribs, some with tiny crying babies inside. The two young girls, neither much older than twelve themselves, ran backwards and forward, trying to comfort the squalling infants without much success.

They stopped and Rosa looked down into the crib, squeezing Thomas's hand as she did so.

'She's not got any hair,' Michael observed from his position on his father's shoulders.

'Some babies don't have any hair for the first few months.'

'Why not?'

Rosa blinked, then smiled at her son, 'Because everyone is different. Some babies have hair, some don't. Just like some have blue eyes and some brown.'

'I've got your eyes,' Michael said, then frowned in a way that made Rosa's heart swell with love. 'But you've got your eyes, too.'

'That's right, darling.' Turning to Mr, Pitt Rosa asked, 'Can I hold her?'

The governor of the orphanage shrugged and stepped back, as if he didn't want to get too close to an actual child.

Rosa leaned over the small baby, taking a minute to stroke her head and feel the silky smooth skin.

'Would you like a little sister?' Thomas crouched down so he was level with Michael.

'Will I have to share my toys?'

'Yes.'

'Even Ted-Ted?'

'Ted-Ted is just for you.'

Rosa cradled the little girl gently, feeling a warm gush of happiness as her eyes flickered open and focused on Rosa's.

'I wouldn't *mind* a little sister,' Michael said. 'As long as I'm the big brother.'

'Always.' Thomas stood, ruffling their son's hair before moving closer to Rosa. 'What do you think?' he asked.

'She's perfect.'

Six months ago Rosa had been watching Thomas and Michael chase each other across the lawn when she'd been struck by the desire to add to their family. She'd nurtured this wish in private for a few weeks before Thomas had wheedled it out of her. Rosa had always known their family would be limited to three and she knew she was blessed to have such a wonderful husband and son, but sometimes she yearned for a little baby to take care of, another child to raise through infancy and beyond.

Despite her desire for another child, Rosa had tried to put the idea from her mind. Thomas had remained healthy in the five years since their marriage, but still they were both very aware the Hunter family curse could strike at any time.

He would not risk fathering any children, and as such Rosa had attempted, albeit unsuccessfully, to put aside her broodiness.

When Thomas had suggested adopting an orphan Rosa had almost cried with happiness. She longed for a little brother or sister for Michael, someone for him to play with and protect, and now it looked as though they'd found just the child.

'Biggins is satisfied the adoption will be legal,' Thomas murmured quietly.

The first time they had visited the orphanage she'd wanted to take Elizabeth home with them straight away. The thought of the little girl suffering in the cold, starved of affection, was distressing, but Thomas had insisted they make everything legal first. He didn't want them to get hurt, to attach their affections to a child who one day might be claimed by an errant parent or relative. Once Elizabeth left the orphanage with them he wanted it all to be final.

'If you are happy we can sign the papers today,' Mr Pitt said. 'Then, of course, there is the matter of the fee…'

Biggins had waved his hand dismissively when Rosa had questioned the legality of this fee Mr Pitts was asking for. 'Think of it as a donation to the orphanage,' he had said. 'Or a bribe to the governor to let things run smoothly.'

Rosa knew all too well that the money they paid would not be spent on the struggling orphans, but would instead line Mr Pitt's own pocket, and reluctantly she had agreed not to make a fuss. Only her desire not to jeopardise the adoption made her keep quiet.

'Let us complete the formalities,' Thomas suggested. 'My wife will dress the child for outside and follow in a few minutes.'

With a wink Thomas led the governor back through the nursery, leaving Rosa alone with her son and his new baby sister.

Carefully Rosa stripped Elizabeth down, removing the rough, abrasive smock she was dressed in and replacing it with three layers of soft cotton. All the time Michael stood watching his new sister intently.

'Now you are a big brother you will need to look after your sister,' Rosa said.

Michael nodded, his expression serious. He looked as though he were standing guard over the crib, protecting the baby girl inside.

'She will need you to show her how to do things as she grows up and to protect her from harm. Can you do that for me?'

'Yes, Mama.'

Rosa pulled Michael into a cuddle and kissed the top of his head. 'You're my special little man. I'm so proud of you.'

Cradling Elizabeth in one arm and holding Michael's hand with the other, Rosa made her way through the nursery and back downstairs. They'd just reached the bottom step when a bundle of pure angry energy came running at them.

'You can't take her! She's not yours!'

Rosa swept Michael behind her protectively as a small girl, red-faced with anger, shot out of a side room and started pummelling Rosa's knees.

'Stop hitting my mummy,' Michael bellowed, refusing to stay behind Rosa and charging at the little girl.

Conscious of the delicate little baby in her arms Rosa crouched down and did her best to separate the two small children.

'What's the commotion?' Thomas asked, striding from Mr Pitt's office, closely followed by the governor himself.

'Emily, stop that at once,' Mr Pitt shouted.

The little girl fell still and looked up pitifully at Rosa.

'Get back to your lessons.'

Her bottom lip began to tremble, but she stood her ground.

'Why don't you tell me what is the matter?' Rosa asked softly.

'You're stealing my sister.'

Ten seconds of silence followed the statement as Rosa and Thomas glanced at the orphanage governor before looking at each other.

'She's *my* sister,' Michael piped up.

Before the two young children could launch themselves at each other again Rosa held up a warning hand.

'Elizabeth is your sister?' she asked the little girl.

A nod. Followed by a few tears rolling down her cheeks.

'Mr Pitt?' Thomas asked, his voice strained.

'Ah, well. The thing is, you see...'

'*Is* this Elizabeth's sister?' As the governor opened his mouth again Thomas fixed him with a hard stare.

'Yes,' he mumbled eventually.

'Older sister,' Emily clarified.

Rosa looked down at the bundle in her arms and felt the tears building in her eyes. They had been so close, so close to completing their family, so close to finding the perfect little addition, but she knew she couldn't take away this poor little girl's only living relative. Sisters needed each other.

'Emily,' Thomas said, crouching down so he was on the little girl's level. 'Is it just you and your sister now?'

Emily nodded. 'Mama made me promise to look after her.'

Rosa felt a lump in her throat as Emily looked earnestly at her little sister.

'How old are you?'

'Four and a half.'

'I'm five,' Michael piped up.

'But girls grow up quicker than boys,' Emily said with a sage wisdom beyond her years.

'Do not.'

'Do so.'

'How do you like it here, Emily?' Thomas interrupted.

She shrugged. 'It's horrible.'

'I can't see—' Mr Pitt began to speak, but Thomas held up an imperious hand.

'But I've gotta learn to live with it because older children never get adopted. That's what *he* said.' She pointed to Mr Pitt.

'Well, it—it *is* the truth,' Mr Pitt stammered, 'The babies often catch a childless couple's eye, but older children…' He let the rest of the sentence hang in the air.

'But I promised Mama I'd look after Elizabeth.'

'Then you can come and be my sister, too,' Michael said simply.

Everyone froze.

Rosa saw Thomas recover first and glance quickly at her.

'Emily, we were hoping to take Elizabeth home with us, to look after her as part of our family,' Thomas said, speaking slowly but seriously, as if he were conversing with an adult. 'If you would like, you could come and stay for a little while, too—see how you and your sister like it at our house.'

'And if we don't we can just come back?'

'If you don't you can just come back.'

'We'd be together?'

'Always. We're not trying to take your sister away from you.'

The serious little four-year-old bit her lip and considered the offer, then held out her hand for Thomas to shake.

Thomas stood up, slipped an arm around Rosa's waist, and quickly kissed her on the cheek.

'So now I have two sisters?' Michael asked.

Rosa opened her mouth to reply, but her son continued.

'Maybe we could choose a brother next?'

Thomas flung his head back and laughed, and Rosa couldn't help but join in with him.

'What are they laughing about?' Emily whispered to Michael.

'I don't know. Sometimes they're strange,' Michael replied, shaking his head.

'This really isn't what we agreed,' Mr Pitt said, stepping forward.

'You never told us Elizabeth has a sister.'

'An oversight…'

'Mr Biggins, here, will sort out the paperwork,' Thomas said, dismissing the orphanage governor with a look. 'And I'm sure a further donation to the orphanage will help smooth the way.'

That night in bed Thomas pulled Rosa close to his body and began planting kisses along the nape of her neck.

'What have we done?' Rosa asked. 'Are we mad?'

'Most probably. You, at least.'

'We never even talked about adopting *two* children.'

Thomas gently turned her over so she was looking into his eyes.

'But we have enough love for two,' he said softly. 'Surely that's what matters.'

Rosa smiled. Whenever she was doubting herself, whenever she felt unsure of what to do or what to think, Thomas would look at her in that loving way and make everything seem simple.

'Michael seemed to like them.'

'He likes being a big brother.'

'And your mother is spoiling them already.'

'There's no harm in that. Those little girls won't have had much chance to be spoiled up until now.'

'It'll be harder to travel with three.'

Thomas shrugged. 'We managed it with Michael. We can manage it with two more.'

When Michael had turned two Thomas had declared it was high time they saw a bit more of the world and the three of them had set off on an eight month adventure to India. They'd vowed to do the same every couple of years, to choose a destination and travel. It had never been explicitly said, but Rosa knew Thomas still had some of his wanderlust from all the time he spent travelling before he'd met her.

'I can't help thinking of all the other children left behind in that horrible place,' Rosa said quietly.

'Three children I can cope with, but I'm not sure I have it in me to adopt over a hundred.'

'There must be some other way we can help,' Rosa said, looking up at her husband hopefully.

‘I’ll talk to Biggins, see whether we can find a way to support the orphanage.’

‘It’s such a grey and miserable place. I don’t like to think of the children growing up there.’

‘Then we shall not rest until those children are happy and smiling and laughing.’

‘Don’t tease me. I know you feel the same way.’

Thomas grinned at her. ‘I’d have them all here in an instant if I could, but maybe it’s better to make the orphanage a better place for those there now, as well as those who will arrive in years to come.’

‘I love you,’ Rosa said. ‘I can’t believe we left the house today with one child and returned with three.’

‘We can do this,’ Thomas said, running his fingers across her forehead and tucking her hair behind one ear. ‘You, me, Michael and those two beautiful girls. It sounds like everything we’ve ever wished for.’

* * * * *

If you enjoyed this story you won't want to miss these other great reads from Laura Martin:

THE PIRATE HUNTER
SECRETS BEHIND LOCKED DOORS
UNDER A DESERT MOON
AN EARL IN WANT OF A WIFE
GOVERNESS TO THE SHEIKH
HEIRESS ON THE RUN

MILLS & BOON®

EXCLUSIVE EXTRACT

Georgiana Knight accidentally auctions her innocence to ex-soldier Frederick Challenger. In order to protect her reputation, she must marry him, but if Frederick hopes to tame her he'll have to think again…

Read on for a sneak preview of
A CONVENIENT BRIDE FOR THE SOLDIER
by Christine Merrill
the first book in the daring and decadent series
THE SOCIETY OF WICKED GENTLEMEN

Mr Challenger dropped to his knee before her. 'Miss Knight, would you do me the honour of accepting my offer of marriage?'

Georgiana had heard the phrase, 'without a trace of irony'. This must be the opposite of it. The proposal was delivered without a trace of sincerity. And yet, he did not rise. He stared at her, grim-faced, awaiting an answer.

'But, I do not want to marry you,' she said, staring back at him incredulous.

'Nor do I want to marry you.' If possible, his expression became even more threatening. 'But as you said before, if word of this gets out, I will be called to offer for you. I see no other way to save both of our reputations.'

'Your reputation?' Did men even have them? Of course they did. But she was sure that it did not mean the same thing as it did for girls.

'If you do not marry me, I will be seen as the villain

who threatened you, a seducer of innocents. Bowles, on the other hand, will be cast as your rescuer. In either case, your future is set. You will have to marry one of us to avoid ruin.' The statement was followed by the audible grinding of teeth. 'Please, my dear Miss Knight, allow me to be the lesser of two evils.'

The idea was insane. 'But then, we would be married,' she reminded him. 'For ever,' she added, when the first statement seemed to have no impact upon him.

'That is the way it normally works,' he agreed. 'You must have understood the risk when you undertook this desperate mission. As I told you before, if you do not marry me, then you shall wed Bowles.' He looked at her for the length of a breath, then added, 'For ever.'

'For ever,' she repeated. It sounded so final. Eventually, she had known she would have to marry someone. She'd just never imagined it would be to a man who had never been willing to give her the time of day, much less a proposal.

HP0817_2